MW00327171

LAST CHRISTMAS

FOR WHO?

MARIA FRANKLAND

AUTONOMY
PRESS

First published by Autonomy Press 2021

Copyright © 2021 by Maria Frankland

All rights reserved. No part of this publication may be reproduced, stored or transmitted in any form or by any means, electronic, mechanical, photocopying, recording, scanning, or otherwise without written permission from the publisher. It is illegal to copy this book, post it to a website, or distribute it by any other means without permission.

This novel is entirely a work of fiction. The names, characters and incidents portrayed in it are the work of the author's imagination. Any resemblance to actual persons, living or dead, events or localities is entirely coincidental.

Maria Frankland asserts the moral right to be identified as the author of this work.

I am a participant in the Amazon Services LLC Associates Program, and earn a commission from qualifying purchases.

First edition

Cover art by Darran Holmes

For my sons, Sam and Matthew,
with whom I've spent
many happy Christmases.

JOIN MY 'KEEP IN TOUCH' LIST!

If you'd like to be kept in the loop about new books and special offers, join my 'keep in touch list' by visiting www. autonomypress.co.uk.
You will receive a free novella as a thank you for joining!

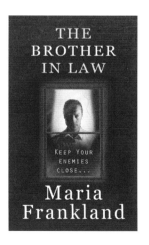

PROLOGUE

IT'S something of an honour to visit a person when they're at the end of their life. When you know you're one of the last people they'll sense at their bedside. Particularly when they're slipping in and out of consciousness.

You've been told they can hear you, but can they? *Really?* You know you can tell them anything you want, and it will never be repeated. How many people can you say that about? A catholic priest at confession? A GP? A counsellor?

But even those professionals will warn you that they may have to break their code of confidentiality, should you pose a risk to life. Your own or someone else's.

But someone on their deathbed? You're safe with them. They can't tell anyone anything.

PART I

NEIL

1

I TRUDGE TOWARDS THE CAR, wishing we were going *anywhere* but to where we are.

"Come on, Neil."

My wife cannot seem to disguise the irritation in her voice as I slide into the passenger seat.

"From the look on your face, you'd think we were heading to the gallows."

"I might as well be."

"For goodness sake, they're not that bad." Sacha rests her arm on the back of my seat as she reverses from our drive. "Look, you've got out of coming with me for the last two years. You could at least *pretend* that you're looking forward to spending Christmas with my family."

"I'm not pretending anything. At least I can relax when I spend it with my Dad." I twist my wedding ring around and around. I've lost that much weight, it's a wonder I haven't lost it. "With your bloody lot, I'll spend the next three days completely on edge."

"Look Neil." With a shake of her head, Sacha flicks her dark hair behind one shoulder and glances at me. "If you feel you need space, there'll be plenty of places at their new house to retreat to."

"I hope so. Look, I'm sorry Sacha. You know I'm not myself right now. I need space, not a crowd of people."

"You haven't been yourself for months." There's the usual weariness to her voice. "It affects me too, you know."

I know I'm dragging her down with me, and this knowledge is more than I can handle sometimes. "Hopefully, I'll get back to normal when these tablets kick in."

"At least you're finally taking them." She turns into the petrol station. "I'll fill. You pay."

"You know I'm broke right now." Something inside me sags even further. "It's not my fault I've had no work over the last couple of weeks."

Sacha sighs as she drives alongside the pump. "The last couple of months, you mean. You need to get it sorted Neil." There's suddenly a sharper edge to her voice.

"Alright. Thanks for reminding me. As you do at every opportunity." I reach into the carrier bag by my feet and pull out a can of beer.

"You've got to be joking Neil." She pulls the handbrake lever with such force, I doubt she'll be able to release it again. "It's not even lunchtime and you're drinking already. What are you bloody playing at?"

"Do you want me to survive the next few days with your family?" I pop the can open and lift it to my lips, immediately feeling calmer. "Besides, it's Christmas. If I want a beer, I don't need your permission. I'm a grown man."

"Couldn't you at least wait until we get there?" She seems to have trouble even looking at me. I've noticed that a lot lately. "You know you need to cut down. If we want..."

"Alright Sacha, don't start. Again. We know I'm a..."

We both jump as the driver behind us sounds their horn.

"I'd better get on with it, hadn't I?" Sacha swings her legs out of the car door. To say we're only visiting her family, she's very done up. In fact, I don't think I've ever seen her wear so much make-up. And I don't know how she drives in those heels she wears. It should be illegal. As she fills up, I scroll through Facebook.

There's a picture of my friend, Ash, basking in his garden hot tub with his wife, Lisa. They've each got a glass of fizz and he's written, *can't think of a better way to spend Christmas Eve.* Their young daughter, the image of Lisa, is dangling her feet in the water between them. Ash told me when we went for a pint the other day that it's just the three of them spending Christmas Day together. Lucky sod. Not just because of how he's spending Christmas Day. He has a successful company, is secure in his own skin, and has a wife who doesn't nag him constantly. But then he's been able to give her a kid. There probably isn't a lot she could nag him about. I'm sure she respects him too. I can't remember the last time my wife looked at me with any respect in her eyes.

A notification flashes in the corner of the screen and I realise my brother-in-law, Adam, has tagged me in a post. I can't believe we're Facebook friends. It must be an old thing. Out of all of Sacha's family, he's the person I'm least looking forward to seeing. Three hours would be bad enough. But three days...

A Merry Christmas with the outlaws, he's written, posting a photograph of a generously filled tumbler of whiskey. He's already on the sauce as well. His wife Christy is much easier-going than Sacha.

I can't stop comparing her and our marriage with other people lately. We're really hanging by a thread. I wish I could make more of an effort over Christmas – bring Sacha back to me, but I haven't got the energy for any of it anymore. Sometimes I wonder how much longer I can go on. I catch sight of myself in the wing mirror. I'm looking more and more like my dad. My face is puffy and my eyes are dark.

If Adam and the rest of the family weren't going to be there – if it was just going to be Sacha's parents, I wouldn't have minded going so much. I might have looked forward to seeing the bungalow they've just bought and having a walk along Bempton Cliffs. But for obvious reasons, my father-in-law wants the whole of his family around him this Christmas. It's certainly not going to be easy spending time with someone who's terminally ill. Like I'm not depressed enough as it is.

I sigh in the quiet of the car as I watch Sacha talking to an elderly man in front of her. Wherever she is, she strikes up conversations with people. Being an introvert, I'm in awe at how easily she makes friends and connections. She's five-deep in the queue to pay. We risk getting stuck in traffic as it is, especially at this time of day on Christmas Eve. The drive up the A64 to the Yorkshire coast is always a popular one. Not that I'm in any rush to get there.

"Finally," I say as Sacha returns to the car. All around us, drivers are sounding their horns. I look behind our car, surprised to see six cars queueing for this one pump. They'll all be getting away to spend Christmas with family and friends. Though I bet none of them will be experiencing the misery I'm feeling about it. I should be able to have a say in how I spend my time and not be forced into things by my wife.

"Have you seen it in there?" She glances in her rear-view mirror as she tugs the seatbelt around herself. "That's why I suggested you pay. We could have saved ourselves ten minutes."

"You should have filled up yesterday if you're in that much of a hurry." I scrunch up the can I've finished and reach into the bag for another.

"You're going to be half cut by the time we get there." Sacha rams the gearstick forward. "You don't give a toss, do you? Your tablets say *avoid alcohol* Neil. Oh piss off," she yells into the mirror as once again, the driver behind us sounds his or her horn.

"I've decided to take a few days off my tablets, actually." I'm calmer now I've got onto my second beer. As though an anaesthetic is coursing through my veins. *Who needs antidepressants?* "Just whilst I get through this next couple of days."

"Whilst you get through *what!* God, is spending time with my family really that dreadful?" The tyres screech as we leave the forecourt. "Anyway, what was all that crap you were spouting this morning? About not wanting to drive because the antidepressants were making you drowsy. You just wanted a drink, didn't you? I'm absolutely sick of it, Neil. You've got a problem, do you know that?"

"Yeah – it's called being married to you. Does putting me down make you feel better about yourself? Leave me alone Sacha. I didn't want to be coming at all."

She doesn't answer me, and I notice her gaze linger on a woman around her age, pushing a pram along the footpath. Being around her two nieces and her pregnant sister over the next couple of days won't do her any favours either. I take a large swig of beer, then hit the button on the car radio to drown out the silence between us. *Merry Christmas everyone.* I change stations. *I wish it could be Christmas every day.* I hit the off button.

"It stinks like a brewery in this car." At least her voice has lost its edge. "You've got to sort this out Neil. You're not looking after yourself at all, and until you do..."

"Yeah, yeah. I know." I should do by now. Sacha reminds me at least three times a day of the criteria we need to hit for one try at IVF. One is improving the mobility of my little swimmers. I'm drinking so often that they're probably swimming backwards. But I'll be honest, drink is my crutch right now. It keeps my anxiety at bay, and I couldn't get through the day without it. And I definitely couldn't get through these next three days without lots of it. I'm in a vicious circle and sinking fast. But when Sacha says *I'm not looking after myself,* it's not *me* she's bothered about, only the baby I'm not giving her. I really think our days are numbered.

"If not for me, then can you at least try to act like a reasonable human being for my dad's sake? Especially with all he's going through." The gears crunch as she turns out of our little town onto the open road. "We both know it's a matter of months and I want to make the most of the time I've got left with him."

"I'd have thought he'd have wanted a quiet Christmas under the circumstances." I press a button on my phone to check it. Not that I'm expecting any calls or messages. Not really. It's just a habit. God, these next few days are going to be an absolute barrel of laughs.

"Well, he doesn't, does he? He wants his family with him. You know as well as I do that this will be his last Christmas. And Mum's gone to a lot of trouble for us all to make it special."

Ah, my po-faced mother-in-law. She used to be decent company, but these days she always seems to be moaning about her weight, her voluntary work, or her former neighbours. Who hasn't done something they should, or who's said something they shouldn't. Maybe with a terminally ill husband, she'll have put these more trivial matters to one side and will leave me alone. It's difficult to feign interest in her conversation. I tried to when Sacha and I first got together, but I guess I was out to impress them all then.

So much has changed in these five years that it's impossible to remember a time when the two of us had fun. It seems like a distant memory when we could go to bed together spontaneously because we actually fancied each other, and not just because it was the peak time of the month. Or when we couldn't wait to see each other at the end of the day – those were the days when I'd ring Sacha during my lunch break just to hear her voice. Nowadays her voice grates on every nerve ending I've got.

We've become so distant – especially since I received the result about my low sperm count and its poor mobility. Sacha was heartbroken when we got the news, then became angry with me. I felt like such a failure and she made it worse. Although two days later, she was forced to apologise when she was told she had over-production of one of her hormones. It was, the consultant said, little wonder we weren't conceiving.

Though, as things stand, if a miracle happened and Sacha got pregnant, I'd probably be a rubbish father. I can't hold a job down for five minutes, I'm drinking like a whale, I can't sleep, my appetite is shot, and I'm permanently knackered. What a list. I bloody hate my life. But I hate myself even more. Whatever the coming days may bring, things can't possibly get any worse.

2

I RUB at my eyes then wipe the steam from the window. I must have dropped off. There's a crick in my neck as I glance at Sacha. I wipe the drool from my chin and hope she didn't notice it. Nice.

"You were snoring," she informs me, disgust written all over her face.

"Sorry." She used to make me feel like ten men. Nowadays, I just want to shrivel up and die.

"It's not like I'm not used to it Neil. You snore every time you have a drink."

I sense that she's itching to add to that comment. Probably with something like *every day.*

"We're nearly there anyway."

"Great." Why the hell did I agree to this? I should be at my Dad's. OK, so I might have had to go to midnight mass with him, but that beats being here.

We pass the sign saying "Bempton." There should be a subtitle sign saying, *where nothing ever changes.* Usually, there's something comforting about this quaint seaside village which appears to be stuck in a time warp. But, this time, as we drive along the coastal road leading towards my in-law's new house, I feel as bleak as the sky which is now darkening to dusk. I hate this time of year. The drizzle and the gloom. Desolate December.

"At least we've gone past the shortest day." It's as though Sacha has read my mind. Despite the problems we're having, she's still good at that. "Thank goodness the nights will start drawing out again soon. Oh look, everyone's here before us. I said we should've set off earlier."

My heart is hammering inside my chest as we pull up on the kerb outside the newly built bungalow. There's no room for us on the drive. Sacha's parent's Mercedes, Greg's family estate and Adam's Audi have claimed the spaces available. If I didn't know better, I might say that the house looks inviting, with the lamps in the windows and Christmas lights around the door. Now we're here, I'm ready for something stronger to drink. Four beers haven't touched the sides.

"Try to smile, for goodness sake," Sacha hisses at me. "Think of my poor dad, will you?"

"How could I not? He's all I've heard about for weeks."

The sarcasm in my voice isn't lost on Sacha and she gives me a look as though I've just shot a small rabbit. I can't help it – I'm sick of hearing about Stuart's deteriorating condition, and I'll be hearing much, much more about it over the next couple of days. I just hope everyone won't spend the three days weeping. If they do, at least there's a cliff nearby for me to jump off.

For all my reluctance to be amongst Sacha's family, I do feel sympathetic towards Stuart, and the rest of them - I couldn't imagine life without my own dad. Though with the way I'm living my life, I'll probably die before my dad anyway. God, I'm a cheery soul at the moment.

.   .   .

"Hello! Better late than never," Sacha calls into the echoey hallway. She beckons me in, and I'm taken aback by the spotlessness of everything. It won't be like that for long, not with Greg and Rebecca's two hyperactive daughters. I expect they'll be even worse than normal with it being Christmas Eve. I find it difficult to call Matilda and Freya my nieces – I've always felt on the outskirts of Sacha's family. Even at the night do of our wedding, her family were all laughing and dancing together, to the point where I felt like an outsider. I'm cut out of a completely different piece of cloth to them, and can never think what to talk about once topics such as the weather, the itinerary, and the *what was the drive over like* conversations have taken place. If I'd met any of them in the normal walk of life, without having known Sacha, they wouldn't have given me the time of day. Any of them, but some less than others.

"Nice place Mum." Sacha approaches Wendy in the kitchen. "I love it. What do you think Neil?"

"Erm. It's very homely." I glance around the spacious open-plan kitchen and dining area, separated by a large breakfast bar, then watch as Wendy swings around and pulls Sacha in for a hug.

"Thanks. We like it." Wendy smiles at me over Sacha's shoulder. "We've settled in very easily. At least it's all on one level for Stuart."

They say when you want to know what your wife will look like in the future, to look no further than your mother-in-law. Wendy is tall and wide-hipped, and always wears shapeless trousers and thigh skimming tunics to disguise her recent portliness. Her hair is short and wiry now but still dark – she must dye it. However, I've seen photographs from when she was younger, with the bikini-perfect body and long dark hair. She looked like a young Cher, and Sacha. So maybe there is some truth in what 'they' say. Sacha is gorgeous and for the millionth time, I wonder how much longer she'll stay with me.

I loiter, not really sure what to do with myself as Sacha and Wendy become engrossed in one another's company. I could head to the lounge, where the rest of them seem to be, from the noise I can hear. But I'd rather poke my eyes out with a hot poker than integrate myself with the rest of them. I wouldn't be welcome, anyway. Hopefully Wendy will tell us which is our room before too long. I'll pour a whiskey and take refuge in there for a while.

"Stuart." I stiffly hold my hand out as my father-in-law emerges from the conservatory and walks towards me. He accepts the gesture, though there is no strength in his grip. It can barely even be called a grip. Our gazes briefly meet, then he quickly lowers his. "It's a great house," I say. "Have you settled in OK?"

"As well as can be expected... for whatever time I'm going to have left here." He glances at Sacha, then looks back at me. I notice how watery his eyes have become. "How's work going?" he asks. It's always the first thing Stuart asks me. What he ought to say is, *when are you going to provide for my daughter? How much longer are you going to allow her to take the strain for everything?*

"You know. It's quiet at the moment. It always is in the building trade at this time of year. No one wants workmen around at Christmas, do they?"

"I would've thought there'd be plenty of work at any time of year for a plumber." Stuart looks past me as he speaks. He's easily lost two stones since the last time I saw him. "If they want work, that is? Surely there's more plumbing emergencies in the winter, not to mention people getting new bathrooms and kitchens in time for Christmas."

As I open my mouth to defend myself, Greg, my brother-in-law, sidles up behind Stuart.

"Well, my mate's a plumber too." Greg catches Freya as she

bounces up behind him and swings her off her feet. "And he's got work coming out of his ears."

Prick.

"Would you like a beer Neil?"

Music to my ears. Saved by the mother-in-law. "I'd love one." I accept the bottle and stride towards the conservatory to get away from Stuart and Greg. I sink into an armchair.

"You smell like you've already had a few mate." Adam, my other brother-in-law, throws himself into the chair beside me. "Me and you both."

I came in here to drink my beer in peace. I follow his gaze to the window out onto the patio where a heavily pregnant Rebecca is waddling around in the garden. We watch as she throws a ball for their young spaniel who is more hyperactive than both girls put together. Adam points at Rebecca and grins. "The first thing Christy said when she saw Rebecca was *why would anyone want to do that to themselves?*"

"Do what? Who?" I take a long swig of beer, concerned to realise that I've already drunk half of the bottle. I'll have to locate the drinks stash, so I can discreetly help myself. We should've probably brought some beer and wine, but Sacha's parents are minted. It wouldn't have made much difference if we had.

"Rebecca. She looks like one of those flump-type characters that used to be on TV. I could never imagine Christy being that huge. You know her take on things, don't you Neil? She can't understand why anyone would want one kid, let alone three." Adam claps his hand over his mouth in a mock grand gesture. "Oh, sorry mate – I forgot."

"Yeah. Course you did." I drain the last of my beer and get to my feet, desperate to get away from him. I've been in his company for less than five minutes and already I feel like punching him.

. . .

"So, do we get a guided tour then?" I load as much cheer as I can muster into my voice as I approach Sacha and Wendy. They're coming out of what must be the utility room. A cursory glance behind them tells me all I need to know about where the drinks supply is.

"Of course." Wendy looks pleased at my interest, but really, I'm only hoping that this 'tour' will reveal the location of our bedroom. I don't fancy waiting until bedtime to find out. I need to know I have an escape from Greg and Adam. "Are you coming too, Sacha?"

"Try to stop me!" Sacha grabs her glass of wine from the kitchen counter and smiles at her mother. "So I've seen in here and in there. That is obviously the conservatory. It's gorgeous. Oh, hello Adam." She smiles at him, but her smile looks forced. I wonder if she overheard his 'baby' comments a few moments ago.

"How's my favourite sister-in-law?"

"Don't let Rebecca hear you say that." Wendy laughs.

Adam walks towards us and hugs Sacha. How anyone could hug him is beyond me. And he lingers a moment too long until Sacha pulls away.

"The garden looks good Mum. I like the fairy lights." Sacha knocks on the window, but Rebecca doesn't respond. She's definitely heard Sacha knocking, but seems to be pretending not to. She's always been strange, Rebecca, and ridiculously jealous of her more vibrant older sister.

"So this is the dining area." Pride is written all over Wendy's face as she gestures towards a polished oak table that wouldn't look out of place in the Queen's drawing room. It's decked with candles, crackers and flowers, and for a moment, makes me wish I had an appetite. Not to mention company I'd want to sit and enjoy a leisurely Christmas dinner with.

"This must be the lounge," Sacha says, opening the door and laughing. "She must've started early."

"She sure did." Wendy laughs too. "The girls have been running in and out of here and she's even slept through that."

I glance in to where Sacha's older sister, Christy, is fast asleep on the sofa. I want to swap places with her amidst the Christmas lights and roaring fire. The screams of the kids echo from the kitchen. I don't know how anyone sleeps with them around. We're shown the office, cloakroom, porch, then Wendy and Stuart's bedroom.

"Very nice. Very nice," Sacha keeps saying.

We walk further down the hallway to see the pristine main bathroom, then another bedroom with an en-suite, where camp beds have been put up for the girls. Then a smaller room where Christy and Adam must be. They look to have already unpacked.

"And that," Wendy says, "concludes your guided tour."

"Have you not got a fourth bedroom?" Sacha looks puzzled. "Where are we sleeping?"

"Ah well." Wendy looks from Sacha to me. "With all that's been going on, I didn't even consider that until yesterday."

"Consider what?"

"That with us all spending Christmas together, we'd be one bedroom short. So luckily, I've been able to get an airbed for you both. The woman said they're quite comfy."

"For three nights?" I think of my back and the lack of anywhere to escape to. Something inside me plummets. "Where do you want us to put it?" I do a mental scan of the bungalow, trying to consider where could be out of the way. I can't believe this.

"The lounge, I guess, though obviously you'll have to fit in with everyone going to bed and getting up in the morning." And... at least Wendy has the grace to look slightly apologetic. "I dread to think what time those girls will get up in the morning."

"Why is it us that have drawn the short straw?" I'm glad

Sacha's asked the question. I'm fuming. She doesn't look happy either. Bad is going to worse.

"I'm sure you wouldn't expect your sister to sleep on an airbed in her condition."

"Of course not."

"And Christy and Adam arrived before you, so it was a case of first come, first served."

"You snooze, you lose," Adam chuckles as he passes us and heads towards the bathroom.

I edge away from Wendy and Sacha towards the drinks stash in the utility room. The plan now is to find a quiet corner and get steadily pissed. Then I won't care where I sleep. And I don't give a toss what Sacha thinks. Or what any of them think.

3

I SLUMP on a beanbag in the corner of the lounge, wondering what the hell I'm doing here. I'm an interloper, watching as my wife and in laws laugh their heads off at some film that's not funny.

Stuart went to bed straight after dinner – he looked knackered. He usually becomes sociable after a few drinks – and even speaks to me like I'm a fully paid-up member of society. At the moment he doesn't seem to be drinking though. One of the side effects of being terminally ill, I guess. He spent the meal even more subdued than usual, and seemed to be just observing everyone else. I can only imagine what must've been going through his mind.

Before he disappeared to his room, I walked in on him and Rebecca, huddled together in the conservatory. She was bawling her eyes out and I caught her saying something about his grandchildren growing up without him. Like that would have really made him feel better. She looked at me as if to say *do one*. So I did.

I don't have a clue what to say to him anyway – I've always been crap with finding the right words in delicate situations.

Foot in mouth and all that. Though it must be horrendous, badly wanting to live and knowing that you've no choice and you're going to die.

Personally, I've been having all sorts of thoughts along the lines of it might be better if I was dead too. At first, I passed them off as intrusive thoughts and wrestled with them, but more and more, I'm giving in to them, and allowing this thinking more credence.

It's the inability to give my wife a baby that's mainly pushing me over the edge. But it's not just that – I feel like a complete failure in so many other areas of my life too. Drinking both numbs the pain but intensifies the awful thoughts. I can't get control of that either. Perhaps I should talk to someone, a counsellor, they're always banging on in campaigns on the TV about getting help when you're depressed. I think it's getting beyond help though. I can't seem to find the joy in anything; life's become one long, hard slog. I've thought about talking to Sacha, but I can't see her being interested. She's too concerned with how much I'm letting her down.

Dinner has sobered me up slightly, which is just as well whilst I'm in Adam's company. I need to be on guard. His face is illuminated in the fire's glow as he laughs his irritating laugh. He's hogging the armchair closest to the TV with his feet up on a stool. I just want to lie down, wallow in my misery, and be on my own. But I can't even do that – I have to wait for them all to clear off to bed. It's a bloody joke – we should never have come here.

"Right I'm turning in." Rebecca shuffles to the front of the sofa and looks as though she could do with a hoist to raise her from it.

Lucky you, I want to say.

"I need to settle those kids of mine. Have you heard them?"

"Aww, don't worry, they're just excited about Santa coming." Wendy pats Rebecca's arm. I'm reminded how early they'll be getting up and wonder whether there'll be room in the office for the air bed. I wouldn't have thought so.

"I know Mum, but I don't want them to disturb Dad. He needs his rest. I can't believe how exhausted he was before."

"Poor Dad." Christy drains her glass. "I don't think what's happening has sunk in with me yet. How are you coping Mum? It's hard enough for us, so I can't imagine what it must be like for you."

"Not too good, if I'm honest. You all being here is helping us though. We've just got to make this Christmas as special as we can."

Greg lowers the volume of the canned laughter on the TV like the dutiful son-in-law he is, and Rebecca sits back again on the sofa to put her arm around her mother.

Here we go, I think to myself, considering how rude it might look if I were to leave the room now to escape the morbid conversation. I really can't cope with it. Not in my current frame of mind.

"Why don't you ring us more Mum?" Sacha says from the other beanbag at the side of Greg.

We've really drawn the short straw today. Relegated to sleep on an airbed and also to sit on beanbags.

"You're not on your own with this," Sacha continues. "We're all here for you, you know."

"Mum rings me most days." Rebecca looks to tighten her embrace around her mother's shoulders. "Don't you Mum?"

She has a smug expression on her face as she glances from Sacha to Christy, as if to say, *at least Mum rings me.* I'm well up on the politics of this family and notice a look pass between Sacha and Christy.

"That's more to check on you dear, with you being so close to your due date. Not to have a moan." Wendy tugs a tissue from the box on the table next to her. "It's just so - well you can see how thin he is. He's a shadow of who he was. I just feel useless."

"Oh Mum." Christy rises from her chair and shuffles along the floor towards Wendy. She looks as though she would have trouble standing if she tried. After her sleep this afternoon, she seems to have got back on the prosecco. Not that I'm in a position to judge.

"It's not only about me." Wendy dabs at her eyes and strokes Christy's hair as she arrives at her feet. "Seeing him with you girls, and his granddaughters – it's killing me, knowing we've got such a short time left. It's all so unfair."

"I haven't told Freya and Matilda what's happening yet." Rebecca now reaches towards the tissue box. "I don't know if I should. They just know Grandad isn't very well."

"He's being so brave about it," Wendy goes on. "He rarely complains. I think what's really worrying me is how I'll look after him when we get closer to the end."

"Does he want to stay here Mum?" Sacha's eyes widen as she looks at her mother. "When he gets to that stage?"

Bloody hell, what a Christmas Eve conversation. I glance from Greg to Adam, both displaying expressions that swing between sympathy and bewilderment. *Why can't I be a bloke who has some idea of what to say in this sort of situation?* Mind you, they're not doing much better.

The girls shrieking from along the hallway breaks the silence. Then a bang.

"I'd better see what they're up to." Rebecca groans. "Kids."

"Tell them Santa's waiting for them to go to sleep before he'll come." Wendy gives Rebecca a shove to help her up from the sofa.

"They might wait until next Christmas Day then." Christy laughs.

"I'll see you all in the morning." Rebecca's hand flies to the top of her bump. "I need some sleep. It's hard work, this baby growing business."

I glance at Sacha. Her eyes meet mine and I see the longing in them before she looks away.

I settle on the sofa in the conservatory with a whiskey, glad to have found an opportunity when Rebecca left the room to make my exit as well. As I slide the tumbler onto the glass table in front of me, I shiver. I've got used to the heat of the fire in the lounge. In the rest of the bungalow, the heating seems to have clicked off. I stare at the Christmas tree in the corner; the lights blurring in front of my drink-infused eyes. There are presents everywhere, and I childishly wonder whether any of them are for me. Of course not. I'm an outcast here.

Once again, I long for the comfy armchair in front of the fire at my dad's house. There, I can be me. He doesn't know any of my shit, nor would he want to. That I'm an infertile, alcoholic, and skint total waste of space. Dad's 'old school.' Out of touch, some might say. His world is small. Being the son of an Irishman, it comprises church, and playing a few hands of cards with his friends. Like Sacha, he's a sociable person. Not like me. If he knew of the thoughts I've been having, he'd just tell me to pull myself together. There'd be no sympathy. Depression is a fallacy as far as Dad's concerned.

"Bit heavy in there, isn't it?" Greg curls his head around the door of the conservatory. "Mind if I join you?" He sits on the adjacent sofa without waiting for a reply. "How's it going? Are things getting any better between you and Sacha?"

"What?" Blimey. He's straight in for the jugular. "What do you mean?"

"I've heard things haven't been too good between you both."

"What things? Who's told you that?" In my drink and depression-fuelled haze, I can do without being quizzed by this jumped-up twerp, barely taller than I was as a young teenager. He thinks he's God's gift just because he's got his wife up the duff three times. He's even wearing a bloody Superman t-shirt. Idiot.

"Ah, you know how women talk to each other. Especially this lot."

"What's Sacha been saying ?" My jaw tightens, and my breath shortens. I cannot believe I'm being grilled by Greg about my marriage. Nor can I put up with Sacha going around slagging me off. I wouldn't do it to her.

"Christy's mentioned a few bits and pieces to Rebecca – what Sacha's told her. Earlier, whilst we were waiting for you both to get here. It sounds rough. Is there anything we can do to help?"

"Things aren't bad, actually." I wouldn't choose to confide in either of my brothers-in-law. "Nothing that we can't sort out ourselves. But cheers for asking. It's much appreciated." I hope my words convey the need for him to shut up.

"How far are you away from getting on the waiting list?" What he really means is *how far away are you from being a man who is as competent, virile, and successful as me?* Prat. I wish he'd leave me alone.

"I don't know. I really don't want to talk about it." *Especially not with you*, I want to add, but I don't. I take a large swig of whiskey. I'll suffer for this tomorrow. Spirit hangovers are the worst. I should've stuck to beer. Perhaps I'll just push on through and carry on drinking through the night. I believe there's such a thing as being able to drink yourself sober.

"I can't imagine..." What looks like forced sympathy crosses his pudgy face. I stare at him, willing him to clear off.

"Just leave it, will you Greg, of course you can't imagine." My tone should be sharp enough to close the subject this time.

"Easy mate, he's only showing an interest." Adam appears in the doorway next, the top of his head illuminated by the light behind him. I've noticed for the last couple of years that it's thinning. "It's no wonder you're so bloody miserable Neil, you snap at everyone who comes near you. Aren't the happy pills working yet?"

"What would you know about those?" My voice really rises now. "What the hell would you know?" I sound even less coherent than I feel. I came in here to be alone, not to be cornered by these two.

"Well, I know a good divorce solicitor if you need one." Adam grins as he steps into the conservatory.

I get to my feet and lurch towards him, surprising myself at my sudden movement in my inebriated state. "What did you say?" The room spins, and I feel like I've left my stomach in the chair.

Just as I stagger back, the overhead light is snapped on. Sacha appears in the conservatory with an expression on her face that I know all too well. It's the expression she always wears when I'm pissed or knackered. It becomes more pronounced when it's her window of ovulation, as she calls it, when she realises not even Viagra could raise my ship.

"Don't you think we've enough shit going on Neil?" She looks squarely at me, ignoring the other two. I expect her to sit next to me, but she sits in the single chair opposite. "Without you getting into this state and picking fights with everyone."

"I'm not the one picking fights." I'm seeing two of her. "Anyway, you knew the score Sacha. I didn't want to be here. And I certainly don't want to sleep on some crappy airbed."

"Well, you can sleep in here then, can't you? Ask Mum for a blanket."

"It's freezing in here." I wrap my arms around myself, momentarily comforted by the slight warmth from my hands against the chill of my bare arms.

"Heater there pal." Greg gestures to it.

Sacha leans forward in her seat. "That's settled then. As if

I'd want to sleep in the same room as a drooling, drunken, snoring..."

"You're not selling him Sacha!" Adam laughs.

"Can't you all piss off?" I could cry right now. If only I could drive back to Leeds. But I'm that drunk, I'd probably drive the car into a wall. Maybe that would not be such a bad thing. No one would give a shit anyway. And Sacha would be free to find someone she deserves. Someone who can give her everything she wants, including a baby. "I need to get some sleep."

"All in good time." Adam laughs again. "Merry Christmas to you too."

"I'd probably better be getting to bed. Those girls are still going strong. Rebecca will be pulling her hair out." Greg drains his mug and gets to his feet. Saint Greg, drinking tea.

"I bet you hope you get a boy this time," Adam says.

"That would be cool. But I guess we'll get what we're given."

"Have you not found out what she's having?"

"Can you lot continue this somewhere else?" I stretch my legs out on the sofa. I want another drink and some kip. Then in the morning, I'm going to leave them all to it and drive over to Dad's. It's not as if Sacha wants me here.

"Night then." Greg bends over Sacha and I watch as she raises her arms around his back. It's the first time I have ever seen them hug one another. It's brief though. Sacha pulls back quickly, looking from me to Adam.

"And it's a good night from me." Adam gets to his feet but before he reaches Sacha, she is rushing from the room muttering, "I'll get you a blanket." Evidently Greg is the only brother-in-law she wants to hug this evening.

I stare into the darkness, willing sleep to put me out of my misery. I've laid here for what feels like hours, feeling like death. I wanted to get blitzed earlier, now I'd give anything to feel sober. I need to pee. I should've stayed away from the spirits. Whiskey and beer – never a sensible combination. I need water. I could be sixteen again, the way this room's spinning.

I'm going to hurl. In this pristine conservatory with its cream rugs and gifts stacked up around the tree. Shit. There's no way I can make it to the toilet in time.

I lurch towards the door and into the garden in time to turn my guts out all over the patio. When I finally stop retching, I'm on my knees on the concrete. Then, in horror, I realise the force of puking has made me pee myself. *Oh my God.* I finish it over the drain and shiver violently in the darkness.

I've no idea what time it is but am beyond grateful that no one seems to have heard me. Well, at least, no one has come out to investigate. I spot an outside tap so go inside for my empty glass. I fill it with water a few times, which I throw at the pile of sick on the patio. Then fill the glass with water a couple more times to drink. I'm beyond freezing but feel better after puking. As though I've purged myself. I go back in for my phone and shine it around looking for a hose. The beam falls on a plant pot, so I fill that a few times to swill the mess. Shit. Shit. Shit. I can't believe what I've done.

Back inside, I'm beyond grateful that Sacha chucked my bag in with the blanket. I peel off the wet jeans and boxers and scrunch them into a zipped compartment of my holdall. Then I tug on a pair of joggers and a clean t-shirt. Exhausted, I slump back to the sofa. Thank God I made it outside. I daren't lie down again in case the spinning continues. Maybe I won't make it outside again. Tears roll down my face. I can't go on like this. I never cry, but once I start, I can't stop. *What sort of a man am I?*

4

Freya bounces up and down in the doorway, her voice grating at the inside of my brain like metal on metal. "He's been. He's been."

I blink in the emerging dawn, tempted to tell her to do one. That would go down well.

"Ugh. Grandad. There's an awful smell in here." Matilda appears at Freya's side and looks back over her shoulder at Stuart. Then the dog runs in after them and leaps on me. I think the dog is the only member of this family who gives me the time of day. Even so, his paws on my tender stomach and slimy tongue on my face are not welcome right now. I throw him off, and he lands with a yelp.

"What's that smell?" Freya wrinkles her nose.

Great. I feel like death and have got these three staring at me. I shouldn't have pissed Sacha off. Suddenly the airbed, tucked away in a room unpopulated by Christmas presents seems like a great place to be.

I raise myself to my elbows and tug the blanket up to my chin. It's absolutely freezing in here. As Stuart flicks the heater on, the girls rip into the pile of presents.

"I think you'd better freshen up." He looks at me as though I'm diseased as he pushes a window open.

"Good grief. Has someone died in here? It reeks."

An unfortunate choice of words, dear brother-in-law, I want to say to Greg but obviously don't. Personally, I can't smell anything. Today he's wearing a Batman t-shirt. Who the hell does he think he is?

"I wouldn't come in here just yet." Greg puts his arm out to stop Rebecca from coming in. "The smell won't do you any good, in your current state." She also stares at me, her dressing gown fastened around her bump. As I register their expressions of disgust, I realise I'm going to be sick again. I grab my holdall, push past them and dart along the hallway, praying that no one is in the bathroom.

I don't know how long I lie on the bathroom floor, oddly comforted by the chill of the tiles whilst the heat from the towel rail wafts over me. Sacha is going to kill me. I should just hide in here all day. There are other toilets for the family to use. Though really, I think I'm going to head to Dad's. My head throbs against the hard floor as I consider whether I'll still be over the limit to drive. I try to tot up how many drinks I had yesterday, how many units of alcohol... I can't think straight.

I jump as there's a thumping at the door. "Are you OK in there Neil?" Christy's concern, whether or not genuine, invites tears to stab their heat at the back of my eyes.

"Yeah. I'm just about to have a shower then I'll be out." I've got to pull myself together. I haul myself up and undress before fiddling with the shower dials, gasping under the initially freezing water, then feel comforted as it finally warms up. If only my misery could be rinsed away as easily as the odours, which will no doubt be the talk of everyone this morning.

I brush my teeth, then down several tumblers of water,

wincing as the chill slips straight into my stomach. I'm not going anywhere near spirits today. I'm never feeling like this again. However, I might need a couple of beers to bring me around. Hair of the dog and all that.

As I emerge from the bathroom, the girls shrieking combined with conversation and the dog going mad echoes from the back of the house. No, thank you. I creep into the lounge instead.

Christy is in there, her feet tucked under herself. "I'm keeping out of the way." She looks up from the magazine she's flicking through. "I don't do kids, as you know."

"Thanks by the way." My voice cracks as I speak. "For checking on me." I sit in the armchair where Adam was last night.

"Someone has to." She rests her magazine on the arm of the sofa. "How are you feeling?"

"Rough."

"You and me both." She laughs. "Though I win the contest for being able to hold my drink."

"What do you mean?"

"Well, let's just say you're not winning any popularity contests this morning. Mum and Dad weren't too impressed with the patio."

"Shit. I tried to clean it up. I really did."

"At least you got outside. That's what I told them. See – I stuck up for you."

"Thanks. What's Sacha said about it?"

"I'd give her a wide berth if I was you." Christy laughs again. "She's fuming." Then a pause. "She's not herself though, is she? I've been watching how she's struggling with this baby business. She's barely speaking to Rebecca – in fact, it's like all the happiness has been sucked out of her. I'm so glad I decided not to have bloody children."

"Let's not go there right now." Why does everyone have to

bring up the fact that Sacha and I can't conceive? My shoulders slump under the weight of my depression. The smell of bacon wafts into the room and my stomach churns. Normally it's one of my favourite smells.

"I'm going to get some air." I rise back to my feet.

I sink to the bench at the front of the house and look around the quiet cul-de-sac. Trees twinkle in windows and wreaths hang from doors. It's the sort of street I'd love us to move to. Our house is OK for our first home, albeit poky. The builders clearly packed as many houses as possible onto their plot of land. I imagine the families occupying the homes around where I'm sitting, all festive. I bet there's nobody, *nobody,* who feels a fraction as ill as I do today.

In a couple of hours, I should be fit to drive. Sacha can travel back with Adam and Christy when she's done here. I need to get away from the lot of them. I slide my phone from my pocket and press the call button next to Dad. He usually answers first ring but today it nearly goes to voice mail before he picks up.

"Neil," he says. "Merry Christmas son."

"Same to you Dad. How are you doing?"

"Yeah, fine thanks. I'm just having a tidy round. I've got a few mates from the Irish Centre coming over in a couple of hours. I've got mass first though so I can't talk for long."

"Sounds good." It really doesn't. I wanted to go to Dad's for some peace and normality, not to sit with his mates from the Irish Centre. Still, it's better than being here. "I was thinking of driving back, actually."

"Driving back? From where?"

"I told you we were spending Christmas with Sacha's family, didn't I?" I watch as a bird of some description lands on the grass in front of me. I can hear echoes of the family coming from inside. I'll stay out here for as long as I can stand the cold.

"Yes. As well you should. Especially with what her dad's facing."

"It's a nightmare Dad. So depressing. It's all any of them are talking about. I ended up getting blitzed last night."

"That was sensible son. I bet Sacha is over the moon with you this morning."

"Tell me about it. Anyway, I could do with escaping from here and was thinking of coming to yours."

"Like I said Neil, I've got company this afternoon. And I think it'd be best if you stay where you are. With your wife."

Great. Even my dad doesn't want me. "Are you saying I can't come?"

"I'm saying I don't think it's a good idea. Come round when you get back in a couple of days."

"Cheers Dad." My voice wobbles. "Have a good day." I end the call, wondering what to do. I might just drive home. Yes, that's exactly what I'll do. Then my heart sinks towards my feet as Sacha emerges from the side of the house. Here we bloody go.

"I wondered where you'd gone." She sits beside me, leaving a greater distance than she usually would.

"Well, wonder no more." I force a smile. "I'm right here."

"Aren't you cold?" She points at my bare feet.

"I think I'm too hungover to be anything."

"I can't believe how you've behaved Neil." Her voice is calm, and she doesn't look angry. More *disappointed.* That's probably worse. "This is my dad's last Christmas with us all. Meanwhile, you get wasted and throw up all over his garden." The bench creaks as she turns to look at me with tears in her eyes. She's got the knack of making me feel like a piece of shit every bloody time. I'd definitely prefer her anger to *this.*

"Getting drunk is hardly crime of the century is it?"

"It's not the behaviour of a grown man spending Christmas with his in laws, especially his terminally ill father-in-law."

"Sorry Saint Sacha. I keep forgetting how perfect you are." I squint in the sunshine which illuminates the top of her head, the light almost forming a halo. *Saint Sacha*. I notice she's got a face full of make-up again. She looks better without it, but she won't be told. I press my hands together in my lap, trying to evaluate how I'm feeling and how long it'll be before I can drive home.

"You're supposed to be taking antidepressants." Her breath forms clouds in the air as she speaks. "I thought we were meant to be improving our chances of getting onto the waiting list for treatment."

"And, as my wife, you're meant to be more understanding. Do you know how awful I feel at the moment?" Maybe it's time to spill my guts to her. Figuratively, not literally. There's been enough of that. Perhaps what's happening is the universe's way of saying I'm not fit to look after a baby.

"You deserve to feel awful. Sorry Neil but I've got no sympathy with you." I notice a new bracelet glittering from her wrist. One of her family must've given it to her. I remember then that I haven't bought her a Christmas present and feel even more of a shit.

"I don't just mean hungover - I'm talking about the depression." The heat of the tears returns to the back of my eyes. Suddenly, I need to talk about it. It's the first time I have.

"Which is why you've been prescribed antidepressants."

"But I don't want to be on them."

"If you'd broken your arm, you'd get it treated, why not your mind?"

"They're not going to work. They just make me drowsy. I can't go on like this Sacha. I need your help." I wonder if she picks up on the tremble in my voice.

"They *are* going to work and you're just feeling sorry for yourself because you're hungover. Look, Neil, pull yourself together and stay off the drink today. Then get back on the tablets. Mum and Dad will calm down - maybe we can salvage something of Christmas, for Dad's sake if nothing else."

It's all about Stuart. She's swatted how I'm feeling away, like an insect. "I'm sorry Sacha. I'm going home."

"What do you mean – you're going home?"

"I can't stay here. I want to go back to Leeds."

"To your dad's?" She crosses one red leg over another, and I notice she's wearing some all in one trouser thing that I haven't seen before. And heels again. Who wears heels when they're inside all day at their parent's house? Who's she trying to impress? Not me, that's for certain.

"No, my dad's got company. I'm just going to drive home and have a quiet one. The way I'm feeling, that's all I want to do today."

"Get pissed again, you mean?" Anger glitters from her eyes.

"I didn't want to be here in the first place. I told you."

"It's not all about you, Neil. Don't you think I'm struggling at the moment too? When are you going to support me instead of moaning about yourself all the time?"

"I'm sorry Sacha. Please, just let me go home. You'll have a far better time without my miserable mug hanging around. I'll make it up to you, I promise."

"If you think I'm going to let you drive in that state, you've got another thing coming. After all the whiskey you put away last night, you'll still be well over the limit. God, you're an idiot. When are you going to grow up?"

"I'll be good to go after a coffee. And stop slagging me off. I'm sick of it."

"Well, I'm not letting you drive. No chance."

"It's my car as much as yours."

"So when you kill someone, or yourself, I've got to live with that on my conscience?"

"I won't kill anyone. Apart from Adam or Greg if I stay here. You're being melodramatic."

"I know you won't because you're not getting your hands on the keys. I'm telling you."

"And I'm telling you. You're trying to control me Sacha. I'm not having it. And I'll get Ash to come and pick me up if you hide the keys from me."

"So you'd ruin your mate's Christmas and drag him away from his family for a four hour round trip? Are you really too selfish and cowardly to go in there, apologise to my parents, and start again?"

"Will you please stop with the name calling and insults? Talk about kicking a dog when it's down."

Sacha falls silent for a moment. "Look, do what you want Neil, but I'm warning you now, if you clear off and leave me on Christmas Day and humiliate me even more than you already have done in front of my family, we're over. You can move out of the house. Have you got that?"

"Out with the ultimatum!" Although I've been considering that Sacha would be better off without me, her threat fills me with a cold fear. Being married is lonely and depressing enough. But how would I cope on my own? On some level, Sacha actually cares about me. Where would I be if nobody did?

In a box, that's where.

5

THE BLAST of warmth as I enter the kitchen through the back door is comforting. I might try to manage some toast and coffee soon, now I'm feeling slightly more human.

"Wendy. Stuart. Can I have a word please? In private?"

"Neil's come to eat humble pie." Adam throws his head back as he laughs. I want to knock it off. "Let's hope he doesn't barf it over the patio."

I ignore him and also ignore Greg and Rebecca sniggering. I glance through to the conservatory where the girls are for once, quiet, immersed in some game together, whilst the dog slumbers on the sofa.

"I'll take charge of the dinner Mum." Christy comes up behind her mother. "Whilst you and Dad speak to Neil."

I smile at her. I've definitely got an ally in Sacha's sister. She's the only one.

"We'll go through to my office," Stuart says stiffly, as though he's going to fire me. This is going to be such a fun conversation.

I look at Sacha to see whether she's going to take part in this conversation with her parents, but she gives me a cold stare before sitting down with the others.

Wendy, Stuart and I follow each other along the hallway. I notice the photographs of the three girls at various life stages as I lag behind. Sacha with her untroubled smile before I came along to wipe it from her face. Stuart opens the door to his office, and I feel the same sense of foreboding as yesterday when I got into the car to come here.

"Have a seat." Stuart gestures to the corner sofa, which I perch on the edge of. Wendy sits on the other side of it, and Stuart sits behind the desk. There's nothing on it apart from a pen pot and a computer. I'm not really sure why he'd need an office in his house, particularly when he's terminally ill. If he'd turned it into a bedroom instead, at least Sacha and I would've had somewhere to escape to last night. Things might have been better then.

"I feel as though you're about to interview me." My laugh sounds hollow in the sparsely furnished room.

Stuart doesn't raise a smile. "Well, if it was for the role of being my daughter's husband, I'm afraid you wouldn't get the job."

Ouch. I glance at Wendy whose expression is passive. Clearly, she agrees with him. An apron covers her trousers and tunic, and she has a sprinkling of flour on her sleeve.

"That's harsh Stuart." I squint in the direct sunlight as I try to look at him, though I find eye contact with anyone difficult these days. Any self-confidence I had has drained from me. I wish I could go home. I'm ashamed I've allowed myself to be told what to do this Christmas.

"I'm not liking what I'm seeing or what I'm hearing Neil." Stuart rests his elbows on the desk. "Not one bit. It sounds as though you need to sort yourself out. And quickly."

"What is it you're seeing and hearing?" I'm not sure who he

thinks he is, sitting behind his poxy desk in judgment of me, but I'll run with it for now.

"We all saw what you are capable of first-hand last night, and I gather that this out-of-control drinking has become a regular occurrence."

I'm not sure whether it is a question or a statement. "Who told you that? It's rubbish. I haven't been as drunk as I was last night since I was a teenager." That's not strictly true, but I'll tell him what I want him to hear.

"Never mind who told me what. Do you have a drink problem Neil?"

"Whether I have or I haven't Stuart, with all respect, you'd be the last person I'd talk to about it." It's true. He doesn't give a rat's arse about me and obviously wishes his precious daughter had chosen better for herself.

"You could always try Alcoholics Anonymous." Wendy's voice is gentler than Stuart's as she clasps her hands together in her lap. Perhaps she means well, but I don't need this right now. My head's pounding. I remind myself that it's Christmas Day, a day of supposed happiness. It feels more like Doomsday.

"I'm also hearing that you're unable to hold down a job." Stuart massages the bridge of his nose under his glasses. The shirt he's wearing must be new. It's creased from its packet and hangs off him. He's a dying man and is becoming a flicker of the person he was. I won't get into an argument with him, not that I've the energy for an argument. Instead, I'll allow him his moment of power and authority.

"I've had a few problems lately, admittedly." My voice is shaky. I wish they were talking to me because they *did* give a toss about me. They're only talking to me because of Sacha. It feels shit. I want someone to care about *me* for a change.

"What problems?" Wendy tucks her hands under her legs and leans forward on the sofa.

"Look I don't want to go into things too much." I stare at the pattern on the carpet. "Not on Christmas Day. All I'll say is that I'm going to get it sorted. Once and for all."

Stuart clears his throat. "As you know, I won't be around much longer Neil. I need to know my daughter is alright with you."

"Of course she's alright with me." My voice rises now. "What do you mean by that?" *What sort of lowlife does he think I am?*

"Sacha's lost all her sparkle," Wendy says. "She's very quiet. Both Stuart and I have noticed, and we're worried about her. And you." That's crap. She adds the words *and you* as an afterthought. "We want to help, if we can."

"You know we've got all this fertility stuff going on, but to be honest, it doesn't feel appropriate for me to discuss it with you." I'd rather boil my head. "Look Stuart. I'll sort it."

"Well, you better had. I'm going to be watching you, and I'll tell you now..."

God, my father-in-law is threatening me. What's so awful about me that makes people think they can judge, threaten, and look down their noses? I've had enough. I'd better say something to appease him, so he'll let me go. Right now I'm a disgusting specimen under his microscope. "Look I'm really sorry about last night. Getting drunk and throwing up in your garden was unforgiveable, and I'm truly ashamed of myself." It's true. I really am sorry for that one, but what else can I say? I can't turn the clock back, no matter how much I want to.

"OK Neil. Let's put it behind us, shall we?" Wendy pats my hand. "We just want to make this a special Christmas, don't we Stuart? It means a lot to us to have our family around."

"I'd thank you not to get into a similar state today Neil," Stuart says stiffly. "I hope you'll show a bit more respect for our home if you're continuing to stay with us."

Like I have a choice in the matter. "If you don't mind, I'm going to get some toast to settle my stomach." I get to my feet and look from Stuart to Wendy. "I really am sorry, and I really will sort it." I don't care if he has anything else to say to me. I've apologised and need to get out of this oppressive room. It looks as though I'm stuck here for the next couple of days. It's not worth the hassle it will cause with Sacha to go anywhere.

I'll have to find myself a quiet corner again. But not get so drunk in it this time. I'll probably fall asleep as I didn't sleep properly last night. In between being ill, I think I probably fell into some sort of whiskey-induced coma. Right now, I wish I could fall asleep and never wake up.

"Neil. Neil." I wake to find Christy tugging at my sleeve. The bloody dog runs up behind her, lands on my belly and licks frantically at my face. I like the dog, but he only seems to give any attention to me when I'm waking up or feeling like death.

"Gerroff." I raise my head and blink in the light of the fire. If the truth be known, I don't want to get off this comfy sofa and wish everyone would leave me alone. "How long have I been asleep?"

"Oh, about three hours," she laughs. "We thought we'd better leave you be, though it's been tricky keeping the kids out of here."

"Thanks. I needed a kip to be honest." I swing my legs around and put my feet on the floor. "Blimey, it's getting dark already."

"You've had a fun Christmas Day, haven't you?" Christy sits in the space I've created.

"I'm not really bothered to be honest. It's not about me. It's about you three spending time with your dad, isn't it? And the kids." I rub at my eyes, picking the sleepy crusts from the corners. My mouth feels like something has rotted in it. I reach for the glass of water I poured before I fell asleep.

"I guess so. It's pretty rough for us all right now." She looks down at her hands. "Dad's holding up well today, but it's horrible, knowing this is his last Christmas." Christy pulls an elastic band from her wrist and twists her hair into a ponytail. Her hair is exactly the same brown as Sacha's. They're very alike, though Christy is more relaxed in leggings and a jumper, not a bloody trouser suit get up. She hasn't got a face full of make-up either.

"How's Sacha doing?"

"Not too great. She's had a few tears with Dad this afternoon. She's just helping Mum serve up now."

"Dinner? Already?"

"Yep, that's why I'm waking you. You didn't want to sleep through dinner, did you?" She gives me a look though, which says she knows I would probably have wanted to.

I wonder if anyone else would've bothered to wake me. If it were not for Christy, perhaps they would've just enjoyed their Christmas meal, and maybe stuck a plate in the microwave for me. I wouldn't have been missed, not even by Sacha. Not that I'm even sure I can face a big Christmas dinner. But what choice have I got? After everything else, it will look pretty bad if I boycott it. I drink the last of my water and get unsteadily to my feet. "I'll nip to the bathroom and then I'll be through."

"Good stuff. See you soon. I'll save you a place."

I feel spaced out as I head towards the chatter and clinking of glasses and crockery. I'll definitely need a couple of drinks to bring me round, but I'm going to be sensible. The sudden glare of light makes my eyes ache and I look around the room to see where I'm supposed to sit. In between Sacha and Christy by the looks of it. That's probably the best I could hope for. All I've eaten today is a slice of toast, so my stomach inadvertently rumbles in response to the smell of Christmas dinner.

"Uncle Neil. Pull my cracker with me." Freya thrusts it into my face. I'm comforted by her choosing me and by the fact that she's referred to me as *uncle*. It's a small comfort, but I've got to hang onto whatever I can at the moment. I've read up on depression, and one way of coping is to try each day, to look for simple, positive things. Though often, they're hard to find. Sometimes I feel as though this black hole will devour me. I look around at those already seated, laughing and chatting, wondering what they could find to laugh about. I can barely raise a smile at the moment.

"Are you feeling better after your sleep?" Sacha's tone is stilted, but at least she's making conversation.

"Yeah, I'm fine now. Thanks for asking." I reach for her hand, but she pulls it away. So I reach for the glass of fizz at the side of my plate and down it.

"That's supposed to go with dinner," she hisses. "No one else has drunk theirs yet."

"Sorry, I'm dehydrated. It's do or die for me today." I force a laugh. "A couple of drinks with dinner will help me feel human again and then I'll leave it alone for the rest of the day, I promise." I sense we're being watched and as I look up, the eyes of Stuart and Greg are boring into me. Then they look at each other. I feel so utterly disliked and wish for the millionth time I wasn't here.

"You OK?" Greg mouths at Sacha from across the table.

She nods at him and looks away. Rebecca is watching everyone intently. It's probably the most excitement she's ever known.

I want to tell Greg to mind his own business and I sit for a moment, wondering what to do for the best. Instead, I call out. "Can I help you with anything Wendy?" I force some joviality into my voice. At least if I'm in the kitchen, I can snaffle a beer or two from the utility room.

Adam laughs. "Neil's trying to earn himself some brownie points. You can't beat a spot of grovelling."

I ignore him and slide my chair back.

"It's fine. All under control thanks." Wendy wipes her hands on a towel as I approach her. "Sacha and Christy have helped. You just relax for now. You can help with the clearing up afterwards if you want to make yourself useful."

"Done." I grin. "Is it alright if I get myself a beer?"

"Is that a good idea Neil?" Wendy pours gravy into a jug.

"It's Christmas. I promise I'll take it easy today! Besides, a couple might help me feel more human." I force a laugh, though the situation is far from funny.

The conversation at the table fades and I realise everyone is listening in to what Wendy and I are saying to each other. As I return to my place, I notice my glass has been refilled. Christy winks at me and I start to feel more settled in myself. Maybe Christmas dinner won't be too bad after all.

6

REBECCA HEAVES herself up and grips the table. "A toast." Her belly is absolutely enormous. I can't imagine Sacha ever looking like that if we got the miracle that's required. Though often, I'm unsure whether I still want us to have a baby. After all, I can barely look after myself at the moment, let alone have a baby depend on me. I watch as Sacha turns her attention to her sister. The same look of hunger is in her eyes that I saw yesterday, which makes me feel even less of a man.

"To our amazing dad." Rebecca raises her glass of orange. "We all love you to pieces, you're the most amazing father and grandfather in the world, and I don't know how..." Her voice trembles as she notices Freya and Matilda. They're both watching her, having lifted their gazes from the electronic devices which have been keeping them quiet since they finished eating. Whatever Rebecca was about to say, she's evidently changed her mind about it, and eases herself back into her seat instead. Greg places his hand on her arm and Sacha watches on, looking more miserable than I've ever seen. We're officially a million miles away from each other.

Stuart stands from his seat at the head of the table. Of

course, where else would he sit? Oh no, he's going to make a speech. Here we go. He sweeps his gaze over the table and everyone falls quiet. "First, I'd like to thank you all for spending Christmas with Wendy and myself."

He was a chief executive of some company or other before he went off sick last year, and he runs his family like a business too. Look at how he called me into his office earlier.

"It means a lot to us that you're here after what has been an incredibly difficult year - one that I could never have coped with without the support of my wonderful wife, and of course, you, my family. I'm so proud of each and..." His gaze falls on me and his expression hardens. Prick.

"I'm so proud of you all, and proud to call you my family. When I'm no longer around, somehow, I'll still be here with you."

"Oh, Stuart." Wendy dabs at her eyes with a napkin. She's still wearing her apron from cooking.

I'll still be here. He's probably going to haunt us all. He said in his office, *I'll be watching you...* However, that look he just gave me. I'm not part of this family. I never have been. This will definitely be the last Christmas I spend with these people.

Adam taps his glass with a spoon next. He has to get in on things and likes nothing more than the sound of his own voice.

"Right, since we all seem to be making speeches, I'll say a few words as well." He holds his glass aloft. "To the best in laws, Stuart and Wendy." He spills prosecco from his glass as he jerks it higher. He looks to have had plenty to drink. "To family, and to Neil."

My face flames as several pairs of eyes turn to me. As I scan the room, I notice that Greg looks amused whilst Christy's mouth has twisted itself into an angry pout directed at her husband.

"Ignore him." Sacha finally reaches for my hand, probably

trying to placate me. It's taken Adam's behaviour for Sacha to throw a few crumbs of attention my way.

"No, I will not ignore him. Why should I?" My voice rises. "What do you mean, Adam - *to family, and Neil?* Whether or not you like it, I'm married to your sister-in-law. I *am* family." I really hate him, the narcissist piece of shit. He's going to get what's coming to him.

"Not for much longer by the look of you both." Adam drains his prosecco, his eyes not leaving my face, his mouth contorted into a sneer.

"Shut up Adam. I mean it." Sacha now. I wondered if she'd get involved.

There's an eerie quiet around the table, and a look passes between Sacha and Greg. This is why I didn't want to spend Christmas with Sacha's family. Perhaps, *now*, she'll finally give me the car keys and let me escape.

"What's up Neil? Cat got your tongue?"

"What's your bloody problem Adam? Why can't you leave me alone?"

"I wish I could leave you alone. For good. The sooner Sacha sees the light and kicks you into touch, the better." He drops back into his seat.

"You're nothing but a fucking prick, Adam." I don't give a shit anymore. The red mist of rage has descended on me. I hope they throw me out into the night. As long as it's with the car keys.

Rebecca's mouth drops open and a gasp rises around the table. Stuart rises with it, glasses and cutlery rattling as he thumps the table.

"Right," he booms, like the company director he was. He doesn't scare me one bit, and if he sides with Adam after that little display...

"Girls, go to the lounge." I hear Rebecca's voice in the pause as Stuart presumably decides what words of authority he's going to impart. "Now."

He watches as the girls scuttle from the room, then looks from Adam to me over the top of his glasses. The situation would be almost amusing if I didn't feel so low. "You both know this is the last Christmas we'll have together as a family," he begins. "You know how ill I am. And yet..."

"As a *family*," I snort. "I've been made to feel anything but part of your bloody family. And as for that dickhead..." I point at Adam.

"I won't have your sort of language at my table." Stuart thumps the table again. "Who do you think you are, coming into my home and behaving like you do?"

"Well said Stuart." Adam refills his glass. "If anyone's a dickhead, it's Neil."

"Calm down, for goodness sake," Wendy sobs. "All of you."

Greg is nodding in agreement with Adam. I glare at him. He's too cowardly to say what he thinks as an individual, but always happy to hang onto Adam's coat tails. They would have made a good pair of bullies in their childhood.

"Enough Adam." Christy speaks for the first time in all this. I imagine she'll give him some right grief later. She's the only person who has shown any sort of solidarity towards me since we've been here. Mostly, Sacha has looked as though she can't bear to be anywhere near me. And deep down, I don't blame her.

"You're like a pair of children. Both of you." Wendy wipes her eyes with her napkin, the ink of the holly leaves leaving green streaks on her face. "I can't sit at this table with you any longer. Aren't things difficult enough?" There's a moment of silence then she says in a louder voice. "In fact, you can both clear off."

"Clear off? Chance would be a fine thing? Sacha's made it quite clear that she won't give me the keys to the car."

"You and Adam, you can go for a walk - sort out your differences once and for all. I don't care how long it takes, but don't come back here until you can act like a pair of grown-ups in our home. I mean it."

"Well said Mum."

I glare at Rebecca now, who I've never been fond of, then turn to Wendy. "You really expect me to go for a walk with *him*? Give over."

"Between you, and especially *you* Neil, this Christmas, which was supposed to be special for us, has turned into a fiasco. I want you out of my sight until your differences are resolved, or at the very least, shelved until you get back to Leeds. I've had enough, I really have."

I turn to Sacha, wondering whether she'll stick up for me.

"You heard what Mum said." A curtain of her hair hides her face. She won't even look at me.

I thrust my hands into my pockets as we stride away from the bungalow, walking as far apart as we can along the pavement. There's a momentary comfort from the early evening chill as I warm my palms against my legs through my jeans pockets. My jagged breath forms clouds in the air.

The surrounding houses have drawn their curtains against the darkness, and I feel envious of the Christmases they're probably enjoying behind them. My dad enters my mind and I feel envious of the Christmas he'll be enjoying as well. Probably even more without me there. I feel as though I'll enjoy nothing again.

I stride away from Adam once we've left the cul-de-sac and have got onto the main street. He's the last person I want to go for a walk with, and I'm shocked that Wendy has cast us out like a pair of naughty kids. I really have nothing to say to him.

I don't know how Sacha and I are going to come back from

this. Trying to recall a time when I felt any joy or purpose is like bringing to mind the life of another person. I can barely recall when we last slept in the same bed.

The pub and village store are shuttered up, and the sight of them somehow adds to my sense of desolation. I can hide in the hustle and bustle of normal life, but the darkness and quiet will only ever devour me.

From the main street, I find myself in the pitch black of the coastal road and decide to head towards the clifftop. The sound of the waves might help clear my jumbled thinking. It's certainly a relief to be alone. There's no truer saying that you can be in a roomful of people and still feel lonely. These last twenty-four hours have definitely forced me to admit how low I have sunk.

After a few minutes, I check to see if Adam is still following. There's no sign of him. Whilst one part of me is relieved, the other knows I probably can't return to the bungalow without us at least trying to speak to each other. Although surely Wendy can't refuse to let us in. Adam and I will have to agree to lie about having discussed our differences. That means finding him though.

He's certainly the brother-in-law from hell, and Greg isn't much better, although more covert. He just sits there, agreeing with Adam and sneering at me. I know I'm a mess right now, but the two of them are making me worse. I wonder if they'd lay off me, if Sacha was to tell them the extent of the depression I'm drowning in. Although I'm not even sure she really believes me or if she's even interested. As far as she's concerned, I'm using it as an excuse not to go to work and to keep drinking. Yet I would give anything, *anything* to feel better.

I have two choices. Either I try to find Adam, or I disappear. "Adam," I shout into the night, my voice sounding strange. I hate even having to verbalise his name. I stop for a moment and am taken aback at how silent it is now that my footsteps have stilled. I look up, noticing the plough formation in the sky and the intermittent beam of the lighthouse from Flamborough Head, just up the coastal road. Maybe I'll walk along the cliff path to Flamborough for old time's sake. I used to stay there as a kid. My parents would rent a caravan, well they did before my mother left us. It's probably not a good idea walking up there now. I'm wearing my thinnest jacket, and my hands are like blocks of ice. I've given up trying to keep them warm in my pockets. The cold has got into my bones.

As my eyes become accustomed to the dark, I'm drawn to the inky black void ahead of me. I walk towards it, the longer I walk, the more my thoughts are lulled as the sound of lashing waves gradually becomes louder. There's something bleak about the coast in the winter, especially at night. I let out an audible sigh, as though trying to dispel some of my melancholy into the sea several hundred feet below. The chalk of the cliff top path grinds under my trainers as I walk. l head towards a bench I can recall being here. I need to think. I need to work out what to do next.

I'm not sure how long I sit here but am suddenly aware of tears warming my numb cheeks. At least I've finally stopped shivering and seem to have become accustomed to the cold. Usually, I love being beside the sea, well at the moment, I'm three hundred feet above it. But tonight, its vast blackness and overpowering echo makes me feel even more insignificant than normal. I know what I need to do.

"Good one prick." Adam's voice grates into my thoughts. "We're supposed to be calling some sort of truce and you piss off into the night."

"Call a truce. With you? In your dreams. Get lost Adam. I've got nothing to say to you."

"Do you know something Neil? You're just a fucking charity

case." Adam sits at the other end of the bench, his angry voice sounding even louder in the silence. "You leach off other people. What have you ever achieved in life? What do you contribute? Absolutely sod all."

He emphasises the last two words to the extent that I want to rip his head off. I take a deep breath. He has got to me enough. I won't give him the satisfaction of retaliating.

"Do one, will you? Go back to the house. You'll get no conversation from me."

"Sacha's only with you because she feels sorry for you. She's scared to leave you because she thinks you'll do something stupid."

"That's not true." Though deep inside I know it probably is.

"Yet it wouldn't be stupid, would it Neil?" His voice is dripping with pure hatred. "Maybe you should dive off this cliff right now."

"You know nothing about my marriage."

"Do you want to bet on that? I could teach you a thing or two about your wife."

I turn to him. "Go on then. Teach me, you lying arsehole."

"Nah. It's far more fun watching you stew in your own juices. Parasite."

My hands curl into a fist. I'll deck him if he says much more, especially about Sacha. But maybe the top of one of the highest cliffs in England isn't the best place for a fight. Although, maybe Adam's right. Perhaps it would be best all round if I went over the top of it. Maybe that's what I deserve.

"What's it like not being able to get your wife up the stick?" Oh God, he's still going. And he's going for the jugular. "How do you cope with disappointing her month in, month out?"

"That's not true. And anyway, how I live my life is none of your business Adam." My voice is a snarl. I can't remember ever feeling this livid.

"It is when your wife turns up at our house every five minutes moaning about her shitty life with you."

"You're lying." Although, I know he isn't. It's not the first time I've been told that Sacha is gossiping about me.

"I'm not. Look mate."

"Don't ever call me *mate*." It's a good job we're not near any houses. Our raised voices would be enough to pique anybody's interest. They'd probably call the police.

"Why don't you do everyone a favour Neil, and just disappear. Let Sacha get on with her life."

My anger suddenly dissipates, and I'm more in despair than I've ever been. "*Disappear?* What are you talking about? What have I ever done so bad to you Adam? Or maybe you're after Sacha for yourself?"

"At least I can give her what she wants." He laughs, though it's more of a cackle. "Maybe that could be our truce. Our way forward. We can go back and tell Wendy."

"Tell Wendy what?" I jump to my feet, anger blinding me. He really is the vilest human I've ever encountered. I've sometimes wondered if it's just a clash of personalities between us, or if I'm overreacting to how he is with me. But no, he really is an absolute bastard.

"We can tell her I'm going to solve all your problems by inseminating your wife. I reckon we might need a few tries at it though."

Did he really just say that? I grab him by the scruff of his coat and drag him from the bench. Simultaneously, I release my grip and hurl my fist into his face. "You scumbag." I spit the words out. "You stay away from my wife."

"It's a bit late for that." In the moonlight, I watch as his hand flies to his face where I've just smacked him.

"Are you telling me you've already shagged each other?"

"What do you think?" In the moonlight, I can see his smirk.

I punch him again, feeling his nose explode under my icy fist. "Fucking bastard."

"You're gonna regret that." He throws one back at me and misses.

"That the best you've got?"

He comes at me, grips me by the top of my arm and brings his knee up between my legs, hard. I fall backwards to the floor in agony. What sort of bloke does that to another bloke? We all know the pain of being booted in the balls is worse than dying. For a few minutes, he watches, panting, as I writhe around on the floor, coughing and retching. Then he grabs my wrist and yanks me back to my feet. Normally I could fight him off, but after a kick in the balls, I'm at a huge disadvantage.

"Get the..." I can't breathe, "hell away from me." I gasp, as he pushes me along the chalk path, gripping my arms in the same way as before. I'm still winded from the blow, and am struggling to get any breath in. "This has gone," I gasp again, "too far now." I still can't get a full breath. "Leave it."

Suddenly he stops. He releases his grip on me, and I'm amazed he's listened. We turn towards the sea, both puffing and blowing in the silence. A wave of nausea washes over me, followed by more waves of pain. I don't know which is worse, the physical or the mental, and can hardly tell them apart. I can't live like this anymore. I'm not going to...

PART II

SACHA

7

For the millionth time, I pull the curtain to the side and look down the dimly lit street. "They left ages ago."

"Relax Sacha. They'll be fine." Mum turns back to the puzzle she's helping Freya with. Matilda is curled up next to her mother, fast asleep, the lights from the Christmas tree casting colours across her face. "And hopefully, they'll start acting like adults when they get back."

"I don't know if it was a good idea Mum, sending them off like that. They'll probably kill each other." However, I have to admit there's a calmer atmosphere since they left. Initially, after the front door slammed, I was in tears, but a glass of wine and a hug off Mum and Christy has brought me around.

Lately, I've been forced to accept that my marriage is in big, big trouble. I don't feel the same about Neil as I used to. The attraction I once had has waned, along with any respect. But even after all that's been going on, I'm not ready to completely give up on us. At least not whilst he's in the state he's in. If I can just get him to sort himself out...

Despite my jumbled thoughts, I smile as I notice the dog

stretched out in front of the fire. I wish I could have his peace and simplicity.

Dad's gone for a lie down. He gets so tired and all this, well, it's no wonder he can't cope with it, especially with everything else he's facing. Even though he said he's not blaming me, guilt is eating me up.

"I've just tried Adam." Christy rests her phone on the arm of the sofa. "It's going straight to voicemail."

"It's a poor signal around here." Wendy looks up from the puzzle. "There's one network that doesn't get any coverage at all. Rebecca, have you tried Greg's phone since he left? I wonder if he's found them yet."

"I'm sure he will have done. I just hope he hasn't become involved with it all." Rebecca rests her cup on her bump and shuffles back in the armchair. I'm sure she draws attention to her baby bump on purpose, to upset me. *Look at me. I can have babies.* She's always been the same. Anything you can do, I can do better – anything you can't do, I definitely can. My smug sister maybe needs a reminder about karma.

"I know Greg's not Neil's greatest fan at the moment. Not after the way he's carried on. But I want him to keep out of it."

"Alright Rebecca." My voice rises as I glare at my sister. I don't see her face or her clothes or anything about her anymore. All I see is her enormous belly. And I hate her for it. Maybe Neil was right. Perhaps we shouldn't have come. I could have spent some time with my parents in the new year when the rest of them aren't here.

"Just saying Sacha. God."

"Why didn't Greg go in his car to look for them?" I look out of the window... again. "At least he would have had some light to find them."

"He had a couple of drinks with his dinner," Rebecca replies. "If he has even a drop to drink, he won't drive. He's not really used to drinking."

Unlike Neil, her expression seems to say.

Mum must notice the look that passes between us. "Right," she says. "There's no point worrying and gawping out of the window." She finishes the last piece of the puzzle and grips the edge of the sofa as she rises from the floor. "Let's just relax and remember it's adults we're talking about here, despite how they carried on at the table. All will be well. Why don't I cut us all a slice of my lovely Christmas cake?"

It would take a hard heart not to love my mum. She's always so cheery and optimistic and there's never much that can't be solved with cake. God knows how she'll handle things when my dad passes though. I close my eyes against the thought. Our family's got an absolute nightmare to face. No wonder they wanted to spend a peaceful Christmas with us. Next year we'll probably all be here like this, but without Dad. She won't be able to solve that one with cake.

Personally, I think he should fight harder, as I've discussed with Christy, but he's been told it's terminal, no matter what. He could have prolonged his life by trying different combinations of treatment, but he chose to have what he sees as more of a quality end of life, free of sickness and hair loss, albeit a shorter life, as a result.

"Not for me, thanks Mum." I couldn't eat a thing. I've been feeling waves of nausea all day. I always do when I'm stressed. And it's all Neil's fault. He's been a complete idiot whilst we've been here. The writing was on the wall when he was pouring cans of beer down his neck in the car when we were driving over. I should've let him go to his dad's. Bringing him here for Christmas has been like sticking an Elastoplast over a broken leg. I can't imagine him being here next year. I don't think I would want him here anyway, not after all this. Then I wonder if we'll even still be together by then.

"Well. I'll cut some up anyway. Then, if you fancy some later, it's there. How about a nice drink?"

"I'll have a glass of red please Mum." Christy holds her glass aloft. "That last one didn't touch the sides."

"I'll have another one." I drain what's left in mine and pass it to her.

"Go easy love," she says. "You'll probably need a clear head when they come back."

"I wonder what's going on out there." Christy glances at her phone. "Bloody men. They want their heads banging together."

"I wish I could have a glass of wine." Rebecca rubs at her bump. "I can't wait until I've had this baby and can get back to normal."

I can't even look at Rebecca. Instead, I pull back the curtain and say, "perhaps you should try calling Greg. See if he's found them."

"They can't have gone far." Mum walks towards the door and looks back at us as she opens it. "Bempton is literally a few streets, the main street and a cliff."

I look at Christy. I wish I was as comfortable in my skin as she is. She lets nothing rattle her. "Do you reckon they'll sort it out?"

"Look Sacha. Whatever's going on between our idiot husbands, as long as it doesn't come between us, I'm not bothered."

"Of course it won't."

Rebecca sniffs, her expression suggesting she feels left out. As the youngest, I suppose she often has been. There are only a couple of years between Christy and I, and we were inseparable growing up. Even when we were offered our own bedrooms, we continued sharing. Rebecca is four years younger than me and the spoiled, favoured one. Even more so now that she seems to be the only daughter willing or able to produce grandchildren for Mum and Dad. After three daughters and two granddaughters, they're really hoping for a boy this time. Despite the resentment I have towards Rebecca, I hope this too. Anything to bring Dad some happiness in his final months.

"Here you go girls." Mum breezes back into the room with a glass of red in each hand, which she passes to Christy and me. "What can I get you Rebecca? You'd be alright with a little drop of wine you know, maybe a spritzer."

"No chance." Rebecca rubs at her belly again, reminding me of a sumo wrestler. "My baby's far too important to risk drinking alcohol."

"Orange juice it is then." Mum starts back towards the door. She's amazing. Even with all she's got going on with Dad, she still seems to enjoy looking after us.

I jump as the front door bangs. I didn't notice Neil and Adam coming up the street. Or it could be Greg, having given up on finding them. We all look at each other. Mum steps away from the door, evidently expecting the men to show their faces in here, but the footsteps and voices go straight past and continue along the hallway. We all file out of the room after one another towards the kitchen. Adam and Greg are pouring whiskey into two tumblers.

"What happened to your face?" Christy lurches towards Adam. His cheekbone is swollen, there's crusted blood around his nose, and he has a thick lip.

"Did you and Neil...?" Despite my fury towards my husband, his face swims into my head and I imagine him lying somewhere, having been beaten up by my sister's husband. Surely not. I'll thump Adam myself if he's just left him outside. I took the bin out earlier and it's below freezing already.

"Neil got a couple of lucky shots in." Adam inspects his face in the chrome surface of the oven. "Don't worry. It looks worse than it is." I notice the top of his coat is splattered with dried blood too.

"Where's Neil?"

"I didn't retaliate, if that's what you're asking. I let him have a couple of shots. He obviously needed to get it off his chest. But I'm the bigger man than he is."

"And what about you?" Rebecca grabs Greg's arm. "Were you there whilst Neil and Adam were scrapping like little boys?"

"Nah, I got there afterwards. People are hard to find in the dark you know."

"That looks as though it needs some ice on it." Mum steps towards the freezer.

"You haven't answered my question." I catch Adam's eye. "Where's my husband?"

"He stormed off." Adam accepts the bag of peas from Mum. "After he'd punched me, that is."

"Stormed off where?" I look at Greg who shrugs with a nonchalant air and an expression that suggests he doesn't give a toss.

"Don't ask me." He raises the bag of peas to his face. "I expect he'll come back when he gets cold enough."

I look at the kitchen window, which returns only darkness. "It's only going to get colder out there. Is Neil even wearing a coat?"

"Don't start acting like you care now." Adam says from behind his bag of peas. "You've ignored him all day."

"Yeah," Greg adds. They're turning into a right double act and there's nothing endearing about it.

"Of course she bloody cares." Christy passes my wine, which she's retrieved from the lounge. "Sacha is Neil's wife. She's every reason to be worried. Look, we'll have these sis, and then look for him ourselves."

"Have you tried his phone?" Mum pours herself some wine now.

"I'll do it now." I glance around for my handbag. It's still hanging on the back of the chair from dinner. The girls are swinging from chairs at the other side of the table. "Sit on your chair properly," I tell Matilda. "You'll crack your head open if you fall backwards."

"Yes, Auntie Sacha. Sorry."

I slide my phone from my bag but as I do, I notice Neil's phone still in the place where he was sitting for dinner. I briefly check the home screen which displays all the missed calls he's had from me, then hold his phone in the air. "His phone's here Mum," I call to her across the buzz of conversation about *who hit who, where and how hard.* "So that idea's a dead end."

"I don't want you and Christy going out in the dark," Mum calls back over the noise.

Christy laughs. "It's lovely you care Mum, but we're all grown up now."

"You won't be able to see a thing anyway, not once you get away from the houses. Look Neil's a grown up too. He'll just be having a wander around, feeling sorry for himself. He'll come back when he's good and ready, you'll see."

"I'm sure you're right." I take a bigger gulp than I normally would of my wine, trying to mask the uneasiness that's steadily building within me.

8

It's after eight and there's still no sign of Neil. I'm onto my third glass of wine since dinner, and it's doing little to calm my nerves. Normally I'd feel squiffy after this amount of drink, but tonight it's not touching me.

Christy, Mum and I are sitting in the lounge. They're distracting themselves with some Christmas night sitcom crap, whilst I can't sit for more than a couple of minutes without looking out of the window. I've opened the curtains so I can keep a proper lookout.

I hope to God Neil is alright. Perhaps he's punishing me for giving him the cold shoulder for most of the day. Or for making him come here in the first place.

"He'll be fine, I promise love." Mum pats my hand as I sit back on the sofa with her.

"I wish I hadn't drunk so much this evening Mum. I could've had a drive around myself. At least with the car headlights, I'd have had a chance at spotting him. I can't shake the thought that he's lying unconscious somewhere."

"He'll be OK sis. And we've all drunk too much today," Christy says. "Especially Tweedle Dum and Tweedle Dee." She jerks her head towards the door. Adam and Greg have taken themselves, along with a bottle of whiskey and some cigars, into the garden. They don't seem bothered about Neil's disappearance.

The girls are supposedly getting ready for bed and Rebecca's gone for a soak in the bath. She doesn't drive, so I can't ask her to take me, and according to Mum, Dad isn't allowed to drive anymore because of the sedative effect of his pain relief. So we've no choice other than to wait. Dad's got up once to see what's going on, and returned to his room, muttering about Neil being even more irresponsible than he could ever have imagined. I've never known Dad to sleep so much, but Mum says the painkillers make him even more tired with alcohol and I think he had a couple of drinks with his dinner. How I wish I could turn the clock back to dinner. I would have stopped Mum from ordering Neil and Adam out.

"Has Adam said much to you about the fight they had?" I look at Christy. "Him and Neil?"

"Only what he told us all in the kitchen. All he really said was that they were arguing, and Neil swung a couple of lucky punches at him. Then he stormed off."

"I sent them off to sort themselves out," Mum sniffs. "Not to brawl all over the village. Whereabouts were they when Neil hit Adam?"

"Adam said he's not sure," Christy replies. "Apparently it was too dark."

"And Greg wasn't there at that point?"

"I don't think so."

"I've got a terrible feeling Christy." I place my glass at the side of me, rocking forward on the sofa so my knees hug into my chest. "I'm going to have to do something. I'm wondering whether I should report him missing."

"What time did they go?" Christy pulls the elastic from her

hair and lets it fall around her shoulders. "I've got such a headache."

"It was just after five, I think." Mum looks at her watch. "I'm starting to feel guilty for sending them packing like that."

"It's not your fault Mum." I squeeze her arm. "But he's been gone well over three hours. I think he's wearing his jacket as I can't find it anywhere, but it's only a thin one."

"It's below freezing out there," Christy says. "Not that you'd think that with Greg and Adam. They've been in the garden for over an hour."

"They've got the patio heater," says Mum. "And they look like they're out there for the night. Which is maybe just as well, judging by the state of them."

"Not to mention whiskey insulation," I add. "Look, I'll give it another half an hour and then I'm ringing the police."

"That sounds drastic Sacha." Christy gets to her feet. "I'm not sure they would look for him yet, to be honest. I think an adult has to be missing longer than three hours before the police would get involved." She glances at the clock. "Anyway, I'm going to have a word with them two before they get much drunker – ask them again, *exactly* what happened."

I'm pacing up and down in front of the fire when Rebecca comes into the room and lowers herself into the chair which Christy vacated. Even the dog has got fed up with my pacing and has retreated into a corner, out of my way.

"Well, that's the girls settled hopefully." She tugs at the towel wrapped around her head and rubs at her hair. "You'd think they'd be shattered after the time they were up this morning. Any sign?" Her tone conveys nosiness more than concern.

I shake my head.

"Have you seen the state of them two out there?" Rebecca

goes on. "They were sitting in judgment of Neil last night, but now I'm thinking it won't be long until they're throwing up all over the patio as well."

"They'd better not." Mum's expression hardens. "Your dad would go berserk. What is it with these husbands of yours? Can't you keep them under control?" She sighs. What she's just said should be funny, but nothing in our family is amusing at the moment.

"I hope I don't go into labour tonight." Rebecca strokes at the bulge beneath her fluffy dressing gown. "How would I get to the hospital? Everyone's over the limit."

"It's all about you, isn't it, Rebecca? My husband's been out there in sub-zero temperatures for over three hours and all you can think about is yourself, as usual."

"And my baby." She looks at Mum, possibly for some backup. "So shut it Sacha."

"If you started in labour dear, we'd call an ambulance for you."

"But who'd come with me? He's in no fit state, is he?"

"We'll cross that bridge if we come to it, shall we? You wouldn't be on your own."

I feel like telling her I certainly wouldn't go with her, but don't. I'd get lynched, and Mum's had enough without Rebecca and me falling out.

Christy's return to the room puts an end to the conversation anyway. "They're not saying anything they haven't already told us." She lets the door close behind her and sits on the rug in front of the fire, facing us. "They're just more incoherent than they were earlier. Leave them to it, that's what I say."

"Well, if Greg thinks he's sleeping in our room whilst he's that drunk, he can think again." Rebecca pulls a comb from the pocket of her dressing gown and begins tugging it through her hair. "Not stinking of whiskey and cigars. No chance."

I glance up at the carriage clock on the mantlepiece, which

was a wedding gift to Mum and Dad. Twenty to nine. "I can't sit here any longer doing nothing." I stand, trying to quell the feeling of foreboding. "I'm going to have to report him missing."

"Just leave it until nine." Mum follows my gaze to the clock. "Your dad will have a fit if police turn up at the door."

"Sorry Mum. There's something wrong. I can feel it in my bones. I'm ringing them. Should I call three nines or that one zero one number?"

"It's hardly an emergency, is it?"

I glare at Rebecca for what feels like the millionth time today. "It might be if Neil's lying injured somewhere. Or if he's lost in the dark."

"Lost," she scoffs. "How can you get lost in Bempton?"

"Dad." I tap on the door of my parent's bedroom. "Can I come in?"

"Humph, what?" His voice is thick with sleep as I push the door open.

"It's me. Sacha."

"Are you OK love?" He flicks his bedside lamp on.

"I'm sorry to wake you, but I've had to report Neil missing. I wanted to let you know."

"I'm sure that's not necessary." He raises himself onto his elbows and I notice how thin his arms have become. Arms that used to throw me and my sisters around the room whilst we shrieked with laughter. "To have got in touch with the police, I mean."

Dad's voice brings a lump to my throat. I recall the days when he could make anything better for me. "It's freezing out there Dad, and he's been gone for nearly four hours now." I lower myself onto the edge of his bed. "He and Adam had a fight, then he apparently stormed off."

"A proper fight?" His face bears a look of bewilderment. "You mean they actually hit each other?"

"Well, it sounds as though Neil hit Adam. But Adam,

thankfully, didn't fight back and just let Neil stomp off somewhere."

"It's a good job one of them saw sense. Look love, I'm not blaming you in the slightest, but this... well, it's all we needed. I'm glad Christmas Day is over with."

"I know. I can't believe it either. I'm really sorry Dad." I reach for his hand and am taken aback at how crepey his skin has become.

"I can do without police cars outside our house as well. We've only just moved here. What will the neighbours make of us? When you lot go home, we still have to face them."

I know where he's coming from, but this is the least of my concerns. "They're not going to turn up with sirens and blue flashing lights. They're just sending a car and a couple of officers to get some details."

"And they're on their way now? I'd better get up, hadn't I?"

"No, you stay where you are Dad, you look exhausted. I didn't want to wake you really, but I figured you'd want to know."

"Of course." His voice falls. "I'll stay here then as the painkillers have wiped me out, but you know where I am if you need me."

"Yes, but I can sort it. I'm just worried about Neil."

"And I'm worried about you." He squeezes my hand, but it's a weak squeeze as though it's an effort. "You're not happy. Neil is far from happy. I need to know you'll be OK when I've gone."

"Oh Dad." I drop my chin to my chest. "I can't bear to think about when you've gone. I still keep hoping and wishing the doctors will have made a mistake."

"Me too." He leans back against his pillows. "You'd better get that." He nods in the direction of the door as the doorbell sounds. "Keep me posted, won't you?"

·   ·   ·

"Mrs Young?" A male police officer with kind eyes says as I open the door. He looks to be around the same age as me.

"That's right. Thanks for getting here so quickly."

"No worries. We're based in Bridlington, so we we're not too far away. And it's a quiet night tonight. I'm PC Martin James and this is my colleague, PC Ruth Taylor. Can we come in?"

"Of course." I stand to the side. They walk past me and wait in the hallway as I close the door. "Come through."

"Thank you."

"Have a seat." I stack some place mats and coasters from the edge of the dining room table as Mum, Rebecca and Christy appear.

"This is my mum and two sisters." I gesture to them. "And I'm Neil's wife – the man who's missing."

"So it was you who made the call to us?" PC James tugs a notebook and a pen from his top pocket, and they both place their hats on the table.

"That's right. My husband's been gone for nearly four hours. He's a bit down and he's only wearing a thin coat, and..."

"OK. Let's get some details from you. What's his full name?"

"Neil David Young."

"Age? Date of birth?"

"15th September 1987. He's thirty-two." I watch as PC James scribbles the information down. His handwriting is terrible. I used to be a secretary a few years ago, so am used to bad handwriting. But even I couldn't decipher that.

"And you live here?"

"No, this is my parent's house." I nod towards Mum. "We've come here for a few days, as a family. It's my dad's last Christmas. He's ill, you see." I don't know why I feel the need to add that.

"What's your name and home address?"

"Sacha Young. 13 St Ive's View, Farndale, Leeds."

"And you live there with your husband?"

70

"Yes."

"Any children?" PC Taylor asks.

"No." A word loaded with sadness as I glance at Rebecca's protruding belly. I don't even know why she's sitting here. She doesn't like Neil; she doesn't even like me. And I'm not sure what difference it makes to the police, whether Neil and I have children.

"Who else is in the house? Here, I mean?" She sweeps her gaze over the room, the bun on the back of her head not moving. She looks as though she'd have really long hair if she let it down.

"My husband's in bed," Mum says. "As Sacha just mentioned, he's not too good and is needing lots of rest."

"My two daughters are asleep." Rebecca gestures towards the door. They're six and four. And my husband, Greg, is outside in the garden."

"With my husband, Adam." Christy frowns as she looks towards the conservatory. Greg and Adam are just about visible in the glow of the patio heater. Adam looks to be refilling their glasses. I hope the police won't want to talk to them. They'll be slaughtered by now.

"It's very cold to be outside," says PC Taylor, dimples forming in her cheeks as her mouth curves into a smile. Although, I haven't got a clue what there is to smile about.

"I know," Christy says. "But in the state they've got themselves into, they can stay out there all night for me."

At this PC Taylor's smile broadens. Then she turns back to me. "Right." She appears to straighten herself up. "If you could explain to us why you're concerned about Neil first, then go through the events leading up to his earlier departure. Then we'll take it from there."

9

PC JAMES GLANCES towards the conservatory. "OK, thanks for all that. I can certainly see why you're concerned. Particularly with the altercation that's taken place. We'll need to ask your brothers-in-law a few questions next."

"I'll see what state they're in." Christy pushes her chair back with a scrape against the wooden floor. "Do you need to talk to them now?"

"Ideally." He turns to Sacha. "Meanwhile, I need a description of your husband." His pen is poised above his notebook. The room still smells of Christmas dinner and extinguished candles. It's now approaching five hours since Neil left. I feel sick as a picture of him forms inside my head. He's a handsome man, but I've lost sight of that. At best, our relationship has become conservative. At worst, well – I'm not even going to go there right now.

"He's about six foot, dark brown hair, brown eyes, and was wearing jeans, trainers, a hoodie, and a dark blue jacket."

"Do you have a photograph?"

I rack my brains, trying to recall if I have one of him on his own. We haven't taken many photos over the last few months.

There have been very few happy moments between us to capture. My eyes fill with tears at this thought.

"I should have one on my phone, somewhere." I slide the phone towards me and begin scrolling through. "There's this one from July." Ironically, it was taken just down the road in Filey. At Mum and Dad's old house.

"I'll give you a text number to send that to. Does he have any distinguishing features? Tattoos, scars, piercings?"

"Um, no. No tattoos. He's got a scar above one of his eyebrows. He got it in fight when he was young."

"So, is he much of a fighter then?" PC Taylor asks.

"No, not at all," I reply. "My brother-in-law must have really riled him for him to have hit out like that."

"They've never got on with each other," Mum says. "Family get-togethers are always spoilt with them sniping at each other. They're best kept apart. Though, having said that, I'm feeling like it's all my fault for sending them off to sort their differences."

"What about the other one, Greg? Does he get on with Neil?"

"They're not as bad," says Rebecca. "They're civil, at least. Greg and Adam have a business arrangement, but none of them are normally close. Which is why I'm quite surprised at that little display outside." She watches Christy as she returns to the room.

"They're absolutely wrecked," Christy says. "You won't get any sense from either of them. Greg can hardly string a sentence together."

"Great." Rebecca's hand flies to her bump. "If I start with this baby tonight..."

"When are you due?" PC Taylor asks.

"In just over a fortnight."

"So any time, really. Although my youngest was a fortnight late."

My husband might be lying frozen to death somewhere and they're wittering about bloody babies and due dates.

"We can't take a statement from them if they're heavily in drink." PC Martin puts an end to their baby conversation. "But I'll try to have a word if that's OK? See for myself." He stands.

"Be my guest," Christy says. "Good luck."

"Can I just ask." PC Taylor looks at me. "How things are in your marriage? Are there any reasons your husband might have taken off like this?"

I glance at my sisters and my mother, wondering whether to spill the beans in front of them. Neil's depression, his drinking, his lack of work and our fertility problems are not exactly news to them. I suddenly remember Neil's threat to get his friend Ash to collect him. As PC Taylor writes this down, PC James returns to the room, shaking his head.

"No chance." He retakes his seat at the table. "I've respectfully asked them not to drink any more, and to get some sleep. We'll need to talk to them first thing in the morning."

My stomach flips. *Surely Neil will be back by then.*

"Before we circulate your husband's information," PC Taylor begins. "Is there anyone else your husband could have gone to, or asked to collect him? To begin any kind of search, whether it's tonight, or we wait until morning, will use a lot of our resources, so we need to check all other possibilities first."

"He can't be left out all night."

There's no way I'll get any sleep until I know he's safe. When they've gone, I'll go looking myself. I can't just sit here, waiting.

"There's literally only his friend Ash, who I've just mentioned, or maybe his dad. The thing is though, Neil's phone is here. He can't get hold of anyone and he's useless at remembering phone numbers."

"He could've used a payphone or borrowed a phone from

someone." PC James looks thoughtful. "Do you know if he has any money on him?"

"Probably not." I recall him pleading poverty whilst we were at the petrol station yesterday, which makes me feel even more miserable. "He's been out of work for two or three months. And like I say, he's useless at remembering numbers even if he has."

"Can you check with his dad and friend before we take things any further?"

I pick my phone back up and get to my feet. I ring Neil's Dad first. I haven't spoken to him for months so he'll be surprised to hear from me.

"Joe, it's Sacha," I begin. "You haven't heard from Neil tonight, have you?"

"Erm, hello Sacha, Merry Christmas. And no. Not since this morning." His speech is slurred, and I can hear the raucous laughter of several men in the background. No wonder Neil wanted to spend Christmas there, rather than here. They don't sound like Joe's church friends though, more like his friends from the Irish club.

"So he's definitely not there with you?" Neil could have told Joe to cover for him. "Please Joe, it's really important. He's gone missing and I've got the police here."

"*Gone missing? The police?* You're joking, aren't you? No, I've not heard from him since this morning, like I said. What do you mean, *gone missing*?"

"I don't know." My voice finally cracks. I've held it together so far. "I'm so worried about him."

"Look Sacha. He's a big boy. I'm sure he'll turn up safely. Have you rowed or something?"

"Kind of. But there's more to it than that. Will you let me know if you hear from him?"

"Yes, of course I will. And you let me know when he comes back. He's probably sulking somewhere. He's always been the same. To be honest, he sounded a little off this morning." The background laughter has faded. Joe has clearly moved away from his friends. "You keep your chin up Sacha. He's not been right for a while as far as I can gather."

"OK. Thanks Joe. I'll keep you posted." Feeling slightly brighter, I turn to everyone sat at the table, relieved that Joe has been OK with me. "Well, he's definitely not with his dad. I'll try his friend now."

I get the same response from Ash. I don't know him well, but luckily, he picks up when I call him via the Facebook app. I don't have his number and can't get into Neil's phone for it. Ash sounds more worried than Joe though when I tell him how long Neil has been missing, and hasn't heard from him. He's unable to suggest anywhere he might have gone. Neil's always been a solitary person, not needing many people in his life. I promise to keep Ash informed too, and hang up.

"So what now?" I sink to the chair and Christy puts her arm around me. Glancing at the clock, I can see it's now after ten. "Something's happened to him. I know it has. I can feel it."

"We really need to speak to Greg and Adam," PC Martin says. Right on cue, they stagger from the patio into the conservatory, flopping down on the sofas at either side of the Christmas tree. "Though looking at the state of them," he adds, "You're going to need a couple of buckets."

"There must be something you can do whilst you're waiting to talk to them," I say. "You must be able to look for him?" I'll get on my knees and beg them to look for him if I have to.

"I'm going to call it in now. Is there a room we can use to liaise with our control unit?"

"I'll show you into the lounge." Mum gets to her feet. She looks knackered now, and unless he's found quickly, this shows no sign of abating.

"We won't be long." PC Taylor squeezes my shoulder as she

passes me. "Try to stay calm Sacha. We'll do everything we can to find him, I promise."

"I'll straighten things up out there." Christy gets to her feet. "Move the whiskey out of their way. They need to sober up. They haven't even switched the heater off. Idiots."

"I'll get some buckets and glasses of water," Rebecca says. "There's no point trying to move them from there. Not that I'd want Greg anywhere near me or the girls in that state."

"I'd better find some blankets." Mum walks back into the room. "Your dad'll have a fit if he sees the state of them."

I watch as my sisters bustle around for a moment, then drop my head into my hands. I don't know what to think or what to feel. *Where the hell is my husband?*

"Are you sleeping in the lounge again tonight Sacha? On the airbed?" Rebecca returns to the table, followed by Christy who slides the conservatory door shut behind her.

"I can't imagine sleeping anywhere unless Neil turns up."

I look up as the two constables return to the room and sit at either side of me.

"Normally," PC James begins. "We wouldn't launch a search for an adult until they've been missing for twenty-four hours. But from what you've told us of your husband's depression and drinking, we're classifying him as a vulnerable person."

"Therefore," PC Taylor continues, "his description is being circulated to all our units and we're going to get the helicopter up. If he's out there, the infrared will find him."

"The coastguard helicopter?" Mum gasps. "Do you think he could be hurt? Oh gosh, this is all my fault."

"Possibly. That might explain why he hasn't come back. Obviously if we wait until first light, it could be too late if he's lying unconscious somewhere. It's the coldest night we've had this winter - we must start looking straightaway."

"You will find him, won't you?"

"The Search and Rescue Team are amazing," she replies. "If he's out there, they'll pick him up.

"You don't think he could've gone..."

I can't say *over the cliff*. Adam says Neil stormed off but in the state of mind he was in... He could have fallen.

"We've got to look everywhere Sacha. It's going to be trickier in the dark, but we'll do everything we can."

"Thank you."

"I'll be in touch as soon as there's any news, or if we need any more information." She puts her hat back on.

PC James slides his notebook towards me. "If you could just write your mobile number and a landline number down for us."

"What do I do now? I can't just sit here. I should do something to help. Can't I join in the search?"

"You need to wait here in case he turns up." PC James takes a card from his pocket. "Let us know straight away if he does." He scribbles a number on the back of it and slides it towards me. "Quote that number when you call."

"Will he be in trouble?" I sniff. "If Search and Rescue are out on Christmas night and he's just hiding somewhere. He's been very depressed lately and just might not be able to face coming back."

"We would much prefer that scenario," he replies. He doesn't need to mention the alternative. "Try to get some rest Sacha." He nods at Christy and Rebecca in turn and says, "We'll be back to see your sleeping beauties first thing. Hopefully, they'll be coherent by then."

"I'll see you out," Mum says, then to us, she adds, "I'd better let your dad know what's happening."

"Well, bloody hell," Christy says as the front door bangs. "I'm worried as well now sis."

. . .

"What did Dad say?" I look at Mum as she enters the lounge and takes up her usual space on the sofa. Normally by now, she'd be cosy in her dressing gown. She's only just got around to taking her apron off. This certainly is not the Christmas she'd hoped for.

"He's very concerned love. Let's just hope Neil's found soon, safely." She emphasises the last word. "Gosh it's eleven o'clock already." She rubs her eyes. "This'll be a Christmas we won't forget in a hurry."

"You should try to get some sleep Mum. And you Rebecca." All prior resentments towards my sister have evaporated for now. "As you keep saying, you could go into labour at any time."

"Yeah, you two go." Christy turns the fire up a notch and the flames leap higher. The room smells of the huge pine tree in the corner, and the cinnamon candle that's still burning on the mantlepiece. "I'll stay up with Sacha. I couldn't sleep a wink anyway."

"I don't know how I will either," Mum says. "But if I don't try, I'll be useless tomorrow. You'll let your dad and I know the moment you hear anything, won't you? No matter what time it is?"

"Of course we will." I wipe at hot tears with the back of my hand. "I'm so sorry for all this Mum. I really am."

"Hey." She gets back to her feet and sits on the arm of my chair beside me. "It's not your fault love. I'm not blaming you for a minute. If it's anyone's fault, it's mine for sending them packing." She puts her arm around my shoulders and draws me towards her. I breathe her familiar, comforting scent and for a moment, I'm eight again, knowing she'll fix whatever needs fixing. But yet, I know in my heart of hearts that I've had my part to play in all this. Hugely.

"Sorry about those two in there as well." Rebecca shakes her head. "I can't believe the state they're in."

"Me neither. I'll have to hide all the alcohol in the future."

I glance at Mum as she smiles, but it's a sad smile. She stares for a few moments at the Christmas tree.

"Right" Rebecca gets to her feet. "Let me know as well if you hear anything. I'm going to try to get a few hours since I'll be looking after those girls single handedly tomorrow. Come on Benji." The dog hauls himself up.

I don't like Rebecca's use of the word *if*. Fear is eating away at me as it is. "I'm going to get changed out of this stupid outfit." I lean to the side of the armchair and pull joggers and a hoodie out of my holdall. "I look more like I'm going to a party than waiting for news of my missing husband."

"You just look like you've made an effort to look nice for Christmas Day." Mum pats my arm as she gets up. "You always look lovely. Right, I'll see you both in a little while. They'll find him, you'll see."

"God, I hope she's right," I say to Christy as Mum and Rebecca follow each other from the room. "Just pull those curtains across whilst I put these on, will you?"

"I'll make us a coffee whilst I'm on my feet."

I feel slightly better after changing into something more relaxed. I spot Mum's slippers in the corner. I drag the curtains back again and turn off the tree lights as I go to fetch them.

"Aww, why have you turned off the lights?" Christy sets a hot mug in my hands.

"I can't bear to look at Christmas lights right now." The heat of the mug and its steam curling towards me is soothing. "As far as I'm concerned, Christmas is over and done with. Is there any sign of life in the conservatory?"

"I could hear two lots of snoring so at least they're both alive." She sips her coffee. "I think we're going to be needing more of this."

"Thanks for waiting up with me, Christy. You're a love."

"What else would I have done? I wouldn't have left you on your own in a million years, and I wouldn't have got a wink of sleep, anyway. I know Neil and Adam clash with each other, but I like Neil. You might've had your problems, but..."

"He likes you as well. I just hope to God he's OK – he's been so down lately, and I haven't been the wife I should – I should have..."

"Stop 'shoulding' sis. All marriages have their trials. Whatever happens or has already happened is not your fault. Stop it."

"So you think something's happened?" I can't bear this.

"I'm not saying that... oh look."

I follow her gaze to the window. Along with the intermittent beam from Flamborough Head Lighthouse, I can now see the Search and Rescue helicopter in the distance, casting a downward ray of light. I walk to the window and open it. "It's loud, isn't it?"

"Bet the locals will be happy, hearing that at nearly midnight."

"I'm sure they'll know that it wouldn't be up without it being important. I just hope they find him." I don't add the word *alive*. I think of the anti-depressants he's supposed to be taking. If only I'd been more persuasive about them.

"The police said they were circulating his description as well." Christy tucks her legs under her. "And remember, the helicopter has heat-seeking equipment. They're likely to find him with that."

I close the window and join my sister on the sofa. "I can't stand it. What if they don't find him? He has to be alive to be found by heat-seeking equipment. He's been gone for seven hours. I feel so guilty."

"Come here." She reaches out and I lean into her. "What on earth have you got to feel guilty about?"

"Oh, you know. Nothing. Everything. And I feel so useless, just... sitting here."

I open my eyes. The soft snoring of my sister vibrates through the sofa as reality hits me like a sledgehammer. I sit bolt upright and look at the window. The helicopter light has disappeared, and the lighthouse beam has resumed its sole ownership of the darkness. I feel as heavy as a helicopter. It's twenty to five. Still around three hours until daylight. Where is he? Where is he? *Where is he?*

I stiffen as a door clicks shut, followed by footsteps padding along the hallway. I am certain I can hear someone breathing outside the lounge door. Then, with a creak and a dragging of the carpet pile, it opens.

10

"WHAT'S GOING ON?" Adam lets the door close behind him and steps into the room, wearing yesterday's clothes, his hair on end and lines all over his face. I don't think I've ever seen him look so rough.

"We're still waiting for news."

"Of what?"

I stare at him. "What do you mean *of what*? What do you think? Neil hasn't come back all night. He's been out there for nearly twelve hours. Thanks to you."

"Look. We were all drunk. I'm not shouldering the blame for him taking off." He sinks into the armchair. "Are you going to report him missing then?"

"I already have."

He leans towards me in his seat. "What have they said?"

"They've had the helicopter up. They're out looking for him."

"I thought people had to be missing a while before they looked for them." His speech still sounds slurred even though it's been hours since he stopped drinking. He must have had a right skinful.

"He's depressed. And you haven't helped with that. With your constant nastiness. The police want to talk to you, anyway."

"Me? Why?"

"You were the last person to see him. Of course they want to talk to you. And Greg. What happened between you and Neil? I need to know Adam."

"Nothing. He went for me then stormed off."

"Why did he go for you?" It's not like Neil at all.

"If I'm honest." Adam pauses. "I said something inappropriate. Don't push me on that Sacha."

"What did you say to him? I've got a right to know."

"I can't tell you." He reaches up to the mantlepiece for the glass of water I brought in earlier and glugs it down. "It was something really personal and if I'm honest, I'm not feeling proud of myself."

"Does Greg know what you said?" I can only imagine it was something to do with Neil's infertility problems.

"Greg came after Neil had already gone." Adam's voice is flat, and he looks away.

"It might be important Adam. What you said to Neil."

"It's no worse than what I said at the dinner table." At least he has the grace to look sheepish.

"Well, if you won't tell *me,* then you'll have to tell the police. I'll be mentioning it to them to make sure you do."

"Fair enough. But for now, I'm off to get my head down before they come back. I feel well rough."

"You deserve to. Though you'd be better getting a shower and waking Greg. The police will be back before long. They've promised to resume things at first light."

"Oh, it's alive." Adam looks at Christy as she hauls herself up to a seated position.

"I'm surprised we've dropped off for so long." She rubs her eyes. "Is there still no sign of Neil?"

I shake my head.

"It's your turn to put the kettle on sis."

"Not for me," Adam says. "I need some more kip."

Like I'd make Adam a drink anyway. I head to the kitchen, fuming to myself. Not once in that short exchange did Adam express concern for Neil or sympathy for me. As I wait for the kettle, I listen to Greg snore and stare out of the window into the darkness. Somewhere out there, is my husband.

Adam's gone when I return to the lounge. "I'm going to get in touch with the police." I reach for my phone. "See what's happening."

A few moments later, after giving the reference number to the operator, I'm put through to PC Taylor.

"Hello Sacha." She sounds more alert than I'd expect at this time of night. I suppose she'll sleep through the day. "I'm hoping you're calling to tell me Neil's turned up."

"I wish." I close my eyes. "No. I haven't heard a thing. I thought I'd ring and see if there's any news."

"Search and Rescue were out for nearly two hours." Her voice dips, seemingly in response to my lack of good news. "They combed the coastline from Bridlington along to Flamborough. The search was stood down at 1:40."

"What does that mean? They've given up?" I look at Christy, and there's panic in her eyes.

"No, not at all. They'll be back out at first light. So will the lifeboat. All our local police units are keeping a lookout for him too."

"Do you still think you'll find him?" Again, I don't add the word *alive*.

PC Taylor hesitates. "Well the best-case scenario here is that he's taken himself off somewhere. Maybe he's warm in a spare room of a friend you don't know about, with no idea of the worry he's causing."

I sense a *but* coming.

"But," she continues. "We've currently got temperatures of minus four. If he's been out there all night, I'm afraid it doesn't look good. There's still every reason for hope though. Let's hang on to that."

"My brother-in-law's just got up and gone back to bed," I tell her. I don't give a toss if he wants more sleep. "He seems sober enough now to answer some questions. I take it you still want to talk to him?"

"Of course. Two of my colleagues will be along after we've changed shifts. Oh, and Sacha..."

"Yes."

"We haven't put anything out in the news yet, but as it's approaching daylight, we're about to release his description in order that the public can keep an eye out. Early joggers, dog walkers. Is that OK with you?"

"Of course." Tears are rolling down my cheeks. "I just want him found." It's usually dead bodies that early joggers and dog walkers find. This has been, without doubt, the worst night of my life.

"I know you do." Her voice is gentle. "Is there someone with you?"

"Yes, I've got my sister here."

"Well, sit tight Sacha. The search will resume shortly, and my colleagues will be around to talk to Greg and Adam. You've obviously got our number if Neil turns up in the meantime."

"Thank you." I hang up, lean into Christy's warmth, and sob onto her shoulder.

"I can't imagine how you must be feeling." She strokes my hair. "This is absolutely horrendous. If he *is* OK and has gone off somewhere, I'll be having a right go at him for doing this to you."

"I'll be right behind you." We both look up at the door, where Dad emerges, tying his dressing gown and wearing the new leather slippers I bought him for Christmas. I'd give anything to turn the clock back to when we were sitting around opening presents yesterday morning. I'd make sure things had turned out completely differently to how they have.

"Any news?" He sits at the other side of me on the sofa. His presence makes me weep like a child. And soon I'm going to lose him too.

By seven o'clock, everyone in the house is awake. The dog and the kids have no idea that anything is not as it should be, and race up and down the hallway. Dad has bollocked Greg and Adam for getting so drunk and has tasked them with restoring the conservatory to its usual order and making themselves presentable before the police return.

"Shhhh, listen." I point the remote at the TV and everyone in the lounge quietens with me.

Concerns are growing for the safety of a thirty-two-year-old man who has gone missing in Bempton in the East Riding of Yorkshire. Neil Young was last seen at around five-thirty yesterday evening, after leaving the home of his wife's family in Bempton. He is said to have been in a distressed state and was inadequately dressed for the sub-zero temperatures we are experiencing.

The Search and Rescue Service conducted a search last night, and will shortly be resuming this. In the meantime, the public are asked to keep a lookout for him. Neil is six feet tall, of medium build, and is wearing blue jeans, Nike trainers, a dark red jumper and a navy blue jacket. You will see from the photograph being shown on the screen that Neil has short brown hair and brown eyes. If you think you have seen Neil or if you see him today, please call 101, quoting reference 362.

"Bloody hell." Rebecca carefully lowers herself into the chair with her cup of tea. The bigger she gets, the more slowly she moves. "This is serious, isn't it? I heard the helicopter up last night." She looks at me. "Are you OK Sacha?"

"I can't believe you've only just decided it's serious." I rub at my aching head. "And no, I'm not OK actually." Perhaps I should be touched by her concern. But I'm not. It doesn't even sound genuine – it never does.

She gets up and switches the tree lights back on. "I thought he'd be back by now, I really did, but that was before he'd been out all night. It's not looking good, is it?"

Christy gives Rebecca one of her looks. "He might've stayed with someone we don't know about. He might've even hitched a ride back to Leeds. You should ask the police to send officers round to your house when they get back here."

"I'm sure they'll do that anyway. In fact, they probably already have."

"You must stay positive Sacha. Until we know any different. Listen." Christy presses her palm into the air as if to hush us all again.

Dad mutes the TV. The overhead rumble tells us the helicopter is back out.

"They're doing all they can," says Christy. "Are you going to have something to eat sis? You need to keep your strength up."

"You must be joking." My stomach twists at the idea. I look at Rebecca. "Where's Greg?"

"In the shower," she replies. "I've let him know the police will be here anytime."

"Can't you shut them kids up?" Adam sinks lower into the beanbag he is rolling around on. "My head's banging."

Rebecca scowls at him. "Sit in the garden if you don't want to listen to them. You were alright out there last night."

I get up, pace the room three times, then sit back down. I get up again, look out of the window, slide my phone from my pocket and check it for what feels like the zillionth time.

"Have you contacted *everyone* you can think of?" Rebecca asks. "What about Facebook? He's on there, isn't he?"

"He has an account and about twenty friends – and most of them are us." I reply. "He never uses it. Says he doesn't trust all that social media stuff."

"I think you should put something on there, just in case. Do you want me to do it for you?"

I shrug my shoulders, which she will know means *do what you want.*

A police car pulling up behind my car is a welcome, yet dreaded sight. Have they got some news? Good? Bad? It's either that, or they're here to see Greg and Adam. I can't hear bad news. We all look at each other. I'd rather hear nothing. There's suddenly a lot of store in that old saying, *no news is good news.*

As they make their way up the path beside the drive, I watch to see if their expressions are giving anything away. If they'd found Neil alive, they'd probably look happier than they do. It's difficult to say.

"Come in." I hear Mum's voice in the hallway and the children fall silent. I expect they would, at the sight of two police officers.

"Mrs Sacha Young?" One of them says as I enter the hallway.

I nod, searching their faces for what they might be about to tell me.

"I'm Sergeant Hazel Downing," the female police officer announces, holding out her hand, dark curly hair escaping beneath her hat. She's older than PC Taylor, probably in her mid-thirties. "This is my colleague, PC Lee Scott."

He nods at me.

Christy emerges from the lounge and stands at my side. "I'm Sacha's sister. Is there any news yet?"

"Shall we?" Sergeant Downing gestures towards the dining room.

"Yes. Come through." Mum leads the way.

"Is it OK if we sit down?"

"Of course." I sit facing the two officers. Mum and Christy flank me, either side. Dad and Rebecca appear in the doorway. I don't know where Adam and Greg are. I know they're both dying this morning after their overindulgences last night, so probably can't face this. Obviously, I've no sympathy for them.

"Right." Sergeant Downing clasps her hands in front of her on Mum's polished table. "Myself and PC Scott have taken over from PC Taylor and PC James. As you might be able to hear, the helicopter is back out looking for your husband."

So they haven't found him yet. I exhale slowly. At least that means... I can't take much more of this. I lock eyes with Sergeant Downing, and see sympathy emitting from hers. "They've also deployed the lifeboat to join with the search. Neil's details have been circulated throughout our police teams and have now been released to the media. We're doing everything we can to find him."

I nod, slowly. "I know you are." There's a wobble in my voice. "Have you checked our house in Leeds too, just in case."

"Yes. Officers from the West Yorkshire division have checked a couple of times. There's no sign of him there."

"Maybe he's just lying in bed or something, ignoring the door? Or asleep?"

"I hear what you're saying, but it seems unlikely. However, if he doesn't show up soon here in Bempton, we'll be asking you to check your upstairs at home and our West Yorkshire division will look at the surrounding CCTV."

I don't think I could focus on a two-hour drive right now. I'd have to get Christy to take me. We could be there by ten o'clock. I imagine him, laid in our newly decorated bedroom with the duvet pulled over his head, ignoring the door. He said he wanted to go home – I should've let him go.

"I gather he left his mobile phone and wallet here. Have you got access to his phone?"

"No. I don't know his PIN. But I've called his dad and his friend Ash, and they've not heard a thing from him. Neil rang his dad yesterday morning, but he hasn't spoken to Neil since then." I'm suddenly reminded that I ought to update them both. "And my sister has just put a post out on Facebook, not that he really uses Facebook. He doesn't have anyone else who'd know anything as far as I know." I feel heavier than ever, recalling what an insular life Neil has been leading.

"We'll need to take his phone back to the station," Sergeant Downing says gently. "There might be something on it we can follow up. That's what we're hoping for."

"We gather he's been suffering from depression?" PC Scott speaks now. "And that he'd had a run in with his brother-in-law?"

"That's right. What are you thinking?" Really, I know exactly what they're thinking. Depression. Leaving behind of phone and wallet. Thin clothes. Argument. Clifftop. Then there are the ongoing traumas of him being out of work, having a drink problem, and us being unable to conceive. It's not a hopeful picture.

"Whilst the search is ongoing, we need to speak to both his brothers-in-law."

"My husband is in the other room," Christy says.

"Mine is too," Rebecca adds. "I've just seen him go in there."

"Shall I get them," asks Mum.

"Being they were the last people to see your husband," Sergeant Downing turns back to me. "We'd like to get their version of events on record. We'll have a chat with them at the station."

"You're arresting them?" Rebecca gasps. "But I'm about to have a baby. One of them is my husband."

She's at it again.

"Officially," says PC Scott, "it's known as assisting us with our enquiries. So no, we're not arresting them." The radio attached to his jacket beeps. He presses a button. "PC Lee Scott." A faceless voice asks if they are with *the family*. "Bear with me one moment." He jumps up from the table and heads down the hallway, towards the front door, too far away for me to make out what he's saying. I study the back of his head, willing it to be good news.

Whatever has gone before, Neil and I can get through this. If last night has taught me anything, it's that I actually *do* still love him and want to us to put things behind us and move forward.

"What's going on?" Christy looks at Sergeant Downing who's also watching her colleague.

"I'll find out." She rises from the chair and strides towards PC Scott.

11

THE OFFICERS TAKE their conversation into the front garden. The rest of us sit in silence. A cold hand of fear is squeezing at my chest. *Why have they gone outside?* Dad comes to sit with us at the table whilst Rebecca shoos the children into their bedroom to get dressed. When she returns, she's followed by Adam and Greg. They slump in unison onto the couch in the corner of the dining room. Their movement causes the tinsel hung on the picture above them to waft in the breeze. I feel like ripping all the Christmas decorations down. Rebecca takes a seat beside Dad, and Mum reaches for my hand.

"I feel useless," Mum says. "Shall I put the kettle on?"

With a shake of his head, Dad dismisses that suggestion.

"None of this would have happened if it wasn't for me." Mum dabs at her eyes.

"We've been over this Wendy," Dad says. "You only asked them to talk to each other. This is *not* your fault."

"He's right Mum." I squeeze her hand.

The front door opens and closes. My heart hammers in sync with the footsteps that grow louder back towards us, bringing with them whatever news they have to impart. I can tell by the officer's faces what they're going to say before they say it. They stand side by side at the top of the table.

"They've found him," Sergeant Downing begins. "The Search and Rescue Team."

Time goes into slow motion and at first I think I mishear her next words. I nip the skin on the back of my hand, willing myself to wake up from this.

"At the foot of the cliff."

"The. Foot... is he?"

She nods. "I'm so sorry Sacha. It will have been instant. He's gone from the highest point."

"Oh my goodness." Mum's hand flies to her mouth.

"How?" The word catches in my throat. "Did he..?"

"That's what we need to find out," she says gently. "Given his medical history, and the circumstances you've told us about, we're keeping an open mind at this stage."

"You mean he's jumped?" Adam says. His bluntness should shock me, but it doesn't.

"We'll need to get statements from all of you." She sidesteps his question. "But both of you," she nods in turn at Adam and Greg. "We'd like you to accompany us to the station."

"Can we not just make a statement *here* with the others?" Greg's face falls.

"Given the fact you were with Neil shortly before he died, we need your version of events audibly recorded."

"The only version of events I've got is that he'll have jumped." Adam's tone is bordering on a sneer. "Definitely. He was that sort of bloke."

Both officers look taken aback.

"Shut up Adam." Christy jumps up from her seat and rushes around the table to my side. "He could've easily fallen. Especially in the dark. It's pitch black on those cliff tops."

I don't know what to think. I can't think. This can't be

happening. And until I see Neil with my own eyes, I won't believe it. "Will I be allowed to see him?"

"We'll need you to identify him. I'll let you know when that'll be possible."

"He'll be in a right state after falling from there," Greg says. Another idiot who doesn't think before speaking.

Dad glares at him. "Greg. For God's sake!"

"When do you want us to come?" Adam asks.

"Straightaway, if you don't mind. We'll stay here with your family and two of my colleagues will collect you and conduct the interview."

I want to say *they're no family of mine.* But as I open my mouth to speak, no words will come out.

"Can't we just drive ourselves to the station?"

"You're both probably still over the limit" Mum clasps my hands in hers as she speaks, her eyes not leaving my face. It dawns on me that I'm a widow now and before long, Mum will be one too.

I'm numb, absolutely numb. From being utterly pissed off with Neil and unsure whether I even wanted to stay with him, suddenly I'm never going to see him again. Sergeant Downing is speaking into her radio, but I don't hear what she's saying. I can't make sense of anything.

"I think she's in shock," Dad says to Mum, looking at me with concern written all over his face.

"I know. I'll get her something. What's best for shock? Hot sweet tea?"

"A large brandy." Christy squeezes my shoulder.

"It's a bit early..." begins Mum.

"Sod that! What would you rather have, Sacha? Tea or brandy?"

I try to answer, but my teeth are chattering.

"Brandy it is." Christy heads through the kitchen towards the utility room.

"My colleagues will be here in five minutes." Sergeant Downing says to Adam and Greg. "If you could be ready for them, please?"

"Will they bring us back?" Adam stands. "It's just – it's Boxing Day. There won't be any buses."

"Get a taxi." Christy speaks through gritted teeth as she slops brandy into glasses. "Stop thinking about yourself all the time, will you?"

They file from the room like obedient schoolboys. The expression that Adam is wearing says he's taking all this in his stride. Greg, on the other hand, looks anxious. I take the brandy from my sister. It burns all the way to my stomach. Thank God I've got my family around me. As I stare into the brown liquid in my glass, the enormity of what's going on flattens me. *How am I going to get through this? What am I going to do?*

Dad looks helpless as I realise I've said the words out loud. Nobody says anything.

"Why's Auntie Sacha upset?" Matilda and Freya peer into the room.

Rebecca jumps up and rushes towards the door. "Girls, let's put the TV on in the other room."

"Why are there police here Mummy?" I hear one of them say as they walk away towards the lounge.

"Right, we'll see you when we see you," Adam calls from the hallway. "The police car's here."

No one replies and the door bangs after them.

"Are you all up to making a statement?" asks PC Scott. He makes it sound as though we have a choice in the matter.

"The sooner we get them from you, the better," adds Sergeant Downing. "Whilst everything is still fresh in your minds. Then we can leave you alone."

I don't want to be left alone. And I think *fresh* is a strange choice of word to use in relation to someone jumping or falling from the top of a cliff. My scrambled thoughts attempt to assimilate which scenario it could be. It's something I know will torture me over the coming weeks and months. Hopefully, something will come to light that will tell me exactly what happened.

"To be honest, I don't suppose there's much any of us, apart from Sacha, can tell you. Nothing that would be of significance." Dad looks exhausted again, and he's only been out of bed for a couple of hours.

"What you tell us will be more useful than you might imagine," Sergeant Downing replies. "We need to build a clear picture of what happened in the run up to Neil's death."

Neil's death. I can't believe it. I just can't believe it.

"Is there a room we could use to talk to you all?" Sergeant Downing asks. "To take each statement privately. Both of us will sit in for each one."

"Yes, of course." Mum replies. "I'll show you through to the office. Is that OK Stuart?"

He nods. With the girls having taken over the lounge, there's nowhere else for them to go. I can't imagine the conservatory smells too great, with Greg and Adam having inhabited it all night.

"We'll start with you, if that's OK sir?" Sergeant Downing nods at Dad. "It shouldn't take long."

It's probably for the best that they speak to Dad first. Then he can rest. Amidst all this, I've almost forgotten how ill he is. Though when they question him, I can't imagine he'll have great things to say about Neil. Especially after yesterday.

"Would you like some tea?" Mum calls after them.

Whilst they get through the statements, I shower, then force an apple down. Each swallow is an effort and I wonder if I'll ever enjoy food again – if I'll ever enjoy *anything* again.

Mum has apparently given Freya and Matilda the hard word, and we haven't heard a sound from the lounge since they were sent there. Not even from the dog. For the first time, I'm relieved we weren't successful in our attempts for a baby. How would I cope if I were pregnant now? If I had a baby to look after on my own? Then, my thoughts turn to who might have been more at fault out of Neil and I for our inability to conceive. If it was mainly Neil, then maybe now... I scrunch my eyes against this intrusive thought. I know where my thinking is heading, and I've got to put a stop to it.

Dad goes straight for a lie down after speaking to the police. So does Rebecca after giving her statement, complaining she has awful back ache. She's always complaining about something. Christy is in with the police now.

"Can I get you anything love?" Mum's coping with things as she normally would. She's cleaning the kitchen. It's her way of keeping control of her surroundings in an otherwise very out-of-control situation.

"I need to get out of here Mum," I reply. "The walls are closing in on me. I can't breathe."

"Go for a walk Sacha. Fresh air will do you good." Fresh air. Mum's answer to everything. She walks around the breakfast bar and begins stacking place mats from the dining table, wiping each in turn. I watch as she wipes the one where Neil sat yesterday. Guilt is eating away at me for all the things I should, or more to the point, should not have said and done.

"I'll take my phone with me." I unhook my handbag from the back of the chair. "In case the police are ready for me before I get back. Just drop me a text." I glance at my phone. "It looks like I've got some signal." I drop the phone into my bag. "Can I borrow some boots Mum?"

"Help yourself."

I slide my feet into Mum's fur-lined walking boots and tug her coat from the peg. It's the one I've always laughed at for being like a duvet. Now it feels like a hug and I badly need one of those.

I step out of the front door, the biting wind slicing into my face almost immediately. Apart from the police car parked behind my car, all is ordinary in my parent's quiet cul-de-sac. I expect the neighbours are watching the comings and goings and may have linked them to the news reports. I hurry away from the house, no doubt as Neil did in the darkness last night.

I'm trudge along the main street and head towards the coastal road without planning to. With each footstep the sense of dread and sickness builds. Seeing where he died is not going to do me any favours, yet I cannot help myself.

The police presence and cordoned-off area along the cliff path tell me immediately where it happened. Where he fell from. If he fell. I sink to a nearby bench, clinging to the theory that he fell. People *have* fallen from here before, and he *had* been drinking.

But he was so depressed. And Adam was a complete arsehole to him yesterday. He's got a lot to answer for. I want to know exactly what was said between them before Neil stormed off last night. But that relies on Adam telling the truth, and I don't feel as though I can trust him. Maybe no one will ever know for certain what took place between them. And maybe no one, other than Neil, will ever know whether he jumped or just lost his footing. He's taken that truth with him.

The overcast clouds echo my mood and the sound of rhythmic waves below does little to soothe me as they usually might. The police officer guarding the cordon must be freezing. As I rise from the bench and walk towards him, I gasp with the sudden gust of wind. My mouth fills with salt – a combination of sea spray, along with the tears that I didn't realise I was crying until I taste them.

"Are you alright?" The officer must notice my distress as I approach him. I'm probably a right sight with my blotchy face and hair still wet from the shower clinging to the sides of my face. Not to mention my mother's oversized coat.

"I'm his wife."

"Really?" The officer's face falls. "Of the man who..."

We look at each other. He doesn't need to say any more. I nod.

"Is he? Has he?" I try to peer over the cliff from where I'm standing. I don't want to get any closer – it's too windy and I'm also scared of what I'll see.

"We've moved him." The officer tells me. "We concluded what we had to quickly – obviously before the tide was due to come back."

I'm relieved. The thought of my husband's broken body still lying three hundred feet below where I am standing would be more than I could bear. Yet, I've still got to formally identify him. "Do you know where he's been taken?"

"I don't. I'm sorry. You'll have to ask the officers on the case."

Is that what Neil is now? *A case?* Then, once they've drawn their conclusions, decided what happened, it, and he, will be laid to rest. Case closed.

12

My heart is thumping as I pull the car onto our drive and stare at the home we've shared for five years. In a few minutes I'll have to go inside, and all will be as we left it. The basket of laundry. Our unmade bed. Though Neil had spent the night on the sofa before we left, as he did many nights, claiming he couldn't settle upstairs. His beer cans will still be all over the place. And the roll of paper and sticky tape from when I was wrapping gifts for my family will be on the kitchen table.

My gift to Neil still lies forlornly under the tree in the conservatory in Bempton. It was nothing exciting, just a shirt and a jumper. What I'd give to see him wearing them. To see *him*.

The last time I saw him was through a window in the hospital mortuary. From what I could make out, he didn't look as though he had fallen three hundred feet. I'd been terrified that what was left of him would be mangled. They had covered most of his body in sheeting, leaving his face and the side of his head visible. I'd nodded, 'yes that's him,' then fallen into Christy's arms. Tears prickle at my eyes again at the memory.

As we'd left the hospital, Greg and Rebecca had been on their way in.

"The contractions are every five minutes." Rebecca had looked pained, yet her eyes shone with excitement, and in that moment, I hated her with every fibre of my being.

"What happened at the station?" I'd asked Greg.

"Nothing much. Anyway, don't you think I have enough on my plate right now?" His tone and the way he wouldn't look at me were infuriating. A simple *how are you doing* would've made a difference. They must have known that Christy and I were there to identify Neil.

Mum and Dad were over the moon when Greg phoned to say they'd had a son. Dad whooped in joy and for a moment, seemingly forgot about the pain and misery surrounding us. Mum made some crass comment about how strange it is in families that often with a death, there's a birth. Maybe something of Neil, she said, would live on in her new grandson. I don't know how she worked that one out.

I stayed at their house last night but left first thing this morning. I hadn't wanted to come home. Not really, but in no way could I have coped with any sort of baby celebration at Mum and Dad's. I gather the plan is for Greg and Rebecca to stay an extra night or two so Dad can spend some time with the baby.

Christy and Adam are on their way back to Leeds as well. Christy says she'll give me some time to settle at home and then will give me a ring. She's offered to stay with me, but I don't know what I want right now, so I told her to go home. I just want my husband back.

I jump as there's a tapping on the car window. It's Hilary from next door.

"Sacha. I've heard the news." She reaches through the car

window as I wind it down and places her hand on my shoulder. "I'm so very sorry."

"Thank you." What else am I supposed to say. This is probably all I'll hear for the foreseeable future. *I'm sorry. I'm so sorry.* Why do people even say that? As though it's their fault.

"What on earth happened to him?" She tucks her hair behind one ear as she bends towards me.

"I don't really know. They're doing a postmortem today. Then apparently it's up to the coroner to decide if it was an accident or not. I know Neil was depressed but I can't believe he'd have left me like this." I don't know if I should be spilling my guts to my neighbour, but the words are out before I can stop them. Hilary's not exactly a close friend, but someone I have coffee with from time to time.

"I suspected he was depressed," she says. "He hasn't seemed himself at all lately. He barely spoke when I saw him the other day."

What's the saying, *hindsight is a wonderful thing?* In this case, it isn't. And I don't know how they can ever possibly discover *for certain* how my husband's body came to be dead at the foot of Bempton cliffs. With no eyewitnesses, there's no way of knowing for sure. Sergeant Downing told me there doesn't seem to be any suggestion of any foul play. But they need to ascertain whether it was an accident, or a suicide. According to Christy, Adam and Greg said in their statements exactly what they'd told us at the house.

Greg stood by his story of not finding Adam until after Neil had stormed off. Adam confessed to having riled Neil enough to make him lose his temper and punch him. He still won't tell me what he said to him but claims to have included it in his statement to the police. I'm sure Christy will get it out of him, and she's promised to let me know straightaway. I just pray it isn't what I think it could be.

"Is there anything I can do to help?" Hilary's voice cuts into my miserable thinking.

"Wave a magic wand? No. I don't think so. I guess I've just got to somehow get through it."

"Well, you know where we are... if there's anything we can do...anything at all." Another phrase I'll probably hear a lot of.

"Thank you."

"Will you let us know about the funeral arrangements? We'd like to be there."

I nod. I haven't really thought about the funeral. "I don't know what's happening yet. I suppose it depends on when they release the death certificate."

"Will you bring him back here?"

I haven't considered this. "I guess so. Leeds was his home, not Bridlington, where his body is at the moment."

His body. I look at the house again, our house, just a three up, two down semi, but we loved it from the moment we saw it. How things have changed. We moved in right before our wedding, brimming over with excitement about our plans for the future. Now look at us. Well, me. There is no *us* anymore.

I need to talk to Neil's dad. Find out what his wishes are. I offered to visit when I broke the news to him yesterday, but he wanted to be left alone. I'll ring him again later. I just feel so helpless. Ash, Neil's friend, was in a such a state when I told him that his wife had to take the phone.

"Anyway, thanks for checking in with me, Hilary. I suppose I'd better get inside. I can't put it off forever."

"Will you be alright? Do you want me to come in with you?"

"No. I'll be fine. But thanks anyway." My voice exudes a strength I don't feel. My eyes are raw from a two-hour journey, crying. It's a miracle I didn't get pulled over by the police. He was so young. Only thirty-two. It's an utter waste. And I can't shake the hunch that he jumped. For that, I'll blame myself forever.

I lean into the back seat for my holdall. The police took Neil's bag as evidence and haven't let me know whether it yielded anything relevant to their investigation. I wonder if they will. Same with his mobile phone. But I guess today is only the day after Boxing Day. I'll have to be patient.

I walk to the front door and stand for a moment, watching Hilary as she strides up her drive back to her own house.

An image of my sister with her new baby, all pink and happy floods my mind and I try to block it. But at least my parents have experienced some good news and joy this Christmas after everything else that's happened.

I can't put it off any longer. I push the door open, taken aback by the smell of home and the empty doormat. But there wouldn't have been any post over Christmas, and it's too soon for word to have spread about Neil's death – for the sympathy cards to start. *Neil's death.* I still have to chew the words around. I can't swallow them yet. Perhaps I never will. Maybe they'll always choke me.

I wander from the hallway to the lounge, then into the kitchen, noticing things I never have before. The trophies in the cabinet from when Neil used to play football. The graduation picture on the wall from his sports degree. His self-help books, most of them unread, lining the bottom two shelves of the bookcase. I used to laugh at those.

After an injury put an end to any kind of sporting career, Neil trained as a plumber. However, with each passing year, he left the man he had hoped to become further and further behind and endured setback after setback. It got to a point where it was going to take a hell of a lot more than two shelves of self-improvement books.

My eyes fall on the Christmas tree in the bay window. I remember when we put it up a fortnight ago. It was the only decent day we had together in December. We'd shared a bottle of mulled wine and put on some Christmas music, as usual. We had our routine with the tree – he was on lights and I was on baubles. That evening, he'd seemed less depressed – still nowhere back to himself though. That he'd done something, albeit helping with the tree, made me think the antidepressants must be kicking in. But then the next day the subject of spending Christmas with my parents had come up, and he'd retreated into his black hole again.

I drag the Christmas tree box from the cupboard beneath the stairs and begin wrenching the decorations from the tree. I can't look at it. Nor can I look at the cards displayed all around the room. I take ten minutes to clear the room of all festive paraphernalia. I don't think I'll ever celebrate Christmas again. What will the next one look like, anyway? Not only will it be the first anniversary of my husband's death, but my dad will be dead too. Suddenly, my mouth fills with saliva and my stomach lurches. I realise the boiled eggs Mum forced down me before I left her house are about to make a reappearance.

I lie on the bathroom carpet, spent and sobbing. I can't do this. I just can't do it. As I haul myself up, I notice Neil's shaving stuff at the side of the bath and his toiletries on the shelf above it. I catch sight of myself in the mirrored tiles and am repulsed at what I see. My hair looks like rats' tails and my eyes are red and piggy from crying and throwing up. I've never looked worse. I've never felt worse. I need him back. I need to be the wife I should have been.

I jump at the sound of the doorbell. I'm not expecting anyone and don't want to see anyone. But they're not going away. The doorbell rings twice more then I hear the letterbox rattle and, "Sacha. It's me, Ash. Open up." I'll have to see him. My car is on the drive, so he'll know I'm here. Besides, he was Neil's best friend and will know what I'm going through.

He steps forward as I open the door and envelops me in a

hug. It feels strange but good. I can't have enough hugs right now. I look over his shoulder, expecting to see his wife.

"Where's Lisa?" I step back. "Come in."

"She's at home with Emma. I thought I should come on my own. Emma's too young to hear all this."

"Come through. Excuse the mess – I haven't been back long from my parents and I had to get rid of the tree. I couldn't bear to look at it."

"I know what you mean. Ours has come down too. Christmas is over." He sits in the chair Neil normally sits in, and I perch on the edge of the sofa, facing him. His normally groomed fair hair is on end, and his usually clean-shaven face shows the shadow of a beard. He's the same height and build as Neil and other than the difference in hair colour, they have a look of each other. It's agonising to draw the comparison.

"Oh Sacha." Ash sweeps his gaze around the lounge. It seems to rest on our wedding photograph above the fireplace. "I can't bloody believe it. I had a bad feeling as soon as you rang on Christmas night. I didn't sleep after that. It's like, I felt he'd gone – somehow."

"You and Neil were very close. He must have talked to you. In fact, the police might want to talk to you. You were his closest friend. His only friend, in the end."

"It wasn't always like that though, was it?" Ash's eyes are still fixed on our wedding photo. "He'd closed himself off from everyone." Ash wipes at his eyes with the back of his hand. "Sorry for getting like this. I came around to support you and here I am, bawling instead. I'm just totally gutted."

"You've got nothing to apologise for Ash." I wipe my eyes with a tissue then blow my nose. The grief is like a physical pain and I'd give anything to feel normal again. At least what Ash is saying suggests he's not blaming me. Me blaming myself is bad enough. I pass the tissue box to Ash.

"He tried it with me." Ash leans forward and tugs a tissue

from the box on the coffee table. "Avoiding me, I mean. People with depression often do, but no way was I allowing him to, even if he got pissed off with me for 'hounding him,' as he called it."

"Did he ever talk to you? I mean *really* talk to you?"

"You know what he was like. God, I can't get used to saying *was* about him. Not really. He preferred to keep the conversation on things like football. I knew bits and pieces though."

"Such as?"

"Well." Ash looks uncomfortable. "He mentioned the troubles you were having, and the waiting list you were trying to get on, to have a baby."

"What did he say about it?"

"Just that he felt like a failure. He kept saying you'd be better off without him so you could find someone who could…"

"We were both failures Ash. In our own way. His drinking made things so much worse though." My eyes fall on two spent beer cans above the fireplace.

"I know. It was the drinking that interfered with him going to work. Well it does, doesn't it? If I had a skinful on a weeknight, I wouldn't feel like going to work. I can't have more than one or two."

"Neil couldn't stop at one or two though."

"He was running away from himself Sacha. Given the chance, he'd have rather sorted himself out."

"He was running away from me, you mean?" I wrap my arms around myself and rock forwards in my seat. "Did he say anything else to you? You only saw him a couple of days before he died. He must've mentioned how he was feeling."

Ash shakes his head. "People who are seriously depressed rarely want to talk about it. All he talked about was wanting to spend Christmas differently."

I swallow. "He tried to open up to me on Christmas

morning." Fresh tears spill from my eyes. "But I was so angry with him because of the night before, that I didn't even give him a chance. Instead, I gave him an ultimatum. *Oh God.* It's all my fault. I'm his wife and I didn't even listen to him."

"Stop it Sacha. You couldn't possibly be to blame. No one is. Depression is to blame. What happened the night before anyway?"

"We were at my parents' and Neil got wasted. He threw up all over the patio and slept in the conservatory. He tried telling me the next morning how bad things had got for him, but never mentioned a thing about wanting to end it all. I wouldn't have let him out of my sight if I'd have known."

"It's the ones who threaten to hurt themselves that rarely do anything. Those that really want to end it all just do it. As we've found out."

"But we don't know that yet. He still could have fallen."

"Oh Sacha, I know that's what you want to believe, but..."

"It was pitch black out there. And he'd been drinking. Have you ever been up to Bempton cliffs?"

"I can't say I have. Flamborough Head, but not Bempton."

"It's like Flamborough. There are warning signs all along the cliff path. And everyone knows about that part of the coastline. It's been eroding for years. He could have lost his footing. In fact, he should never have been up there in the dark."

"What are the police saying?"

"Nothing yet. They're waiting for the postmortem results."

"How will they know whether he jumped or fell?"

"I've no idea. Maybe in the way he landed." Tears stab my eyes again as I imagine him at the bottom of the cliff. "He was there all night. Cold and alone. He could have laid there in agony before he died."

Ash moves to my side on the sofa and puts his arm around my shoulders. I catch his male scent, which makes me feel more miserable. I'm never going to breathe Neil's scent again. Though affectionate moments, when we were close, had become fewer and far between. God, if I'd hugged him more and told him I loved him, he might still be here. If I hadn't...

"Stop torturing yourself Sacha." It's as though Ash can read my mind. "It will have been quick. That's what I keep telling myself. And he's not in pain anymore – he's free now."

"Nothing you say can make me feel any better." I move away from him, the closeness of our physical contact suddenly feeling uncomfortable. "Would you like a drink? Tea? Something stronger?"

"Stronger sounds good." He sits back on the sofa.

I pluck the brandy bottle from its hiding place in the kitchen and grab two glasses from the cupboard.

"When will you hear more from the police?" Ash calls out.

"They said within the next day or two." I walk back to the lounge, blinking at the sudden sunshine from the window. I want it to be a dreary day like yesterday – more in keeping with my current mood. How can the sun be so bright when I feel so dreadful?

"You'll keep me posted, won't you?" As I place the glasses on the coffee table, Ash reaches for my hand. "We'll help you with everything Sacha - Lisa and me. You're not on your own with this." His shoulders tremble and tears fill his eyes again. "I loved Neil. He was like a brother. I wish he'd come to me."

"So do I. Instead, he came to *me*." I slop brandy into the glasses, unsure whether I'll be able to keep it down. The stress of this has made me feel constantly sick. But more than that, I'm exhausted. I want to close my eyes and never wake up.

13

Even before I answer my phone, the *no number* notification offers an inkling of who the caller might be. I brace myself as I accept it.

"Sacha. It's Sergeant Hazel Downing speaking. Are you OK to talk for a few minutes?"

"Yes. I'm just at home." Work have told me to take as much time off as I need. They had a big spray of flowers delivered to me earlier. As the news has spread over the last few days, this is one of several bouquets that have arrived. Sympathy cards have filled the spaces where the Christmas cards were. They're comforting, yet at the same time, I can't bear the sight of them.

"How are you doing?"

"I've been better but, I'm hanging in there." I'm not going to tell her I'm exhausted, that I have no appetite, and when I eat, it comes back up again. All she'll be bothered about is closing Neil's case as quickly as possible, and moving onto the next one.

Guilt is gnawing at me and the fact that Joe, Neil's dad, won't see me, is making it even worse. He says he can't bear to see anyone right now, especially me. I don't quite know what he means by that, but I suppose I should be reassured that he's at least *spoken* to me. That suggests he isn't blaming me completely for what's happened to Neil.

"I'm ringing with news from the Coroner," Sergeant Downing begins. "I've just heard from them."

I hold my breath, praying they're going to say he fell rather than jumped. He will not come back to me, no matter what, but somehow, him falling will be easier to bear. I'm sure it will be for his dad as well.

"I'm afraid it's not been possible to determine the cause of death from the postmortem, which I suspected would be the case."

"What does that mean?"

"The Coroner has opened an inquest."

My heart plummets. *An inquest.* "Why?"

"They have to be satisfied with a definite cause of death before they'll release a death certificate."

"But maybe we'll never know whether he fell to his death or jumped." Maybe it's for the best if we never know for sure, anyway."

"In cases like this, an unexpected death, they have to investigate. They need to know if Neil's death was accidental or a suicide. They also have to establish whether there are any other relevant circumstances."

"Like what?"

"I've not actually seen the pathologist's report yet but I'd expect its contents to be shared with you when the Coroner's office gets in touch."

"Gets in touch? With me? Why?"

"They'll need to take a statement."

"But I've already given a statement to you. I really can't go through it all again. I don't feel strong enough."

"They'll take their own statements from everyone involved

and inform each party who'll be called to give evidence at the inquest."

"Give evidence? Like at a court?" Oh God. This is getting worse.

"It's standard procedure when a death is unexplained. Try not to worry Sacha."

Try not to worry. That's easy for her to say. "It's just one thing after another. How long will it all take?"

"Because Neil's isn't an overly complex situation, the information should only take weeks to gather, rather than months."

I swallow my anger at my husband's death being described as *a situation.* "But I'm supposed to register his death. What about the funeral?" The thought of Neil's broken body, lying in a fridge for weeks, or even months, is more than I can contemplate. Surely they'll let us lay him to rest and say goodbye to him. I sink to the sofa, my misery feeling as though it's going to suffocate me. I can't go on like this.

It's as though she senses what I'm thinking. "Once they've got all their evidence, if they haven't already, the Coroner's office will register his death and release what's known as an interim death certificate. This will at least allow you to apply for probate and start planning the funeral."

I don't bother telling her that there'll be no point applying for probate. Neil had nothing, which might strengthen their belief that he took his own life. There are no savings, no life insurance, no pension, no property. Even this house was taken out in my name because Neil failed the credit checks for the mortgage. I'm sure when I get around to digging through his paperwork I'll find plenty of debt though. But I can't face it yet.

"So what do I do now?" Days of misery stretch out before me like an abyss. I can't even focus on planning his funeral. Today is New Year's Eve – normally a time of year that I love. But the thought of this new year fills me with dread.

"Just sit tight and wait until you hear from them. From my experience, I think they'll be in touch early in the new year at the latest." I can hear a phone ringing and a male voice in the background. I imagine Sergeant Downing, sitting behind a desk in an open plan office, the type that's shown on crime dramas, her dark, curly hair pinned up. I noticed she wore a wedding ring when I met her at Mum's the other day. I would give absolutely anything to have her normality. She'll finish work, maybe call at the supermarket and go home to her husband – perhaps kids too.

"Are you OK Sacha? You've gone quiet."

"Sorry, erm, can I have a phone number for them, please? The Coroner?" No way am I going to wait around. I glance at the calendar hung on the door through to the kitchen – now spent and ready for recycling. It's one of those humorous couples calendars, given to me last Christmas. When life was normal.

The Coroner's office has got until the third of January, then I'll start hounding them. The thought of all this hanging over me for any length of time is like having a weighted black cloak thrown over my head. I grab a pen from the shelf under the coffee table then scribble the number Sergeant Downing gives me onto the edge of a magazine.

"Are you getting some support for yourself, Sacha? There's plenty of help, all you have to do is reach out for it. Bereavement counselling for a start, and that becomes more specialised with suicide situations."

It sounds as though that is what she thinks. Suicide. It's probably what everyone is going to think – and they'll all blame me. They'll say I drove Neil to his death. That's maybe why his dad won't see me. He's probably scared of what he'll say. But there's a touching gentleness to Sergeant Downing's concern that invites fresh tears. Then suddenly the familiar saliva and stomach lurching. "I'm sorry. I'm going to have to go."

. . .

"I can't stop being sick," I tell my sister as she follows me into the kitchen. "I don't know what's wrong with me."

"Maybe you're..."

"Don't be so stupid," I snap back. "You know what the score is with that. We were told there was absolutely no chance without IVF."

"I know what they've said, but miracles can happen." Christy leans against the kitchen counter.

"It *would* be a bloody miracle. I've got a hormone problem and Neil had a low sperm count. The ones he did have were swimming in circles. And we barely went near each other, anyway." I adopt a different tone. She means well. "Do you want a cuppa?"

"Go on then. I just came to make sure you're OK. You haven't been answering. Mum's been trying you too. Even Rebecca tried the other day. Apparently, Mum told her to."

"I don't want to talk to Rebecca." An image of Greg with a baby floods my mind this time. I don't want contact with any of them until I see them at the funeral and that will be the only time. Surely they won't bring the baby along.

"You can't go through your life avoiding babies. Rebecca's your sister too Sacha. And she's probably worried about you. We all are. What is it between you and her? It seems to have got much worse from what I saw over Christmas. Even before what happened to Neil."

I can't face talking about that right now. Or even thinking about my toxic resentment and jealousy. I don't want to ring her number and hear the baby in the background. And aside from that, all Rebecca cares about is Rebecca. Not me. She never has. "I'll give Mum a ring later. How's Dad?" I slide the coffee tin from the cupboard.

"Ah, you know." Christy hoists herself up onto the kitchen

counter. "He's up and down. The pain relief makes him so drowsy. I expect that'll get worse as they increase it."

"Poor Dad." I could drown in misery right now. There's not even a flicker of light at the end of my darkest of tunnels.

"Anyway, I'm here to find out about you. Have you started with any of the arrangements yet? Do you need help?"

"I'm waiting to hear when I can do anything. The Coroner has apparently opened and adjourned an inquest."

"An inquest. When? Why?" Christy slips from the counter back to her feet, looking concerned.

"I don't know yet, but I imagine they'll ask Adam and Greg to give evidence if it gets to a hearing." Just saying the word *hearing* makes me feel heavy.

"But they've both given statements already, haven't they? From what Adam has said to me, there isn't any more they can tell an inquest other than what they've already told the police."

"That's what I said to Sergeant Downing when she told me about it. Look, I just don't know. You'll be the first to find out when I know more."

"What a nightmare." She sighs and pulls out a kitchen chair with a scrape, sinking heavily onto it. "I don't know how you're coping sis."

"Neither do I."

"Adam seems gutted too. He's been really quiet. Being the last one to have seen Neil and all that. I can't get him to talk about it."

I can't imagine that he's remotely gutted, but I stay silent and take the milk from the fridge.

"Have you been out of this house since you got back Sacha? It's been days."

I pour hot water into two mugs and shake my head. "Part of me can't bear to see normality and houses still with their Christmas decorations up." I swallow. "The other part of me feels too sick to go far from the toilet."

"Is it that bad? You should see a doctor Sacha. Really. That isn't right."

"What's a doctor going to do? Magically bring Neil back? That's the only thing that could make me feel any better."

"You need checking over if you ask me – you look terrible."

"Thanks." I try to smile at her. "It's probably all the stress. Things always seem to affect me in my gut."

"How are you sleeping?"

"I'm not. My mind won't stop going round and round. I keep blaming myself, thinking there must've been something I should have done to stop him."

"You've got to stop it Sacha. You'll drive yourself insane." Christy seems to peer at me a little more closely. "Have you been eating?"

"I keep trying but then I bring it back up. I've never felt so rough. Grief's almost like an illness. And I feel like I'll never get better."

Christy frowns. "Even in the few days since Christmas, you look like you've lost weight. But it's the sickness I'm most concerned about. Where's your phone?"

I nod towards where it's plugged in on top of the microwave. The kitchen is such a mess. The whole house is. I haven't got the energy to do anything, and how I'm ever going to get back to work when I feel like this, I don't know.

"Whilst I'm here, I want you to make an appointment with the doctor."

"But it's New Year's Eve Christy. There's no point. I'll make one in a couple of days."

"They'll be open today. Ring them now. I'm not leaving until you do."

Placing the mug of coffee in front of her, I then reach for my phone. I actually don't want her to leave, so anything to stop her going on at me. "There's a call queue," I say a few moments later.

"Good. Just get an appointment. I'll come with you if you want."

"I'll be fine. You'll be back at work next week anyway, won't you?"

"I guess I'll have to be. I've checked in with all my shops though, and they've been managing fine without me. When are you going to go back? It might do you good to have some sort of normality."

I'm relieved when the doctor's receptionist answers. It's better than my well-meaning sister trying to organise me.

"I've got an appointment on the second at ten past eleven." I sip my coffee, the taste of it making me gag. I've never experienced grief before. I was young when both sets of grandparents passed away, so this is all new to me. The worst kind of new. I guess everyone goes through this in their life. Grief is the cost of love. But it's only since I've lost him I realise that I really loved my husband. I wasn't sure before and no doubt he picked up on that.

"What are you doing tonight?" The diamonds on Christy's earrings catch in the sunlight as she flicks her hair behind her shoulders. Unlike me, she always looks effortlessly good, whether she's all dressed up, or in ripped jeans and one of Adam's jumpers like she is today. She's one of those sickening people who never needs makeup. She's always been the prettiest out of the three of us.

"Trying to sleep, I would imagine. I might have to ask the doctor for some tablets if I carry on like this."

"You can't be on your own on New Year's Eve Sacha. Why don't you spend it with us? We're just having a drink and cooking a meal."

"Nice." I load as much sarcasm as I can into the word. How can they be celebrating New Year after what's happened? And what's going to happen.

"So you'll come?" She sips at her coffee. "Get your stuff together – you can come back with me."

"I'm sorry Christy. I wouldn't be very good company. Honestly, I just need to get myself back together at the moment." I don't tell her I'd rather lay in the dark all night than spend five minutes in Adam's presence. If Christy had been on her own, it might have been different.

"That doesn't matter one bit. You've every right not to be good company. We wouldn't expect you to be!"

"Has Adam said *anything* else about what happened to Neil?"

"Not a thing. Like I said, he doesn't seem to want to talk about it – to the point where he clams up every time I mention anything. Honestly, he's as shaken about it as all of us are." She twists at her ring finger. Her rings are as sparkly as her earrings.

"You should warn Adam anyway, and let Greg know too, that the Coroner's office might be in touch with them soon. The quicker we give them what they want, the sooner we can get this over with."

"Are you sure you won't come back with me Sacha? I can't bear to think of you here on your own on New Year's Eve."

"No, honestly. It's where I want to be right now." I usually love New Year far more than Christmas, which over the last two or three years, has only highlighted my childlessness. New Year always offers the sense of turning the page and starting again.

But right now, it feels like all is ending rather than beginning. I have no hope and nothing to look forward to.

14

It's the first time I've left the house in nearly a week. There's barely any food left, so it's a good job I've not been eating much. I trudge from my street and through the housing estate, noticing houses that haven't yet taken their Christmas decorations down. I bet no one else has had a 'festive' period as horrendous as mine. I've been sick twice already this morning and am missing Neil so much it's like a hole has opened up inside me.

Greg tried ringing me earlier, but I don't want to speak to him any more than I want to speak to Rebecca. She'll probably be moaning that I've not even congratulated them. Mum was wittering on about the baby when I was speaking to her yesterday. Every time I tried to change the subject, she rolled it back around to Zachary or Zach, as he'll be known. Dad is apparently smitten. *Like why do I want to know all this?* My husband's rotting in a mortuary and with him, he's taken our chance of ever having fertility treatment. We were going to get one free go if he could have sorted himself out. That was, of course, the bane of our relationship.

Walking through the park makes me feel slightly better as I

gulp in the cold air like it's a drug. Before long, my monkey mind feels as though it's settling down and keeping in pace with my footsteps rather than my heart rate. There's still a bite to the air, and it's the same sort of grey as it was on Boxing Day, which I prefer right now, instead of the crisp winter sunshine I'd normally favour. The drizzly weather means that only the odd hardy dog walker or jogger is out. With each person I pass, I avert my gaze across the river. I don't want to talk to anyone, or even make eye contact. I don't really want to see the doctor either, and have even considered cancelling, but Christy would have my head on a stick if I did that. I've had her on the phone three times since I saw her two days ago. Still, I shouldn't complain. At least she's looking out for me.

I slump on a chair in the waiting room, wondering how life can seem so normal. Piped music fills the air as I become increasingly irritated, not only by the huge Christmas tree they must be leaving until twelfth night, but also by the woman a few seats away. She's doing everything in her power to appease her tantrumming toddler and failing miserably.

It's a relief when the doctor finally pokes his head from a doorway. "Sacha Young?" I get up and he holds the door ajar for me. "I'm Doctor Metcalf. Have a seat." He points to a chair at the side of his desk which faces the wall. Through his window, I can see the river in the distance. He's got a nice view. Better than mine at work, the view from my office window is literally a brick wall. I'm dreading returning there, to the sympathy and to the desk that will be just as I left it before all this, albeit, with no doubt, an overflowing inbox.

"So how can I help you?" The doctor's voice pulls my attention back into the room. He's roughly the same age as Dad and has kind eyes. I haven't seen him before. Usually, I see a female doctor with all the women's stuff that has been going on for me lately, but when I phoned the other day, I just took the first available appointment. Perhaps this doctor knew Neil.

"My husband died on Christmas Day, well Christmas night." My voice sounds strange to me. It's the first time I have spoken to anyone since Christy phoned me last night. "He fell from a cliff in Bempton, or they're saying he might have meant to. Fall, I mean, or jump. We don't know yet." I'm rambling. I watch as the welcoming smile disappears from Dr Metcalf's face as he seems to make the connection with what I'm telling him.

"I'm so sorry Sacha. I saw the news report. I can't imagine what you must be going through."

"Did you know Neil?" The tears are back again. They're never far away.

"I've seen him a time or two." He nods slowly. "But obviously, I can't discuss any aspect of his appointments with you. We're bound by confidentiality."

"That's not why I'm here," I say quickly. "In fact, I wouldn't be here, but my sister made me come."

"Well, if your sister made you come, it sounds as though you're in the right place. What can I do to help?"

"My appetite has completely vanished, and I'm not sleeping. And I just feel so ill all the time."

"Describe 'ill' to me Sacha." He leans back in his chair and adjusts his tie. I definitely won't be his run-of-the-mill patient today.

"I ache from head to foot. But the worst thing is the sickness."

"Is it nausea? Or are you actually vomiting?"

"Both. And it's constant. It's making things even harder to cope with than they already are. I feel like I could jump off a cliff myself at the moment." I know it is a crass thing to say but there are moments when there seems little point in going on right now.

"We'll come back to the sickness in a moment, but first, are you getting some support with all this?"

"Yes, some. My sister and mum keep ringing. And my husband's friend lives around the corner so he keeps checking in with me."

"That's good, but I wonder if you need something more specialised right now."

"You mean, like tablets." I suddenly realise that's exactly what I want. I would take anything to numb the pain and get some sleep.

"Not necessarily. Grief is something that can't really be masked with tablets. It has to be allowed to run its course. But that doesn't mean there aren't other things that can help, that aren't tablets."

I look at his ring finger – he's married too. He can't possibly know how horrendous I feel. "The worst thing is the not knowing," I continue. "Neil's death is being treated as unexplained, and it's being investigated by the Coroner's office." As I say the words, I realise how surreal it all sounds. Almost far fetched. Yet, this is my life now. "I'm waiting to hear about the inquest that's been opened. I can't plan my husband's funeral, or anything."

"I think you should talk to someone Sacha." He fishes around in his open drawer then pushes a card across the table. "There's a number on here for bereavement counselling, which operates on a self-referral basis, but there's a wait time of a few weeks usually. There always is at this time of year."

His words depress me even more. *There always is at this time of year,* meaning more people die over Christmas. He's right though. I know a few people who've lost their parents at Christmas. Maybe I should feel comforted that I'm not the only person wallowing in grief right now. Though, I expect other bereaved people will know exactly how their loved ones died and aren't having to wait to make their funeral arrangements.

"In the meantime, I could refer you to the Crisis Service for some more immediate support?"

"It's OK. I'll wait. It's not as though anything can be changed. Nothing can bring my husband back, can it?"

"I know, but you have to take care of yourself Sacha." Dr Metcalf glances at his computer screen then back to me. "Do you live on your own?" He pulls a tissue from the box on his desk and passes it to me. Crying has become so normal, I hardly notice when I am.

"I do since last week." Neil's presence in the house often used to get on my nerves. He seemed to take up so much space with all his stuff that I understood the old housewife joke about husbands getting under your feet. However, over the last week, the silence and my aloneness have become a chasm that's trying to swallow me up. "OK, yes, refer me. It can only help, can't it?"

He looks relieved as he taps onto his computer.

"Right, now to the nausea and the sickness. Could you hop onto the couch and roll your jumper up? I'd like to have a feel around on your tummy if that's OK."

I do as directed, feeling a sense of relief at being able to lie down for a minute or two. My eyes burn with misery and exhaustion. Dr Metcalf approaches me from the side, rubbing his hands together.

"I think you've got enough to cope with without having cold hands placed on your belly."

I try to smile as I become accustomed to the unfamiliar sensation of another human's hands against my skin. It's strangely comforting.

"Does this hurt?" He presses the right-hand side of my lower belly.

I shake my head. "It kind of just aches everywhere."

"Well, I'm confident it's not your appendix." He continues pressing in different areas, then steps back. "OK. There doesn't seem to be anything untoward. When was your last period?"

"I'm not sure." My voice rises, probably conveying how taken aback I am by his question. "They're a bit all over the place. Why?"

"I'm just wondering if there's any possibility you might be pregnant?"

I'd laugh if I didn't feel so dreadful. "No. Neil and I, if you look back at my notes, you'll see we've not been able to conceive. We've both had fertility problems."

"I see." He returns to his desk and starts scrolling down his screen. "Ah yes. Obviously, I see so many patients, it's difficult to recall specifics until I'm reminded of them. But even so, I feel we should rule it out. Sickness, as we know, is one of the first symptoms." He reaches into his drawer again and pulls out a sample bottle. "Could you manage a water sample? You know where the ladies toilets are, don't you?"

I stare at him. "There's no point. I won't be pregnant. Not in a million years." My mind flits back over the last four years where I have used no contraception. When Neil and I decided we wanted a baby not long after our wedding, we started out just seeing what would happen. Then, when nothing happened, we actively *tried*, which took the shine off everything. When still nothing happened, I got silly. I kept temperature charts, bought ovulation kits, and would spend half an hour with my legs up against the wall rather than cuddling up to my husband after we had made love. This rigmarole went on for nearly two years until we asked to be investigated. Throughout this time, the cracks had shown in our marriage, and in Neil's mental health.

"It's not just about pregnancy," he says gently. "There could be, for example, a water infection causing your sickness. We've got to rule everything out."

"Fair enough." A water infection would certainly make sense and having had one before, I know they're easily treated. Plus, it made me sick last time. I take the bottle. "Shall I do this now?"

"If you would. Then if anything shows up, we can get it dealt with straight away. I'll see my next patient whilst you're in there and then call you back in."

I've become an expert at filling urine sample bottles over the last couple of years, so I'm in and out of the loo quickly. I return to the Christmas tree and the piped music, clutching my warm bottle of wee. Noticing a man peering at me, I slip the bottle into my pocket. At least the screaming toddler has gone. I pick up a magazine but can't focus, so put it down again. I spend the next few minutes staring absently at the rotating public information screen as it talks about flu, then cancelling appointments, then safe units of alcohol, then..."

"Sacha." I wrap my fingers around the bottle in my pocket and get to my feet. Dr Metcalf smiles as I approach his door. "Sorry to keep you waiting."

"It's not like I have anywhere else to be." It's true. From my normality of bustling around, juggling work with life, everything has ground to a pointless standstill. I hand Dr Metcalf the sample bottle.

"Have a seat and I'll get this dipped."

I watch as he opens a drawer below the examination table and unscrews the bottle. He dips the sample strip of paper into it then lays it on a piece of blue paper. "We just need to leave that to cook for two minutes." I know what that means. It's the pregnancy one. Having a pregnancy test feels like a cruel joke.

He dips two more strips and immediately says, "well you're clear of infection." He glances back at the first strip. "Well." He pauses and picks it up. "I think we might have got to the bottom of what's making you ill." He turns the strip over and looks at the other side.

The expression on Dr Metcalf's face tells me it doesn't appear to be bad news. "What is it?"

"It would appear that you *are* indeed pregnant Sacha."

I stare at him for a few moments, aware that my mouth has fallen open. "What?"

"There's no mistaking that result. The strip changed colour almost straight away."

"But. But I can't be. We couldn't conceive. I can't conceive."

"Well, this bit of paper says you can."

"Are you sure?" I want to laugh, cry and throw up all at the same time. I can't believe it. *Pregnant.*

"I realise you must be stunned." He sits back in his chair and leans towards me. "Maybe, just maybe, this pregnancy will be what keeps you going, you could see it as an unexpected gift."

Dr Metcalf is a lovely man. I knew it as soon as I saw him. However, I can't reply – I don't feel as though I can even speak.

"Are you alright Sacha?"

"Erm." I clear my throat. "I think so."

"Is there anyone I can contact for you? Your sister?"

I shake my head. I need to process this myself before anyone else finds out. "How far along will I be, do you think?"

"It's difficult to say. I couldn't feel anything when I was examining your tummy, so I expect you're not much past the ten-week mark. You'll need to have a think about period dates and intercourse around that time to work that out."

I try to do mental calculations, but I can't think straight. All I know is Neil and I weren't really making love in the last couple of months of his life. He was mostly too drunk. I need to work all this out. "Can I have a scan or something?"

"Not usually until twelve weeks."

"But I'm not really sure of any dates. And I need to know

everything's OK. I was drinking at Christmas and I haven't been looking after myself very well."

"Try not to worry about that too much. A lot of mums don't realise they're expecting and report carrying on as normal in the early weeks. Fledgling embryos are more robust than they might first appear. But still..." Dr Metcalf lapses into silence and taps his pen against his chin as though that might assist with processing his thinking.

A lot of mums. He's categorising me as a mum. And talking about expecting. For a moment, I forget about everything else going on in my life, and a shiver of excitement dances in my belly. Maybe he's right. Maybe there is something to go on for after all. A flood of dread quickly quells this excitement. *What if there has been a mistake? What if I lose it? What if it isn't..."*

"I'll make you an appointment for the Early Pregnancy Screening Unit Sacha." Dr Metcalf returns to his computer. "In view of your history and the stress you've been under, I agree it makes sense to err on the side of caution."

I've noticed the signs for the Early Pregnancy Screening Unit when I've been attending at the Fertility Clinic and often fervently hoped I could go left instead of right when presented with the two signage options.

"I'm also going to book you into the antenatal clinic here at the surgery. You can meet our two community midwives and begin discussing your care."

I nip the skin on my hand as he speaks. If this isn't really happening, then I need to wake up. Dr Metcalf is using words like midwife and antenatal. To me. After all this time. I need a drink. No, I don't need a drink. I can't have a drink for the next nine months. Or however many months until the baby's born. I need to know *when. Until the baby is born.* I can't believe it.

15

I'M MET by several hostile stares as I leave the surgery, having taken up the time of about three appointments. Dr Metcalf has given me cards for the Bereavement Service, the Crisis Centre, The Early Pregnancy Screening Unit and The Ante-Natal Clinic. This is sheer madness. My hand instinctively flits to my belly and I realise, as I walk towards the high street, that I have to look after myself now. I haven't even eaten today.

As I walk along, I wonder whether anyone can tell what I've just been told. Do they see a widow or a mother to be? Farndale is a small market town and word will have spread about Neil's death by now. Will people notice my elation as I walk around, and think I'm a callous cow? I can't help it. A baby is all I've ever wanted. I just wish it were something Neil and I could have shared.

I chew on an apple as I leave the market, feeling the familiar nausea rising. At least I know what's causing it now. There must be something I can do to ease it. I buy a bottle of water, feeling instantly better as its chill slides into my sickly stomach. If something's going down, then nothing can come up. I've hardly drunk today, so am probably dehydrated. I head into the chemist.

"What would you recommend for morning sickness?" I ask the kindly-looking woman behind the counter. "Well, it's more like all day sickness, really." I smile at her, and she smiles back.

"Congratulations," she says, and it feels good. After one of my darkest weeks, it's as though I can see glimmers of the sun. Pangs of guilt are trying to chase these glimmers away, but I will not let them. I've waited so long for this.

I leave the chemist with Sea-bands for the pressure points on my wrist, some peppermint oil and chamomile tea. The lady told me about her daughter's pregnancy and recommended fresh ginger and arrowroot biscuits. That's my next port of call, the herbalists.

I walk home, concerned that my two carrier bags will somehow weigh on my belly, so keep stopping to rest. I want to tell someone my news but feel as though I can't. Not yet. How can I feel any happiness when something so tragic has happened? I yearn for the next few months to pass. To get through the first trimester and for all to be OK with the baby. For the inquest to be over and a verdict of accidental death reached. And for Neil's funeral to have taken place.

I remember when Rebecca was pregnant with Freya; she was sick all the time. Someone told her that feeling sick is a good thing. It meant her hormone levels were doing what they should be. Hormone levels. That was one problem preventing me from conceiving. Christy was right. Miracles really happen.

I settle on the sofa with my sickness cures and pluck my phone from my bag. I type in *pregnant at ten weeks* and feel another flutter of excitement as I stare at the image presented to me. At least I know now why I've been so ill and exhausted. Misery is still drilling away at my edges, but deep within me, something wonderful is happening. I read the words accompanying the image, telling me exactly what stage my baby is at. *My baby.* Then a call. Unknown number.

"Can I speak to Mrs Sacha Young please?"

"Speaking."

"My name's Nigel Mahony. I'm the assistant coroner to Mr Curzon from the Coroner's Court at Hull, calling to make preliminary arrangements in your husband's case."

My breath catches in my throat as I'm brought back to earth. "OK." Though I wish they'd all stop calling what's happened *a case.*

"Having gone through all the statements, along with the pathologist's report, Mr Curzon has decided an inquest is necessary."

"The police have already told me this. How long will it all take though?" My voice cracks. "I just want to lay him to rest. I can't bear the thought of him being laid in some fridge."

"I completely understand Mrs Young."

"Did you say you're in Hull? Is that where the inquest will take place?"

"Yes. Because your husband died in our area."

I make mental calculations of a two-hour drive each way, coupled with coping with the inquest itself. Hopefully, by the time we get to it, my sickness should be subsiding.

"Because the pathology examination is complete Mrs Young." His voice interrupts my thoughts. "We can allow an interim death certificate, which means you can get on with organising your husband's funeral in the normal way. The only thing you cannot do is register his death until after the inquest."

We can lay him to rest. Thank goodness. I take a deep breath. That's something at least.

"We should be able to get the inquest listed for February,"

he continues. "Looking at the reports, Mr Curzon has said it won't be necessary to assemble a jury."

"OK. What do I need to do? I've never been through anything like this."

"We'll need to take statements from yourself, Adam Fox, Greg Watkins, the GP and the counsellor who was working with your husband."

"His friend and his father were also in close contact with Neil before he died. If anyone can vouch for his state of mind, it would be one of them." I don't tell this man that he was far closer, certainly in the last year or so, to them, than he was to me. He said he couldn't talk to me because every time he tried, it ended up with a confrontation of some sort.

"Right, they can certainly be called as witnesses. I'll get their details from you in a moment. And if we could make an appointment for you now?"

"Do I have to come to Hull for that as well?"

"Yes. We'll leave you until after the other witnesses, though. That way, we can go through everything we've gathered with you, and you can look around the court, so you'll know what to expect on the day." He sounds OK, this man, and his efficient, yet calm manner is putting me more at ease about the whole wretched mess.

"I don't need a solicitor, do I?" This is probably a stupid question. It's not as if I've done anything wrong. Well, not in the eyes of the law.

"That's entirely your decision Sacha, but the inquest is to find out what happened, it's not a criminal process. However, of course, if any new information of a criminal nature were to surface at the inquest, we could bring proceedings from that."

"I see."

"Just to set your mind at rest, there's little to suggest at this stage, that will happen."

I notice he says *little,* not *nothing.*

We make an appointment for three weeks tomorrow, and I give him the numbers for Joe and Ash. As I hang up, my thoughts are tumbling over one another. I was going to the supermarket but can no longer face it. I should talk to someone, tell someone everything that's happening, but I feel my words wouldn't even make sense right now.

How can I go back to work with all this going on? In less than two weeks, my husband has died, an inquest is taking place to find out whether it was an accidental death or suicide, I have his funeral to plan and, against all the odds, I have a baby on the way. Then there's the situation with my poor dad. It's overwhelming, and despite knowing I have several people I can pick up the phone to, I'm overwhelmingly alone.

It's dark when the growling of my stomach wakes me. I reach for my phone and am shocked to find I've slept for four hours. As I raise my head up from the cushion, the usual nausea rises too. I'm suddenly reminded of my new pregnant state as I fumble around in my handbag for the packet of crystallised ginger.

As I chew on it, I remember the fish and vegetables I bought, and decide that to cook some proper food is the best way forward. The ginger tastes disgusting, but it definitely helps.

Whilst I've been asleep, I've missed calls from Mum and Christy. Part of me is aching to tell them my news, but I also have an overriding urge to keep it to myself. It's come as a huge shock and I need to get used to the idea on my own first. Perhaps I'll wait until after the scan, when I've made sure everything is alright. I have other things to get straight in my head too.

Maybe I'll get the funeral and the inquest over with before I tell anyone. I have to deal with one thing at a time. If the inquest is going to be in February, it won't be too long until I can start telling people. I'm going to need help, there's no doubt about that. The thought of single parenthood is daunting. My stomach growls again. This little one inside of me needs food.

Normally I'd pour a glass of pinot grigio at this time of day, especially after what's happened to Neil, but instead I fill a glass with water. It's going to be a long few months without wine but it will be so worth it. As I wait for my dinner to cook my phone beeps. Christy.

I wish you'd pick up sis. I'm worried about you. Just wondering how you got on with the doc????

Sorry. I've been asleep. Just catching up.

You OK?

I'm fine, I type back. *It's just stress and stuff. I've got something for the nausea, and he's referred me for some crisis counselling.*

That's good. We got a call from the Coroner's office. Adam's got to go to Hull for a statement. Greg as well.

Me too. Have they both made an appointment?

Yep. Early next week.

Good. Just want all this over. I'm allowed to plan the funeral too.

Shit. You OK with that?

I'll have to be. I'll make some calls tomorrow and get things going.

Do you need some help?

Probably. I'll let you know.

I'm here for you Sacha. Don't be on your own.

I know. Thanks sis.

I love you.

Tears well yet again as I read her last message. Christy never tells me she loves me. Apart from on my wedding day when she was sozzled. Part of me wants to call her, tell her the amazing news I've had today, but something's stopping me, and it's not just her 'anti-baby' stance. It's something else.

I check my salmon. Another five minutes. I move a pile of

laundry from the kitchen table and slump onto a chair, my phone still in my hand. Although I know what I'm about to do is like picking a scab off a wound, I start scrolling through some of the recent messages between Neil and me, looking for clues.

I'm stopping at Dad's tonight. I've had a few too many. Really sorry.

Great. Thanks.

Where are you Sacha? The bed doesn't even look as though it's been slept in.

So it's OK for you to bugger off but not me?

I'm at the hospital for our appointment at the clinic. You should have been here half an hour ago.

Sorry love. Can't face it.

Where the bloody hell are you? I can't take this anymore.

I might as well be on my own.

Can you pick me up? Too drunk to drive. Sorry.

Home soon. Just at the supermarket. Do you want anything?

Just a few cans.

No chance.

Have you picked your prescription up yet?

These tablets are making me feel really funny Sacha. How long will they take to work?

I've just had a look on the internet. A couple of weeks apparently.

I stop scrolling. They make for depressing reading and no doubt the police will have saved all these from when they've inspected Neil's phone. It's obvious to anyone that we weren't in a happy marriage. Certainly not in the last few months. The distance I created and the way I made him feel is something I'll always have to live with.

16

HAVING SEEN who it is through the spyhole, I ignore the door. However, Greg spots me through the lounge window as I dart from the lounge to the kitchen, so I'm forced to answer.

"Can I come in? It's freezing out here."

Saying nothing, I hold the door wider for him.

"Why weren't you answering?"

"Why do you think?"

He follows me into the lounge. "You haven't wasted any time, have you?" He nods towards the boxed up books and black sacks filled with Neil's clothes. Plenty of people would share Greg's opinion on packing Neil's things, but I can't bear to look at them. "I know things were bad between you but..."

"Who are you to judge me? Or my marriage? What do you want anyway?"

"I can't believe you haven't been to see the baby. No matter what's been going on, he's still your nephew." There are shadows surrounding Greg's eyes. It could be sleepless nights with the baby. It could be something else.

"I've had a lot to deal with in case you didn't know." I move a bag from the armchair and sit.

Greg lowers himself to the sofa, facing me. "You could find half an hour to visit your sister and new nephew. You won't even answer the phone to her."

"It's always about Rebecca, isn't it?" I spit the words out like a piece of gristle.

"But you've been speaking to Christy, haven't you?" Like Ash, Greg looks as though he's not shaved for a few days.

I look him straight in the eye. "Christy cares about me. Rebecca only cares about Rebecca."

"Don't you think there's been enough bad blood lately? With what's happening with your dad, you should all be pulling together. Rebecca's really struggling to cope with everything, you know."

"Poor Rebecca. She should try having a funeral to arrange and an inquest to prepare for."

"When is the funeral? She told me to ask you." He tugs his phone from the pocket of his jacket. At least he's not taken his jacket off. I wouldn't want him in my house for any length of time. I'm not in the mood for company. Especially the company of either of my brothers-in-law after how they've behaved.

"The twenty-ninth of January. Half-past eleven at St Oswald's Church." My voice is flat. I wish he'd clear off.

"Did you not think to let us know Sacha?"

"I've posted it on Facebook and put an announcement in the paper. What more do you want?"

"No matter what's gone on, Rebecca's still your sister. You could at least have messaged her, instead of expecting her to see some bloody announcement in the newspaper." Greg's face is pinched with anger. I don't know what's rattled him so much, other than he can probably sense how much I don't want him here.

"Rebecca could've called around to see me herself." Not that I'd have wanted her to, but I say it anyway.

"She's just had a baby Sacha. Plus, she has another two kids to look after."

"Don't I know it? You'd think she was the only person in the world to become a mother."

At that, my hand instinctively flies to my stomach. Quickly, I drop it to my lap; Greg is not the person I'd want to be the first to know about the baby. I have my scan tomorrow and am counting down the hours. I just want to be told that everything is alright. The news has settled in with me now.

"Do you need any help with anything Sacha?" Greg must sense my change of mood and his voice softens. "The catering or anything?"

"Neil's dad is helping with the arrangements, thanks."

"What about pallbearers?"

I can't imagine Neil would have wanted either Greg or Adam to raise his coffin, but I haven't got the energy to discuss that with him now. "We've an appointment this afternoon with the priest doing the service. Me and Neil's dad. So I'll let you know." It'll be the first time I've seen Joe since Neil died and I'm not looking forward to it.

"Priest? St Oswald's? I didn't know Neil was Catholic?"

"Yeah. Just not a practicing one." To my surprise, I realise I'm conversing with Greg normally for the first time in ages. "His Dad goes in for all that though. I think Neil had it all shoved down his throat as a kid."

I guess we've all still got a few things to face as a family, and then I can step back and create some distance. Especially from Greg and Rebecca.

"So Neil's going to be buried, is he?"

I nod. "Look, tell Rebecca I'll ring her in a day or two. Let me get this appointment about the funeral out of the way first." I don't add, *and my appointment with the Early Pregnancy Screening Unit.*

. . .

Joe blocks my car in with his Mondeo, which would normally irritate me. But as he gets out of the car and walks up the path, I'm comforted by the sight of him and realise, for the first time, how much he looks like Neil. I fling the door open before he has the chance to ring the doorbell. He says nothing, and just pulls me towards him.

"Thanks for coming." I sob into Joe's shoulder. "I'm glad I don't have to face these funeral arrangements on my own. Come in."

"Neil was my son. Of course I want to be involved." He lets me go and closes the door behind him. "I'm sorry this is the first time I've seen you since it happened Sacha." He runs his eyes across the lounge and I'm relieved that I thought to move the boxes and bags to the boot of my car. Well, I got Greg to move the boxes, telling him I'd hurt my back. Packing things up might be my way of dealing with things, but it's certainly not everyone's.

"There's nothing to apologise for Joe." I continue through to the kitchen and fill the kettle.

"I haven't seen *anyone,* not just you. It's been hell. Even church can't help me through this right now." I look at him, framed in the doorway, somehow a shrunken version of his former self. Had Neil lived, Joe embodies what Neil might have looked like in twenty years' time.

"I know." I wish I could tell him about the possibility of him becoming a grandad. It might give him something to go on for. But it's too soon. And I need to know that all is as it should be, then work things out and make some decisions...

"He's ten minutes early. Shall I get that?" Joe runs his fingers through his receding hair. I follow his gaze to the shiny black car parked behind Joe's, in full view of my lounge window. It's an appropriate car for someone who conducts funerals.

I nod. Here we go.

"I'm Reverend Francis Hepple." The elderly priest lumbers

towards me, his hand outstretched. He wears black trousers, shirt and a jacket, even his dog collar is black. He's a peculiar sight in my home.

"Sacha Young. I'm Joe's daughter-in-law."

"It's a shame we're not meeting under different circumstances." He grips my hand. His hand is warm and I find myself liking him. He's a portly man compared to Joe and to my dad, but there's something comforting about that.

"My parishioners call me Father Francis." He smiles at me, then turns to where Joe has taken a seat at the kitchen table. "How are you doing, Joseph?"

"Up and down." He smooths out a sheet of crumpled paper in front of him on the table. "But I feel better for getting out of the house."

"You must lean on those who want to help you." Father Francis has a booming voice, again out of place in my usually quiet house. He places a folder on the table, hitches his trousers, and sits facing Joe. His body spills over the sides of the chair.

"Tea or coffee?"

"Tea would be grand if it's not too much trouble."

I like the Irish lilt in his voice. It reminds me of a teacher who took me under his wing when I'd had a massive row with Dad as a teenager. Father Francis glances at the photograph framed above the kitchen table of Neil and I, taken on our honeymoon in Saint Tropez. That had been the most perfect two weeks of my life, though much to Neil's disappointment, I had refused to go topless on the beach like all the other women.

Father Francis looks from the picture to me as I fling tea bags into the pot. "I'm so sorry for your loss Sacha. What a tragic waste."

There's no answer I can give to that. All falls silent for a few moments as I make the drinks.

"You weren't married at St Oswald's, were you?" It feels more like a judgement than a question.

"I'm not actually a Catholic myself," I reply. "I'm not even a churchgoer."

"Have you been baptised?"

"Well, yes, but in the Church of England."

"Do you believe in the Lord, Sacha? Do you think Neil has gone on to eternal life?"

What on earth am I supposed to say to that? "Erm yes, I'd like to think that there is both a God, and an afterlife. I tend to need proof of something before I can believe in it though." It's true. It would be good to think Neil has gone on and is at peace and happy at last. What I don't say is that I'll be more likely to think a God exists if my baby turns out to be safe and well at tomorrow's scan. Certainly so far in my life, I haven't felt much of the presence of any sort of God.

"Have they got to the bottom of what happened yet?" Father Francis sips his tea. "To Neil, I mean?"

"There's to be an inquest." Joe glances at me. "I got the phone call just before I left the house."

"Neil should have come to me." Father Francis shakes his head. "I haven't seen him for several years, but I remember the boy he was at Sunday school. There was so much help for him if he'd only reached out for it."

"We don't know what happened yet," I blurt. "It may well have been an awful accident."

"Quite. Yes. Anyway." Father Francis slides a form from his folder. "We've got the date and time for the funeral. Let's get some more details so we can get a plan together for it shall we?"

I don't know how Neil would feel about having a catholic burial. He'd become all but an occasional churchgoer, and his catholic guilt had fuelled those visits. A guilt which had underpinned his life the whole time I knew him. Joe, on the other hand, never misses a Sunday. It had been Neil's decision for us to get married abroad, something Joe had been bitterly disappointed about. As far as I know, to get married at St Oswald's, I'd have had to convert to Catholicism. And there was no way I was going to do that.

"Are you still OK for me to handle all these details Sacha?" Joe slurps from his cup, a sound that always irritates me and even more so, in my quiet kitchen. Though I'm more easily irritated than usual at the moment.

"I guess so. There's just a song I want playing as he's carried in or out." How I'm going to face watching his coffin being lowered into the ground, I don't know. Cremations are bad enough.

"And you must contribute some details for the eulogy Sacha." Father Francis plucks a pen from his top pocket. "You knew him better than anybody."

"I don't know about that." It's true. In the end, Neil didn't know me either. Or maybe he thought he did.

I leave them for a moment and go to the lounge to have a nibble at my ginger. All this funeral talk has invited the sickness back. I can't be sick whilst these two are in my house and it's so quiet that they'd hear me. Though they'd probably just put it down to the grief. I consider putting the radio on just in case, but that's hardly appropriate.

I fill a large glass of water and re-join them at the table. No way can I drink the coffee I've made. It's soon apparent that Joe has given the funeral some thought already. He's chosen two bible readings, three hymns and a poem. He puts himself and his two brothers forward as three of the pallbearers. I put Adam, Greg, and Ash forward as well. I didn't want to choose Adam and Greg, but who else is there? I wonder whether Dad will be well enough to travel over here and get through a requiem mass. I hope so.

"Where's Neil now?" Father Francis asks and I notice Joe's face cloud over, possibly at the directness of his question.

"He's still in the mortuary at Bridlington." My voice is small as the image of him, shrouded in sheets, swims into my mind. "We're waiting to get him back here, to the chapel of rest."

"Have you made arrangements with an undertaker yet?" Father Francis clicks his pen as he speaks, which is annoying. "And is the transportation imminent?"

I hate the word *undertaker*. "Yes. They're collecting him as soon as they can, tomorrow at the latest, I hope. " I turn to Joe. "Will you want to see him?"

"I don't think I could bear to." He fishes a hanky from his pocket and presses it against his eyes. "I'd prefer to remember him as he was, I think. But even then... he was so... depressed." He gives me a look I can't read. "It's not the normal order of things, this." His tears look to be coming faster.

I step towards him and place my arm around his shoulders, but he doesn't lean into me, rather he stiffens.

"It should be me lying in a mortuary, waiting to be shipped to a funeral home. Not Neil. Not my son. I've lived my life. He should've had years in front of him."

"I know. I know." Father Francis places his hand on Joe's arm. "We'll get you through this. Both of you." He nods towards me.

17

As I TAKE the lift to the third floor, I'm reminded of the times I've stood here with Neil, our haunted expressions mirrored in each other eyes, knowing we couldn't impart one of the most fundamental gifts of being a couple. We'd stand here in silence, before walking along the shiny corridor, usually dazzled in sunlight after the gloom of the lift.

The same corridor I now walk along, sensing a lurch of something in my belly as I ignore the sign saying Fertility Clinic, and for the first time, turn towards the sign saying Early Pregnancy Screening Unit. I ring the buzzer and wait.

As I'm let in, a young couple are leaving. The woman is in a torrent of tears, clutching a leaflet about miscarriage. Seeing her brings home how precarious my situation is. I welcome the sickness as it's a good sign in pregnancy, yet have become obsessed with checking for spots of blood every time I'm in the loo. I'm convinced something will go wrong. This might be my only chance of becoming a mother. It wasn't how I imagined it, but I've got a decent job and a stable home.

The only thing I haven't got is a strong support network. Mum's miles away and Christy isn't interested in babies. I'll never understand how anyone bestowed with the ability to bear children would choose not to. And Rebecca, well, no, I definitely haven't got a strong support network.

"Sacha Young." I stand in response to the woman's voice and walk towards her. "I'm Doctor Leon and this is Nurse Cooper. Have a seat." She gestures to a chair beside her desk in the dimly lit room and flips the sign on the door to *engaged*. She sits at the computer and the nurse perches on a high stool behind her.

"So. You've been referred here by your GP, Doctor Metcalf?" Her tone is brisk, more suited to a boardroom than dealing with women in the most vulnerable stage of pregnancy. Still, she probably has to be detached to cope with all the bad news she will inevitably have to dish out. "I'll start by taking some details before we do the scan." She nods towards a dreadful-looking chair, one that only has half a bottom to it.

"Am I not having an ultrasound?" I had images of being laid on a couch with gel rubbed on my belly, albeit without my husband beside me. That was a scenario we'd dreamed of when we first started trying. We said he or she needed my brains and Neil's looks and we didn't mind what we got. Boy or girl. As long as it was healthy. I feel very alone. However, I'll never be alone once this little one joins me.

"We're told that you can't be any further along than ten weeks, therefore the normal ultrasound won't show up as much as a vaginal ultrasound will." With her tight bun and pursed mouth, she *looks* to belong in a boardroom as well. "OK, firstly, what was the date of your last period?"

"I've no idea. Have you read through my notes? Normally, I'd be attending at the fertility clinic. I can't remember having a period since last summer."

"OK. What about Dad? Is he in the waiting room?"

I would laugh at the irony if it wasn't so depressing, thinking of Neil, in his own waiting room of sorts. "My husband died on Christmas Day." My voice wobbles around the stark room. "We were told our only chance of a baby was through treatment, so this is like a miracle."

"I see." Something in her expression softens. "We'd better have a look and see what's going on then. Apart from the fertility problems, are you fit and well?"

"I guess so. Obviously, I'm going through it at the moment, so I'm praying grief can't harm babies. I'm trying to eat but feel sick all the time."

"That's actually a good sign," the consultant says, echoing my earlier thoughts. "Your hormones are doing their job. If you'd like to pop behind the curtain and remove the bottom half of your clothes. Wrap the sheet around yourself and then come back to the chair."

My belly is churning ten to the dozen as I gingerly lower my bottom to the back of the chair, if it can even be described as a chair. I grip the arms and tense up as the probe searches around inside me, feeling scared it will hurt the baby. The doctor's face is unreadable as she presses buttons and stares at her screen. I brace myself for bad news. It's what I'm accustomed to. Then, after several agonising minutes, she flips the screen around and I'm alerted to a grainy image on my right-hand side.

"Sacha, meet your baby." The nurse smiles and squeezes my hand.

Tears fill my eyes as I stare at the grey blob. "Is everything alright?"

"See that flashing which looks like a dot. Just there?"

I nod.

"That's baby's heartbeat."

"I'll just be a few moments," Doctor Leon says. "I've got a few measurements to take, then I should be able to give you an idea of your due date.

As tears tumble down my face, I can't take my eyes off the screen. "You don't know how long I've waited for this."

"I'm so sorry about Dad." The nurse squeezes my hand again amidst the beeping and button pressing going on next to us. "What happened?"

"He fell from a cliff in Bempton, where my parents live." Even as I say the words, they don't feel real.

"Oh God. That's terrible."

"I saw that report on the news." The doctor looks over the top of her glasses and tucks a stray hair behind her ear. "I'm so sorry."

I want them to talk about my baby. I want a few minutes free from being accosted by thoughts of Neil's death. This is a special moment. It has to be. This baby is my oasis of happiness within a storm of complete misery.

I literally skip from the hospital, clutching the picture of my baby, well a picture of a blob. However, it's a safe blob. All's as it should be and they have estimated me as nine and a half weeks pregnant, meaning my baby is due on August 18th.

I'm suddenly swamped by the realisation that my dad might not still be around to meet him or her and the thought momentarily winds me. But my mood bounces up again. *Him or her.* This is my life now. Up and down. Around and around. It's like being on a fairground ride. I certainly feel sick enough, but since I've discovered I'm pregnant, the actual vomiting has stopped, and only the nausea remains. Which is bad enough.

I've an hour before my appointment with the crisis counsellor. There's still a month before I have an appointment with the bereavement service. At least I'll be able to talk about the baby to the crisis counsellor, instead of keeping it to myself like a guilty secret. I certainly don't want anyone else to know until after the funeral. I might even leave it until after the inquest.

~

"Come in Mrs Young." I walk towards the man with a gingery beard. His eyes are bright and unwrinkled, yet in his brown suit and brogues, he's dressed as someone much older would.

I sit in the easy chair he directs me to. Beams of sunlight fall across the table in between our chairs. A painting of a sunset on the far wall adds to the calming aura of the room. It's what I need right now. Calm. Peace. Space. Most of all, forgiveness.

"I'm Mal Walker, one of the specialist counsellors here. Am I alright to call you Sacha?"

I nod. "Yes, that's fine."

"Right then Sacha." He passes me a sheet clipped to a board. "Before we begin, I need you to fill in this form for me. It's a way to measure the difference these sessions make."

I rummage in my bag for a pen. "I don't have to fill one in at every session, do I?"

"No. Just at this first one then again at the final one. I understand the bereavement counselling will take around a month to get underway, so we'll look after you until then."

I glance at the form, comforted at the prospect of being 'looked after.' Just as Father Francis said to Joe, I need to lean on others too, especially now.

I sit for a few moments, scoring my level of anxiety, ability to eat, sleep and look after myself. I have to score feelings of hopelessness, loneliness and finally, frequency of self-harming or suicidal thoughts. This is too close to home.

"And if you could just read and sign the statement about confidentiality and disclosure."

"I was having thoughts of hurting myself. I would never have acted on them, but I certainly went through a spell of wanting to follow my husband." I can't help a smile erupt as I hand the clipboard back to Mal. "But that was before something wonderful happened."

"If you don't mind parking that, just for a moment. Unfortunately, we need to deal with the bad stuff first. It's just to risk assess."

I feel my joy crumple with his words as he runs his pen down the clipboard before placing it on the table.

"Can you tell me about these thoughts of hurting yourself."

"How much have you been told by my doctor?"

"Not much really. Just that you lost your husband in unexplained circumstances on Christmas Day."

"Yes." I swallow. "It's a Christmas I won't forget in a hurry. Neil, my husband, got incredibly drunk on Christmas Eve and made himself ill. Then on Christmas Day he was even more depressed than normal."

"If you didn't know, alcohol is a depressant. How did you know he was more depressed than normal? Did he open up to you about it?"

"He was trying to tell me something on the morning before he died, but I wasn't listening." My voice shakes. "I was too annoyed with him. I'll never forgive myself for that."

"Tell me first, what you were annoyed about."

"Where do I start? The main catalyst that day was the fact that he'd been drunk out of his mind the night before and had been sick all over the patio."

Mal is scribbling onto a notepad as I speak. "What was he trying to tell you?"

"That he wanted to leave. Not me – my parent's house. That's where we were, you see. My Dad's terminally ill. And Neil was going on about how miserable he was and how we'd have a better time without him." If I close my eyes, I'm back, sitting on that bench in my parent's front garden with Neil sitting barefoot beside me. "I hardly paid him any attention at the time – I could barely look at him, but I've played it over and over in my head ever since. If only I'd offered him some comfort. He was really down. We would have probably split up sooner or later, but at least he'd still be alive. My conscience will plague me forever."

"Why was he down?"

"We had all sorts happening. Neil was out of work and had been for a couple of months. Most of that was down to him having a pretty bad drink problem. And we were trying for a baby, so there was a knock on effect of his drinking there. But we both had fertility problems, it wasn't just Neil."

"It's sounds as though you've had an awful lot going on Sacha. Are you getting any other day to day support? Apart from the sessions we're going to offer you here? Because at best, we can only offer an hour a week until your bereavement counselling begins."

"Not really. My mum has enough on with what's going on with my dad."

"What's the matter with your dad, if you don't mind me asking?"

"He's got bowel cancer. And it's spread. He had a choice between feeling sicker from a more aggressive treatment and possibly being here for a while longer, or pain management and a better quality few months. Or however long he goes on for. He showed some improvement when he first stopped his treatment in the autumn, but he appears to be ailing faster now." I have a lump in my throat the size of a golf ball. It's not often I talk about what's going on with Dad, so to say out loud that he's deteriorating makes it more real.

"I can imagine it must be very tough. Have you got siblings?""

"Two sisters. One older, one younger. Rebecca, the youngest, has just had a baby and I don't like being around her. My other sister Christy is there for me, but I can't stand her husband. Since Neil died, I can't help but blame Adam, that's my brother-in-law, for what happened."

"Why is that?" Mal leans forward in his seat. His eyes don't leave my face.

"He and Neil *never* got on. But Adam was particularly nasty in the hours leading up to Neil's death. And he was apparently the last one to see him."

"The last one to see him?"

"My mother had sent Adam and Neil for a walk to bury their differences after an argument during Christmas dinner. She'd been close to breaking point with them. It was awful. Adam was awful." Dad's face returns to my mind. No matter what I'm going through now, I'll hopefully have more Christmases to celebrate. That was Dad's last one.

"So do you know what happened between them?" The counsellor glances at the clock, and I'm shocked to see we're almost halfway through our allotted time already. "When they went for a walk?"

"Adam says Neil had stormed off after punching him." It's the stuff of soap operas and would almost sound amusing if it hadn't ended in such tragedy.

"Your husband punched your brother-in-law?"

"Twice apparently. That was the last time anyone saw Neil alive. He was so depressed." I take a deep breath. "He could have jumped from the cliff – I think that's what everyone is thinking – even the police. My parents live at Bempton where the cliff is over three hundred feet high."

"I know it well," Mal says. "I've walked along those cliffs several times."

"It's a notoriously dangerous path," I continue, "so I think he could have fallen. It's only fenced along the main viewing points and there are warning signs everywhere."

"From the tone of your voice Sacha, it sounds as though you might have a third possibility."

"Or..." I begin. "And maybe this is what the inquest will find out. I can't get it out of my mind. Adam might have pushed him. He hated him and he's spent the last year trying to persuade me to leave Neil." It's the first time I have voiced this suspicion to anyone. God knows what Christy would make of me if she knew.

"We've certainly got quite a lot to unravel here Sacha."

I nod, wondering whether to tell him the whole truth about the baby as well. I guess I've got to be fully truthful if I'm going to gain full benefit from these sessions. Mal's not allowed to tell a soul what's going on in here unless I pose a risk to myself, or someone else. "There's one more thing." I look into his eyes.

"Now would be a good time to tell me your good news."

"Since Neil died three weeks ago, I've discovered I'm expecting."

"A baby?" Mal's voice rises. "But you said..."

"I know. This is another thing that I'm totally confused about. Not to mention eaten alive with the guilt. I think it's highly unlikely that the baby is Neil's."

18

ANOTHER DAY. Another appointment. Normally, I hate driving on the motorway, but the journey has passed without me noticing it. It's probably dangerous driving for so long, especially on a motorway, with so much on my mind. I've almost gone on autopilot. As I approach my destination, I know I've got to focus on what's in front of me today and tomorrow.

Today I have a pre-inquest review with the Assistant Coroner and tomorrow, it's the funeral. Trying to keep my stress levels down is proving difficult. The counsellor gave me some relaxation techniques at the end of our last meeting, but they're probably not best practised on the M62.

For the millionth time since I set off, I berate myself for not accepting Christy's offer to come with me. When I turned her down, it was partly because I thought this was something I should do on my own. But mainly I'm scared of slipping up about the baby. No one knows apart from Mal, my counsellor. Even though I'm now thirteen weeks pregnant, I've a long way to go before I come to terms with all that's happened and get my head around how I'm going to deal with everything.

· · ·

Hull Coroner's Court is an imposing stone-built building. I stand across the road from it, the towering clock casting a shadow over me. Sickness rises in me again. I've already had to pull up on the hard shoulder to throw up. I recalled Dad's advice from when I first passed my test, to get well away from the car if ever it was necessary to use the hard shoulder. Getting run over is not on my list of things to go through. I've got quite enough going on.

I shiver as I step into the building. It strikes a gloom within me that takes my breath away.

"Can I help you?" The smiling woman behind the ornately carved desk is at odds with her sombre surroundings. Her voice echoes around the tiled walls.

"Yes. I'm Sacha Young. I have an appointment to discuss the inquest of my husband, Neil Young." Saying his name out loud is both a comfort and a curse.

"Ah yes. Take a seat. I'll let Mr Mahony know you're here."

I nibble at the crystalised ginger that's become my saviour and take a large swig of water. I can't wait until this sickness subsides. According to the articles I've been reading, I could still have a few more weeks like this. By then the inquest will be over too. A few weeks can't come quickly enough for me and then I'll start telling people about the baby. I know more than ever now, how precious life is and that I shouldn't wish the time away, but these are not normal circumstances. In the meantime, I'm thinking about returning to work next week, to keep myself occupied until the inquest, if nothing else. From what I can gather, my team leaders have been doing a great job deputising for me, but no doubt my desk will still be piled high with a six week backlog. It will be good to get my brain into something outside of myself though.

"Hello Mrs Young. Thanks for coming over. I'm Mr Mahony, the Assistant Coroner. We've spoken on the phone a couple of times."

"Hello." I stand and shake his hand.

"Would you like to come through?"

I follow him beneath a sign saying *Chambers* into a wood panelled office that reeks of furniture polish and filter coffee. I take another swig of water. Since my pregnancy was confirmed, my sense of smell has heightened considerably.

"Would you like some coffee?" He gestures to the jug on a hotplate on one of the tables.

"No, thank you. I'm OK with my water." Normally I would have snapped his hand off after a two-hour drive, but the thought of coffee makes me gag.

Mr Mahony gestures to a chair in front of a huge desk and flicks a switch on what I think is called a banker's lamp. He slides a file from a tray and thumbs through some papers. "So we've got the date now for the inquest." His thumb rests at the top of one of the sheets. "The twenty-fifth of February. That's already been communicated to you, hasn't it?"

"Yes." The irony of the date isn't lost on me. Exactly two months after Neil's death. It's hard to believe it's been over a month already. In some ways it seems like an eternity and in others, it's passed in a heartbeat. I've been told that I'm lucky to have got a date for the inquest so quickly – it can often take much longer. Even my counsellor has suggested this might mean that our case is being treated as fairly straightforward. I still hate Neil's death to be described as a case. I guess this is all we boil down to after we're gone. A case, a reference number, a gravestone, a fading memory.

"So the purpose of today's meeting is for you to make a new witness statement which will be read out at the inquest."

"Will I have to answer any questions as well? At the hearing?"

"Probably. You certainly need to be prepared to."

I let a long breath out, dreading the day even more than I do already.

"You'll also have the opportunity today to read the statements from the other witnesses who've been called to give evidence at the inquest."

"Which other witnesses?"

"Your two brothers-in-law, Greg and Adam, Mr Joseph Young, Ashley Walker, Neil's friend." He runs his finger down a list. "Then there are two of the officers who attended at the scene when your husband was recovered, the pathologist, your husband's GP and the counsellor he was seeing prior to his death."

"This is going to be horrendous." I wipe at sudden tears with the back of my hand. I keep thinking I'm coping, then realise I'm not.

"We'll do all we can to make it as smooth as possible for you." Mr Mahony pushes a box of tissues towards me. His voice is gentle and I'm grateful. Everyone has been kind. Everyone I've let near me, anyway. I've shut my own family out, but I've been seeing Joe and Ash regularly. At least they loved Neil, which is possibly why I gather strength from them. My family, on the other hand, barely gave him the time of day. "And we'll let you know, every step of the way, what's happening. Before we start on these statements, would you like a look around the court so you know what to expect on the day?"

"Yes please." I stand and follow him to the door. "What I don't understand though, is why I need to make another statement. The police already took a detailed one from me."

Mr Mahony turns as we get to the door and I notice how blue his eyes are. It's strange what you notice about people in certain situations. And this is still so surreal. My life has changed beyond recognition. "When you give your statement to the police, everything is raw," he explains. "Whilst this captures your initial reaction and memories, often things surface after an event in the cold light of day. Taking a second statement means we don't miss *anything*."

"I guess that makes sense." I follow him along the tiled corridor, the heels of my boots clicking against the floor.

"The inquest will be held in here." He unlocks a door. "There isn't a hearing listed until this afternoon so I can show you around."

The stench of lilies and an even stronger smell of furniture polish hits me as we enter the court. I'd expected something less formal, something more resembling a meeting room, but no, this is a proper courtroom. With its oak-panelled walls and rows of desks pointing towards where Mr Curzon, the Senior Coroner must sit, it's an imposing prospect. I look around the rows of blue chairs, then my gaze falls on what must be the witness box. "Have a wander around," he invites.

"Is this where I'll have to stand?" I step into the box, seeing why it's called a box, as I'm totally enclosed by it. I imagine myself, a month from now, my voice shaking as I give evidence to a packed room. The prospect is terrifying.

He nods. "It's the same as a court hearing. If you're called to give evidence or answer questions, they will require you to swear an oath before you're cross-examined. Like I said though, your statement might be just read out. Additional questions may not be necessary." Mr Mahony opens the gate across the witness box and I step back out. "However, what happens here differs from a court hearing in that no one is directly being accused of anything. We are here to establish the facts of exactly what happened, not prove guilt or innocence." At these words, I swallow hard.

"You mean whether my husband jumped or fell?"

He doesn't answer. "Let's return to chambers, shall we, and get your statement. Then we'll have a look through the others."

For what feels like the millionth time I go over what happened at Christmas, and he writes it down, word for word. It seems to take forever, and my bladder feels as though it might explode after all the water I've drunk. I ask for a comfort break.

Mr Mahony tells me that being Neil's next of kin, I'm the final witness he's seeing before he passes everything onto Mr Curzon. As he mentioned on the phone, this is so I can read the other statements he's gathered.

"It's more the professional ones I'm interested in. After all, I already know what will be in Adam's and Greg's."

"Very well." He slides several pages across the polished desk and watches as I scan the first one. I read and re-read words which blur in front of my eyes. I can't concentrate and can only blame this on the combination of grief and baby brain. I can barely remember what normal is these days. And when my eyes finally focus, the police officers' accounts are painful to read. They are reporting no sign of any struggle from the examinations they've carried out at the area on top of the cliff, so the fight which took place between Adam and Neil can't have been that savage.

Next, the appearance of Neil's body at the bottom of the cliff is described - the visible bleeding and other injuries. And his mottled blue skin. They knew well before they got to him that he was dead.

The GP and Counsellor's statements describe Neil's depression and the many reasons behind it. I tug another tissue from Mr Mahony's box and try to read through my teary eyes. Nothing here is coming as a surprise to me. "I still don't understand why there has to be an inquest?" My voice ricochets around the silent room.

Mr Mahony raises his gaze from whatever he is reading. "I know it's difficult, but in situations where death hasn't been natural or expected, we're obliged to investigate. There has to be a precise cause of death recorded on the death certificate."

"I understand all that, but I have to say." I take a deep breath. "Everything here points to Neil having killed himself."

I'd so wanted it to be accidental, for him not to have taken a conscious decision to do this to me, and for me not to have to be wrung out with any more guilt than I already am. But maybe it's time to face facts.

"Have you read the statement from the pathologist?" There's an edge to his voice which suggests I should.

I slide it from under the others, my eyes falling on words like head injuries, fractures, lower limb, pelvis, spinal – all to be expected from a fall of over three hundred feet. But then something else. Faint fingertip bruising on one upper arm, testicular and perineal contusion consistent with genital trauma. I raise my eyes to him.

"Those are injuries not associated with your husband's fall." His voice is soft and I'm not sure if he has just asked me a question or is merely telling me something.

I take a swig of water. "So why has no one been…"

"The injuries weren't picked up until the postmortem examination," he says. "After they had initially questioned everyone. Adam Fox and Greg Watkins have since been asked about them."

"And?" I can't believe no one has mentioned anything to me. Although, I've cut myself off in recent weeks. And if Christy and Mum knew, they're probably trying to protect me.

"Do you have any knowledge of the cause of the testicular trauma your husband suffered prior to his death, or how he may have sustained fingertip bruising on his arm?"

I hope he isn't thinking I did it. "Other than when he was fighting with Adam, his brother-in-law, I've no idea how those injuries could have occurred. And Adam claims not to have hit Neil back, but who knows? No one else was there."

"Adam will be cross-examined and whilst this isn't a criminal investigation, if we're not satisfied with verdicts of either suicide or accidental death, we'll make a referral back to the police."

"Why haven't they already opened a criminal investigation?"

"The contusions were probably not discovered until our detailed post-mortem examination. When they initially referred the case to us, it was to investigate whether Neil's death was his intention or an accident. Even if the police investigation had discovered the injuries, it would not, in my experience, have been enough for the Crown Prosecution Service to allow any charges being brought directly against anyone. They can only prosecute someone when it's likely they will prove their case beyond reasonable doubt, leading to a conviction."

I stare at him as he speaks, watching his mouth but not really hearing the words. I've had a sixth sense all along that Adam knew more than he was letting on. The thought that he actually pushed Neil from the cliff top is becoming more and more of a possibility.

My mind flits back across instances over the last year where I've had to beg Adam to stay away from me. If Christy were to find out, she'd be heartbroken. But if her knowing everything helps bring him to account, then I'm going to have to say something. But I'll get tomorrow over and done with first. Lay him to rest.

19

THE UNDERTAKERS HELP ADAM, Greg, Ash, Joe and Joe's two brothers to raise the coffin to their shoulders. All eyes are on me as clearly, I'm expected to be the first to follow it out.

The one thing I wanted today Father Francis wouldn't allow. He might have said no to a track being played inside his church, but he can't stop me once we get into the churchyard.

As I stand behind the coffin, everyone is probably wondering what I'm doing as I fumble with my phone and portable speaker, trying to find the song Neil loved, one that sums up his final months. *Everybody Hurts.* After today I'll never listen to it again.

As we make our way out into the drizzle, the words of the song sound sadder than ever. The late January wind whips into my bones, and I hope it's not far to Neil's final resting place. I haven't seen it yet but as we turn the corner of the church building, there it is – a gaping void in the ground. The headstone is going to cost a fortune, but Joe has said he'll take care of that.

We arrive at the graveside, and the hum of conversation subsides. They gently position the coffin beside the hole and everyone gathers around. Father Francis looks at me as if to say *turn off that music*. But I don't. The song is going to play out until it ends.

When it does, he speaks. Or should I say, recites. This is the second time I have attended anything Catholic, and I'm baffled by the time it takes to get through the ritual of words.

After five minutes of Father Francis's droning, I'm losing the will to live. I wonder if anyone other than Joe and some of his church friends are even listening. I stare at the coffin. *Neil David Young, 15th September 1987 to 26th December 2018*. I wanted the death recorded as 25th December, the day I lost him. However, the date of his body being found has been officially recorded as his date of death. Apparently, temperature, colour and rigor mortis are indicators of how long a body has been dead, but because it was such a freezing night, these factors couldn't convey whether Neil died on Christmas Day or Boxing Day.

Adam's gaze catches mine in between a couple of sets of shoulders, and I look away. How can Adam even be here after how he treated Neil? Christy must sense something from me and steps through the throng to be at my side. Grateful, I lean into her, the tears freezing with the raindrops on my face.

Father Francis is still going strong. His words blow around and away. I'm too cold to even shiver now, and my feet are completely numb. I get momentary relief from the warmth that breathing into my scarf offers to my face. I stare into the grey sky, then back at Neil's coffin. I can't believe he's in there at the age of thirty-two. If his path had never crossed with mine, he'd still be out there somewhere, happily living his life.

They're moving the spray of lilies now. Four undertakers take their positions around the coffin and take hold of the ropes. This is the bit I've been dreading the most. Ash is sobbing into Lisa's shoulder and Joe wipes frantically at his eyes with a grubby hanky.

"Earth to earth, ashes to ashes, dust to dust." I can hardly bear to watch as they slowly lower my husband into the ground. His face swims into my mind and I see him when we first met, laughter dancing in his eyes, the dimples that he hated deep in his cheeks. I slip my glove off and with numb fingers, accept a handful of the soil from the box that is thrust before me and scatter it into the hole. I close my eyes as it drums against the coffin. "Goodbye Neil," I whisper. "I did really love you. I'm so sorry." I look up to find Greg watching me now. He's another one who's no business being here. Not really.

Mum leaves Rebecca's side and tunnels through the group towards me. So now I'm flanked by Christy and my mother, and I bury myself in their warmth, listening as The Lord's Prayer is chanted around us. I can't join in.

One by one, people move away. I hear *The King's Arms* said repeatedly as they leave. Part of me wants to get as far away from here as I can, the other part can't bear to leave him. I peer at the coffin, now resting at the bottom of the grave. When we've gone, they'll fill it with the mound of earth beneath the astro turf. He's in there forever, alone in the cold, in the dark, in...

"Come on love." Mum tugs at my arm. "You're like a block of ice. Let's get you back to the car. Your dad will have it nice and warm for us." Dad got through the service but had said in advance that the burial, particularly in this weather, would be too much. Today must be doubly hard for him. The attendance at a funeral must surely foreshadow what is ahead. I already know that when it comes to it, Dad's funeral is more likely to be a celebration of his life, not this miserable Catholic requiem mass we've just suffered. It's only inflicted pain deeper than it already was. Surely funerals are meant to bring at least some comfort?

"You deserve a very stiff drink sis. You're holding it together amazingly."

I smile at Christy, my hand instinctively darting to my belly. "I'll see you there. I'll go with Mum and Dad."

"Are you OK love?" Mum steers me towards the car. "I mean, clearly you're not - today of all days. But I've noticed you holding your belly a lot, that's all. You're not in pain, are you?"

I wish I could tell her. Maybe I will. I can just say to everyone, *this miracle baby is Neil's*. Hardly anyone knows that without fertility treatment, we had next to no chance of conceiving naturally. Hardly anyone who's not family, that is. And that is where the problem lies.

"I've got you a large." Christy pushes the wine glass towards me. Under normal circumstances, it wouldn't touch the sides, but in my current predicament I don't want to touch a drop of alcohol. Even if it is my husband's wake.

"I'd rather have a hot drink," I say. "I'm so cold."

"I'll sort it for you." Mum squeezes my shoulder. "What would you like?"

"Milky, weak tea please."

"*Milky, weak tea.*" Christy sips from her glass. "Since when did you drink your tea like that? Call yourself a Yorkshire woman?"

I sink to a bar stool. It's not even one pm and I'm done in. I just want to sprawl out on my sofa in front of the fire and the telly. Me and my baby. Not here amongst nearly a hundred people who barely gave Neil a second thought when he was alive. They're probably only here for the free buffet. My stomach growls at the thought of food. I might not feel hungry, but this little something inside me is having other ideas.

People must be starting to thaw out after the long stand in the graveyard, as they've started hanging their coats on the hooks by the door. It's warm to the point of stifling in here. I slip my coat off and drape it over the back of a chair at the table where Dad is sitting. "How are you doing?" I ask him. He looks exhausted. My familiar friend, guilt, washes over me for putting him through this. I might as well be Catholic, the amount of guilt I allow to weigh on me.

"Ah, you know. We've all had better days, haven't we? More importantly, how are *you* doing love?"

"We're nearly through it now, aren't we? I've just got to survive the inquest in a few weeks."

"Why don't you come back to Bempton with us Sacha? You shouldn't be on your own this weekend."

"You've got enough on your plate without having to cope with me, Dad." His face is greyer than the last time I saw him at Christmas, and he's lost even more weight. He's a far cry from the man whose shoulders I used to ride on.

"Rubbish. What are parents for? All that matters right now is getting you through this."

"What's going on?" Rebecca approaches the table, clutching two large glasses of wine.

"Nothing. I'm just trying to persuade your sister to come back with us and enjoy having her mother look after her for a couple of days."

"I agree." Mum turns up on the other side of me. "I don't like the thought of you in that empty house over the weekend. Not after what you've been through today."

"She's a grown woman." Rebecca bangs a glass on the table in front of me with such force that the red wine slops out. It drips like blood into my lap. It's a good job I'm wearing black, although in hindsight, I should've bought something new. This crossover dress is snug on me. I didn't even try it on before today. My body has certainly altered since the last time I wore it.

Rebecca can never hide her jealousy when either Mum or Dad offer time or attention to me or Christy. She's a mother of three now but appears to still need the special interest she's always had from being the youngest. Pathetic.

"Thanks Rebecca. But I'm not drinking today." I twist

around to where Rebecca is standing behind me. Greg is now at her side, clutching a pint of beer. Christy slides into the seat next to Dad, and Adam stands at her side. I'm aware that rather than cornering myself with my family, I should mingle amongst those who have come today. Whether they're here for the free buffet or not. That is what Joe is doing. He's a more jovial man here than the one who was weeping at the graveside.

"How come you're drinking tea Sacha?" Rebecca sips from her glass. "I'll have that wine if you don't want it. I won't see it go to waste."

"She needed warming up, didn't you love?" Mum leans across the table and rubs the top of my hand.

"What's wrong with you? It's boiling in here."

"What's wrong with me?" I glare at my sister. "What planet are you on? I've just buried my husband. That's what's wrong with me."

"Now, now you two." Dad frowns at Rebecca. "Just drink your wine and leave Sacha be."

Our table falls quiet. It's my cue to get some food. I stand stiffly, my hand unconsciously landing on my belly as I get to my feet. Without meaning to, I'm taking on the stance of a pregnant woman. It's in the hollow of my back and the way I'm standing. I've seen other pregnant women who stand like this. I straighten myself up, but as I glance back to our table, I notice Rebecca watching me.

I fill a plate with salad and fruit. It will be about all I can manage. If I don't eat soon, I'll be sick.

"How are you doing Sacha?" Lisa hurries towards me as I'm heading back to the table. "I know it's a silly question."

"I'm just glad the funeral's over with," I reply. "It was grim, wasn't it?"

She nods. "Cremations are bad enough, but burials are the worst. I'm sorry I haven't seen you since it happened Sacha. I've thought it best to stay at home with Emma when Ash has called around." She glances to where Ash is standing at the bar. "I came with him once when she was at nursery, but you were out. I've been thinking of you though. All the time. I can't imagine what you must be going through."

"Don't even try to." We fall silent for a moment, and it's evident that she doesn't know what to say next, so I move it along. "Are you coming to the inquest with Ash?"

"Hopefully. That's all a mess, isn't it? Ash was telling me things might not be as clear cut as they first thought."

"How's Ash coping with everything?" I'm not getting into talking about the ins and outs of it all. Not now. Not here.

"He's in bits to be honest. I'm hoping the inquest might give him some closure. I keep finding him in tears in the middle of the night."

"Nights are the worst." I turn away from Lisa towards the next couple of people that are waiting to say something to me. "Anyway, if you'll excuse me. I'll catch you soon."

It takes forever to get back to the table, with people continually stopping me to offer condolences, but as I do, I'm aware of Rebecca's eyes still boring into me.

"And your problem is...?" I know I'm snapping at her, but I don't care. She's really getting under my skin. On the day of my husband's funeral, she's as jealous and judgmental as ever, and has not had so much as a kind word to say to me.

"Your belly's looking a little rotund Sacha." She points at it as I stand at the edge of our group.

20

Why did I wear this dress? I'm slim at the best of times but have lost so much weight since Neil's death. Therefore, at my now thirteen weeks stage of pregnancy, a tiny bump is visible to those who know me well, or know what to look for. Rebecca falls into both camps.

"Rebecca!" Mum shrieks at her, but her eyes also flit to my midriff. All the chairs are taken so I can't sit and try to disguise it. I desperately glance around at neighbouring tables for an empty chair. Why won't they all just leave me alone?

"You do look as though you've been at the pies sis." Christy is staring at me now. "Well, your belly does. You look like a stick insect everywhere else. Is it bloating or something? I get a bit of that."

"Yeah, it must be. I get it when I eat bread." My face is burning and I'm stuttering, two regular occurrences when I'm lying. Both sisters and my mother know this all too well. Nor have I put any bread on my plate.

"What aren't you telling us?" Rebecca points at my belly again.

"Weren't you ever taught that pointing is rude?" I hiss.

"You're not… expecting, are you? Your stomach is massive."

"Why don't you get lost." I try to suck my belly in and when this proves impossible I slide my plate to the table and both hands instinctively fly to my middle in an effort to cover it up.

"You are, aren't you?" Rebecca's eyes widen, and she looks at Mum, Christy, and then back to me. "But I thought you couldn't…"

"Mind your own business, will you?" God, I didn't want it to come out yet. And certainly not like this. Everyone at our table is gawping at me.

"Here, have a seat." Greg stands. "I'm off to the bar, anyway. I'll leave you all to it."

"I'll join you." Adam also stands and they both look as though they can't get away from the table quickly enough.

"Don't you two be getting wasted again," Christy calls after them, then turns back to me. "Sacha. Why on earth didn't you tell me?"

"I haven't told anyone." I pick up a piece of melon and bite from it. I've got to quell this churning. "I was trying to get my head around it myself first."

"We could've supported you." Mum looks upset. "Why do you always have to be so *closed up*?"

"I'm not. It's just my way of dealing with things. It's not been the easiest few weeks."

"All the more reason to lean on your family love." Dad sips from a mug – he's also on the tea. Normally, in such circumstances, he'd have a pint in front of him. Mum's on tea as well. She won't touch a drop of wine when she is driving. "Well, you're definitely coming back to Bempton with us young lady. I won't take no for an answer."

"*Young lady!*" Rebecca laughs. "Hardly. And with all the weight loss, she's looking haggard." She takes a huge slurp of wine and I envy her. If I wasn't pregnant, I would have a large glass right now.

"Take it easy love." Mum frowns at her. "You've got those kids to look after when you get back. Who's got them, anyway?"

"Greg's Mum has got Zach. The girls are at school but she's going to pick them up too."

"That's good."

"So. You're going to have four grandkids, you two." Christy grins at Mum and Dad. "Well, I..." she gets up and walks around to my side. "I think it's great news. It's what you wanted, isn't it?" She crouches down and hugs me. "Personally, I think you're mad, but..."

I nestle into my sister's warmth, needing it for a moment, before pulling back. "It's what Neil and I wanted... but now..."

"I still don't understand how it's happened." Rebecca has given herself a red wine moustache. She's on it today. "Maybe you should enlighten us."

"Oh, Rebecca." Dad chuckles as he places his cup down. His laugh is a good sound – and it's been a while since I've heard it. "Do we need to give you a birds and the bees talk?"

"No. I mean. Well, you're infertile, aren't you?"

"Will you keep your voice down?" The surrounding tables fall silent as I blush to the roots of my hair. "Evidently, I'm not, am I?"

"Well, Neil was. He told me about it himself. He had a next to nothing sperm count." She's literally spewing venom as she speaks. "And those he had were all over the place. He even made a joke about it once. We got talking last year when he was drunk."

"Like you seem to be now." Mum slides the wine glass away from her. "I don't know what's wrong with you today Rebecca. You're going too far. What does it matter about the details?"

"Miracles can happen you know." Dad smiles, but it's a sad smile. "Especially at a time like this."

"Of course they can." Christy straightens herself up. "Do

you know – I think some champers is in order with news like this."

"Can I remind you…" I lower my voice. "That this is my husband's wake. No champagne, do you hear me? Please. Can we just change the subject?"

"No chance. Champers it should be. I agree with Christy." Rebecca reaches over the table for my fork and uses it to belt the side of her other wine glass. "Ladies and gentlemen, I have an announcement to make." As she gets to her feet, her voice echoes around the now silent function area. The room is a sea of people wearing black. All eyes are on our table as I stare at my sister in horror. It's as though everything has gone into slow motion.

"Rebecca. Sit down, will you? This is my news to tell. Not yours." Oh no! It can't come out like this. I've got to stop her.

"On behalf of my sister Sacha and my family." Rebecca gestures around at our table. "I'd like to thank you all for coming to honour the life of my brother-in-law, Neil."

Who does she think she is? "Sit down," I hiss again, noticing Joe heading over to our table. He needs to hear the baby news from me. Not like this. *I don't even think Neil is the father!*

"But," Rebecca continues. "There is a saying, that when one life ends, another one begins, and this is a perfect time to bring some light into the darkness and share my sister's wonderful, and some might say, miraculous news." Her words carry a sarcastic edge and I've never hated her more than I do right now.

"Will you bloody shut up?" I snarl at her. "Sit the hell down. I'll never forgive you for this."

"What's going on?" Joe looks from me to Rebecca. "This is my son's funeral. What are you playing at? And who asked *you* to make a speech?"

Father Francis is hot on his heels. "Is everything OK?"

My face is on fire. This is so embarrassing. Even Dad looks

horrified. "I'm pregnant," I say. "There. Are you happy now?" I glare at Rebecca, resisting the urge to slap her like I would have done a few years ago. "I hadn't told anyone yet, but my sister here has guessed and has taken it upon herself to make an announcement." I look at Joe. "I'm sorry you had to find out so publicly."

"Well, that's wonderful news, isn't it?" Father Francis's expression turns from one of bewilderment to one of joy. "Your sister was right about light in the darkness."

I stare at my plate of fruit like it's somehow going to help me.

Joe sinks to the chair Adam vacated and looks at me. "Is it Neil's?"

"What sort of a question is that?"

"I'm sorry. But given the circumstances, I've got to ask. I know about the problems – medical and otherwise."

"I'm going for a walk. I've just about had enough." A sob catches in my throat as I jump to my feet, snatching my coat from the back of the chair. "Of the lot of you!"

"Sacha. You're going nowhere. Sit down and eat your food." My dad sounds as though he's talking to a five-year-old me again.

"I need to get out of here for some air. I'll be back when I'm ready." Tears are sliding from my eyes as I put my coat on.

"Do you want me to come with you?"

"No." I shake my head at Christy. "I'm OK. I just need to be on my own. I won't be long."

It's a relief to get out of the stifling pub and away from the accusing stares. As I get further away from them all, I start to feel calmer and my breathing slows to the same rhythm as my footsteps. It's a good job it's rainy and cold – at least there aren't too many people around to notice the state of me.

~

I don't know how long I wander around for but eventually the tears subside. What a bloody day. The frozen numbness I had in the churchyard has returned and I realise I must have been out here for a while. I've lost all track of time and my brain feels as heavy as the mist that's thickening around me. I've left my hat, gloves and scarf in the pub in my haste to get out of there. I've even left my bag behind.

I take in a deep breath and let a jagged one out, the air in front of my face steaming as I continue walking. I'm not even sure where I am, and really seem to have gone off course, not that I had a course to start with. I simply stumbled from the pub without knowing where I was headed. Story of my life.

I can't believe my news has come out so publicly and that doubts were immediately expressed over whether Neil is the father. I wish nobody had ever known about our business. But they were all aware that nothing had happened on the baby front for four years, and we'd told them that our only chance of becoming parents was with fertility treatment.

I've confided in Christy that couldn't happen until Neil had got himself into better shape with his drinking and his mental health. I bet she's told Adam, and well – that will be how it has got around. Still, miracles do happen – they all know that too. A miracle is definitely my preferred version of events to run with. It's far less painful than any alternative.

Rebecca is evidently more upset with me than I realised. I haven't visited her or the baby yet, and have completely closed off from her since Neil died. But the older we get, the greater the distance becomes between us. As a child, she was always jealous of me, and she was of Christy, but to a lesser extent. Possibly because Christy's that bit older, it was more me that Rebecca saw as a rival. She was upset when it was my birthday, she'd compare what we got at Christmas, she would try to get in the middle if Mum or Dad gave me any attention, and she was immensely threatened of the bond Christy and I had, having grown up sharing a room. Now I'm having a baby and challenging her self-imposed high status of being the only daughter to have blessed our parents with grandchildren, so she won't like that.

I suddenly feel annoyed with myself for these trivial thoughts about my sister. Trivial considering what's taken place today. It's not stopped drizzling since first thing, so dusk is falling earlier than usual. I imagine my husband, laid in his six foot long, six foot deep hole in the ground with darkness descending all around him. A melancholy hits me so hard it's like a punch in the chest. I tug my sodden coat more tightly around myself. I should go back. I have no bag, phone or anything with me. They'll be worried. At least some of them will be. I look around, trying to get my bearings. From which direction have I got here? How long have I been? I stand looking up and down the single track country road, searching in the fog for a sign or a marker. I start walking again, hoping I'm going in the right direction.

I'm startled by the roar of an engine. It becomes louder, then stops, fifty feet or so away from me. I look left and right for somewhere to get out of the way. I blink in its headlights, thankful I've been seen. I should've been paying more attention. As I move to the left, there's another roar. Then a screech of tyres. The car is hurtling towards me. It's not going to stop.

PART III

CHRISTY

21

It's not until something like this happens that you realise how much you love a person. For the last month, I've spent as much time as possible at my sister's bedside, willing her to wake up. We've got a system going between us. Me, Mum and Rebecca are dividing the twenty-four hour stretches up, so there's always someone here.

The person doing the night shift can normally get their head down on the camp bed in the family room. This is usually Rebecca. She has her kids to look after during the day, so she tends to be the one in the family room at night.

That's unless another family is using it. We've seen lots of families come and go from the high dependency unit in the last few weeks. Some go up to intensive care, some go down onto a normal ward. Some don't make it either way and when I see their red, swollen faces emerging from the family room, or from a patient's bedside, I can only pray that this fate is not set to befall our family as well. As if we've not had enough tragedy. We've lost Neil, and we're going to lose Dad. Surely Sacha's life will be spared.

Mum does mornings – she sets off whilst Dad is sleeping

and his morning carers sort him out. I keep making her take a day or two off here and there, but this is how she wants to handle it all. Over the last week though, I've noticed it catching up with her. Her skin has taken on a grey tinge and the poor love has aged eight years in eight weeks.

Yet in some ways, Rebecca has been the most affected of all of us by what's happened to Sacha. I've never known her to be so subdued. The two of them weren't getting along, and Rebecca was a right cow at Neil's wake. She'd no right broadcasting Sacha's news like she did, no matter how drunk she was. So no doubt all of that will be eating away at her.

It's surprised me by how readily she agreed to be the one that stays here at night. Perhaps it's the fact that Sacha is clinging to life – often we don't realise how much someone matters until it's too late – or we face the threat of it being too late.

I can't bear the thought of Sacha waking and there being no one here for her. We've been warned time and time again that equally, it could go the other way, and she might not wake. Ever. If she takes a turn for the worse, then we want to be here for her too. My life revolves around being at her bedside, and I wouldn't have it any other way.

No one has any idea what happened to her on the day of Neil's funeral. It was pitch black when she was found in the road by a driver who had to slam on his or her brakes to avoid hitting her. The thought of her badly injured body being hit again doesn't bear thinking about, and makes me feel ill when I do.

What also doesn't bear thinking about is that somebody, somewhere knows they ran my sister over on that country road and drove away, leaving her for dead. The thought of her lying injured in the rain for as long as she apparently did haunts me.

There were no tyre marks in the road, and typically no CCTV around that area. If the driver saw Sacha prior to hitting her, then he or she did not try to stop. All the police appeals have come to nothing. Whoever did this to my sister seems to have gotten away with it.

News of someone having been seriously injured on the local headlines was the first inkling that something had happened, although by then, dread was already pooling in my stomach. Sacha had been gone for at least three hours since storming away from Rebecca. The attendees of the funeral had more or less left, apart from Joe and some of his friends. They were carrying on drinking, as is often traditional at a Catholic wake, so Father Francis told us.

The initial news report was scant and first came up on my social media feed. Police were appealing for information following the discovery of a seriously injured young woman found on the B514, one mile out of Farndale. They needed to establish her identity given the fact she was not carrying anything to help identify her. At that point as I read out what was on my screen, Mum and I had simultaneously noticed Sacha's shoulder bag hanging on the chair where she'd been sat. I knew immediately that the young woman they'd found was my sister. I've never felt fear like it. Dad looked like he was going to pass out.

We discovered they had rushed her to hospital, and by the time we got here she was already in surgery. She stayed there for several hours whilst they worked to relieve the pressure on her brain. Adam took Dad back to Bempton as he was exhausted, whilst Rebecca and Greg returned home to sort their kids. Mum and I clung to each other in the family room, high on caffeine as we watched the hours tick past, either weeping or in silence. I couldn't have got through that night without Mum, and she couldn't have got through it without me.

When the consultant finally came to tell us that Sacha had survived the operation, Mum had fallen asleep with her head on my shoulder. There were a few broken bones, he said, but it had been her head injury that had caused the most problems.

She's been asleep ever since she was brought in a month ago. They keep doing CT scans on her brain and there's every reason for hope. Without hope, there's nothing.

Our next question was about the baby. Somehow, he or she survived the accident, the tough little thing, and Sacha is now seventeen weeks pregnant. In a few more weeks, the baby could be born and even survive on its own. Sometimes I wonder if that's what the medical team are waiting for. And if once they have saved the baby, they'll let Sacha go. So, we're not leaving her side. As long as she's alive, we're all here, fighting with her.

The bay Sacha's in is partitioned into three. One specialist nurse to three patients. Curtains divide them all. It's day when it's night and night when it's day. Sometimes when Mum or I are here during the day, others come in to relieve us so we can have a break. Ash and Lisa have been amazing. Lots of people have. Bringing us food, and just caring about us. It's heavenly to go home for a shower or even just to sink onto the sofa. But when I'm at home, I can't settle. I just want to get back to Sacha.

I stare at my sister's chest as it goes up and down, down and up. I thought I already knew her inside out before all this. I can now honestly say that I know every contour of her face, every lash that curls from her eyelid. Sometimes her eyes move or her limbs twitch. The nursing staff say people still hear when they're in this comatose state, so I talk to her as much as I can. If she can hear me, I probably get on her nerves.

"You know what day it is today, don't you sis?" I reach for her hand, warm inside my own, and gently squeeze it. "Inquest day. I have to say, this is a drastic way of getting out of it. I'm sure you weren't exaggerating when you told me you didn't want to go, but this is overly dramatic, don't you think?"

I decided I was going to be the one to stay with Sacha whilst the rest of them drove to Hull. Adam is giving evidence and tells me it should be straightforward. There's no difference my presence there could make, and I'd rather be with my sister, anyway.

"I suppose you got me out of it too." My eyes run over Sacha's swelling belly beneath the sheet. "Oh Sacha. I'd give anything for you to wake up and answer me. You've got so much to wake up for. Not just for me but for someone very important who's really going to need you."

I keep wondering what will happen to the baby if it survives and Sacha doesn't. I've never, ever wanted children of my own. They're OK, as long as they're someone else's, but children are something that's never been on my radar.

As a manager, I get irritated at work when mothers demand priority in terms of time off. It's almost like discrimination. I'm all for equal rights, but it goes both ways. People often tell me I'll get maternal urges soon enough, but I doubt it. I also get annoyed when in every walk of life, I'm asked how many children I've got. When I say *none*, that's when the probing questions begin. *Do I want them? Can I have them?* It's as though they're the barometer by which we women are measured.

My over and over again response to these people is that I'm happily child free. I could never understand Sacha's obsession with becoming a mother and ultimately, it crucified her marriage. Her fixation on temperature and ovulation charts, diet and supplements were all-consuming. And she never let up on poor Neil. He delivered in the end though – it's just heartbreaking that he never knew.

If the baby survives and Sacha dies, there are not too many options for it, and I might have to revisit my lifelong stance on having a baby. I even discussed it with Adam a couple of weeks ago. I keep replaying the conversation in my head.

"You've got to be kidding." He'd turned from where he

stood at the sink and looked at me as though I were deranged. "If you don't want kids of your own, why on earth would you want someone else's?"

"It wouldn't just be *someone else's*. He or she would be our family. Our niece or nephew." I couldn't believe I was even arguing for this, but it had tripped a switch inside of me. Call it duty. Call it guilt. Call it whatever.

"Your family. Not mine."

"We're married Adam. Do you not class Freya, Matilda and Zachary as your nieces and nephew?" My eyes had then fallen on a picture Freya had drawn for me at Christmas, which I'd taped to the fridge. Not that I particularly welcome reminders of Christmas.

"Not particularly. They're just irritating kids that belong to someone else, that I'm forced to be nice to."

"Look. I'm not saying I *want* to do this Adam. But Sacha's my sister. And this baby could end up in care if we don't step in to look after it. Obviously, I'm speaking hypothetically here."

"It's not even been born yet. And Sacha hasn't died yet. Don't you think you're jumping the gun Christy?"

I was making sandwiches to take back to the hospital and had slammed the knife onto the counter.

"God. You're all heart. What's wrong with you? You're getting worse!" His sentence about Sacha not dying *yet* felt like tempting fate.

"It's too much to ask of me Christy. It's too much to ask of yourself. I don't want it here. No chance."

"But..."

"The kid's got grandparents, your other sister, friends. Someone will step up."

"But not us?" I could never have predicted this reaction from him. There did not seem to be any scope for softening him either. I'd searched his eyes for something, and all I saw was steely determination.

"No chance. I'm already having to cope without you pulling your weight in the business and being at that bloody hospital every day. It's a good job we got that investment from Greg last year. We would have sunk without it by now."

I couldn't believe what he was saying. *Heartless pillock.* "How am I supposed to work when my sister is lying in a coma? I can't even do my own job, let alone get involved in yours."

"I'm just saying. And you're going to have to get back to normal eventually."

I'd left to come back here then. I was fuming, but at least Adam had told me straight. In doing so he'd also sown a seed that if it came to it, he might not be a factor in my future. Our conversation has highlighted cracks in our marriage that I can't ignore any longer. They've been deepening for a while, well before all this. And he can shove his business where the sun doesn't shine. I'll start again on my own if I have to.

I glance at the clock. The inquest starts in ten minutes. I imagine everyone sitting facing each other in a waiting room, as muted as ever, and wonder if our family is ever going to know happiness again. Dad's attending the inquest. He gets really tired but appears determined to stick around and support us all since he stopped the treatment. Maybe a miracle will happen with him as well.

Mum certainly needs him to stay well right now. Despite his arguments, she's increased the carers to twice a day, and a neighbour helps when Mum is over here. But I worry about her. She isn't getting any younger, and she looks shattered all the time. However, there's a strength that's always exuded from her and I'm grateful for it. She won't accept, not even for a moment, that there's any chance of Sacha and the baby not coming through this.

I'm startled by the sudden appearance of Father Francis in

the doorway. A darkly dressed Catholic priest is not exactly a vision of hope in a high dependency unit.

"Christy, isn't it?" He strides towards the bed. "Joe asked me to visit. Is that alright with you?"

"Erm yes. What for?" I'm worried for a moment that Joe knows something we don't.

"Just to say a few words over Sacha and the baby." He tugs a hanky from his pocket and mops his brow. It's quite a hike from the main entrance to this unit and it's very warm in here. I suppose it has to be with patients who are bed bound.

"You don't mean like *last rites,* do you?"

"No, not at all. But your sister needs everyone on her side right now. Especially him upstairs." He raises his eyes to the shiny white ceiling of the room.

"I'm not sure I believe in all that but..."

"You should try Christy. It might make all the difference here."

This is all I need today. My sister is laid in front of me, her body here, but her brain away on another planet somewhere. And I've got some priest preaching at me.

"It's Neil's inquest today." Time to change the subject from what I do or don't believe. I should've kept my thoughts to myself.

"I know. Joseph is anxious to know for certain what happened to Neil. I only hope the same privilege can be afforded to Sacha here."

Despite my initial irritation at his presence, there's something quite comforting about Father Francis. Something *safe.* And I've sat on my own here all morning.

"She's been wired up here for a month now," he continues, "and we're no closer to finding out who did this to her. It's an utter travesty if you ask me."

Like I need reminding how long it's been. I stare at my sister, tears blurring my eyes. The bruises have faded, and her stitches are dissolving. The broken bones will knit themselves back together and the baby will hopefully be born safely. I just hope the head injuries and the bleeding on the brain she suffered allow her to come back to us. In mind as well as in body.

"Have they said much about the possibility of brain damage?" Father Francis must be telepathic.

"They can't tell properly until she wakes up." I cross one leg over the other and flick my hair from my eyes. I haven't had my hair done since before Christmas. I've lost weight and look an absolute mess. No wonder Adam is treating me like he is. He's certainly capable of being an arse, but not usually to this extent.

"The swelling on her brain seems to have gone down, so it's looking more hopeful." I don't tell him that knowing Sacha as I do, she'd prefer to be let go than to wake up and not be herself any more due to brain damage. That's a whole new argument. But I just want her back, whatever shape she's in. I'll look after her myself if I have to.

"She'll come back to us when she's good and ready." Father Francis looks over the bed. "You'll see. The Lord is looking after her. Why don't you get us both a cup of tea Christy?" He takes a chair from the end of the bed next to ours. The nurse on duty gives him a funny look, but says nothing.

The wife of the man in that bed has gone for a shower. It's strange how we all get to know one another in circumstances such as these. There's kind of an unspoken support and comforting presence between us all. We don't say much, but we don't need to.

Father Francis sits heavily at the other side of Sacha.

I stand. "Can I ask you something before I get us a drink?"

"Ask away." He smiles at me.

"If there is a God, why did he let this happen to my sister?" Perhaps it's a childlike question, but I don't care.

Father Francis looks thoughtful, but I don't give him a chance to answer as he opens his mouth to speak.

"If there is a God, then why did he end Neil's life when he was only thirty-two? And if this God you keep talking about is so wonderful, then why do bad things happen at all?"

22

NEARLY FIVE HOURS have elapsed since the time when the inquest should have started. As I've watched the clock ticking the hours by above the nurses' station, I've become more and more on edge, needing to know what's going on. Maybe I should have attended, but I'm also obsessed in my belief that one of us, Mum, Rebecca or myself, should be here with Sacha at all times. I can't bear the thought of her waking up alone.

"Mum?" I grab my phone. "Has it finished?"

"Yes. We've just come out love." Mum sighs. "It's been such a long day."

"And?"

"They've returned a verdict of suicide."

"Really?" I'm unsure why I'm shocked by this. It was always a huge possibility. However, I know how much Sacha needed to believe that Neil had not wanted to do this to her. She wanted to believe that he'd fallen – that it had been a tragic accident. So I'm disappointed on her behalf.

"Yes. It was the evidence from the GP, as well as the counsellor Neil saw that swayed the verdict." Mum sighs again, and her voice dips. "He was more depressed than any of us realised Christy. I wish I'd have known. I'd have talked to him – tried to help more – I can't help but feel guilty."

"But to throw himself from a clifftop. Surely there are easier ways..." The nurse on duty looks at me. Yes, I know it's not a run-of-the-mill conversation. I expect they hear all sorts in here though.

"They acknowledged at the inquest that what he did was an extreme way to commit suicide, and probably not premeditated. That was the word they used, anyway."

"Meaning?"

"Meaning that Neil throwing himself from the cliff was probably a sudden decision on his part. Something must have snapped inside him to drive him to do something so desperate. They said he would have decided, then jumped before he could change his mind or really consider what he was doing. Obviously, there's no going back once it's happening."

I lower my voice, aware that the nurse is listening intently. It's silent in here apart from the continual beeping from the monitoring machines. "Isn't that what anyone who kills themselves does? Makes the decision then carries it out?"

"He wasn't going to come back from a three hundred foot drop down a cliff face, was he?"

Mum has an air of authority about her. She clearly considers herself an expert after her day at the coroner's court. She was like this when she did jury service. It would be amusing if the whole thing was not so horrendous.

"If what Neil was doing," she continues, "had been a cry for help, he'd have done something to himself that he had a chance of coming back from."

"Did they say what might have made him *snap?*"

"It was thought that everything had mounted up. The fertility problems, the drinking, his lack of work, his marriage to Sacha. And his depression being clinical. It does things to a person's mind that we can only imagine unless we've been there ourselves."

"I know. From what I've read and heard about it, it's up there with having an arm cut off. And men often get it worse. They don't talk to each other like we do."

"I'll have to go in a few minutes love. Your dad's done in, and I need to get him home. Are you OK? You've been there on your own all day."

"I had Father Francis for company earlier."

"I heard." Mum's dark tone turns to one of mild amusement. "Joe mentioned he was visiting today, but I forgot to text and warn you. Was it alright?"

"Yeah, I guess so. Apart from when he was trying to convert me to his way of thinking." Despite feeling so melancholy at the suicide verdict, I smile at the memory of his visit. "I told him that if my sister and nephew or niece come through this safely, me and him can talk again. How's Joe, anyway? It must've been a hell of a day for him."

Mum goes quiet for a moment. "He's not too good to be honest. And erm," she pauses again. "I'm afraid he had a go at Adam after the inquest. I'm sure Adam will tell you about it himself when you see him. He certainly looked shaken."

"Oh God. As if things aren't bad enough for us all, as it is." I shuffle in my seat to relieve my numb bum. Hours in these hospital chairs are no good to anyone. "What on earth was he having a go at Adam for?"

Mum pauses, as if choosing her words. "It all came out about Adam and Neil sniping at one another throughout Christmas Day. And we know about the huge argument they had after I'd sent them to sort themselves out."

The nurse is on the phone now so is thankfully no longer listening. Goodness knows what she must make of our family? Who needs soap operas or films?

"We all knew about that argument, though. Joe did too,

didn't he? And he knew about Neil hitting Adam before he stormed off. He can't just blame Adam for everything – it was both of them."

"Well." Mum goes quiet again. "Yes. I'm just talking to Christy. I won't be long. Sorry love. Just talking to your dad."

"What was said between them Mum? Why did Joe have a go at Adam?"

"To be honest Christy, the spotlight was really on Adam for a time at the inquest."

"What do you mean?" I should have gone. I really should have gone. Lisa might have stayed with Sacha if I'd asked her.

"He was, by far, the longest in the witness box. As we know, there was no love lost between him and Neil, *and* he was the last one to have seen him alive."

"But we knew that too. What about Greg? What did he say?"

"He maintained he didn't find Adam that night until *after* Neil had disappeared. He wasn't questioned for long at all - apart from confirming that Neil didn't get on too well with him, or Adam, and had seemed pretty depressed. They went easy on Greg. He went on and on about how drunk Neil was on Christmas Eve."

"But Neil had pulled himself back together after that. I was sitting in the lounge with him for a while." I think back, recalling how I was the only one to make any effort with him that day. And thank God I did. "I sat next to him at the dinner table as well. He didn't seem *suicidal* to me Mum."

He had seemed more angry. And he had every right to be after what Adam said. I felt sorry for him.

"Like they said at the inquest, his decision to jump probably wasn't planned. But listen love, there's something else."

"What?" Oh God. What now?

"Do you know about the pathology report?"

"What about it?" I frown. The grooves in my forehead will

be as deep as the grand canyon, the amount of frowning I've been doing lately. I feel every one of my thirty-five years.

"Apparently, it had highlighted some of Neil's injuries that were nothing to do with his death. Today was the first I'd heard about them though."

"No." What is she going to tell me?

"Neil had severe bruising in his groin department, and some finger marks on one of his arms.

"Finger marks?"

"Anyway, the man cross-examining the witnesses forced Adam to admit that he'd grabbed Neil and brought his knee up between his legs. The admission had to be dragged from him though."

My throat feels constricted. "Why has he never told us this before?" I stare at my sister's form spread out beneath the sheet. *My husband drove your husband to his death.* How the hell am I ever going to tell her that?

"At one point, it wasn't looking good for Adam to be honest," Mum goes on. "And I think what finally took the focus from him was when he admitted to something else. Without him saying what he said next, who knows?"

"Oh, bloody hell. It just gets worse. What did he say?" *How can there be any more?*

"Adam admitted to saying something that must have been the last straw for Neil." Mum's voice fades. She hates drama and confrontation usually. All Mum's ever wanted is a normal, quiet life. "Without his admission, the inquest seemed to look closely whether Adam might have pushed Neil to his death. And even then, after what he said, they still deliberated for nearly an hour before returning the suicide verdict. Like I said, it's been such a long day."

"So, what had Adam said to Neil?" I should've been at the inquest but at the same time, I am glad I wasn't, especially with this.

"This is going to be very hard for you to hear love."

"I need to know Mum."

"I know. I'd want to know too." She pauses. "Adam had apparently said to Neil that perhaps he should be the one to *do the honours*. Sorry Christy, I'm only repeating what they said. I didn't want to tell you this, but one of us had to."

"*Do the honours*. What's that supposed to mean?" But as the cold hand of fear seizes my heart, deep down, I know.

"Make Sacha pregnant. Like I said, I'm sorry love. I hate to be the one having to break it to you. Adam had insinuated to Neil that something had been going on between himself and Sacha. That's why Neil went for him. That's why Adam came back to us with the thick lip."

I feel like my world has stopped as I continue to stare at Sacha. *Could she? Would she?* I stare at the swelling bump over which the crisp, white sheet has moulded itself. *Could that be...?*

"Oh love, I'm sorry to tell you all this over the phone, and when you're on your own there. Are you OK?"

"Mum, do you think Adam could be the father of Sacha's baby?" Everything feels like it's falling down on me. I stand and walk to the door of the high dependency unit. I can't bear to look at my sister's face. *How could she do this to me?*

"I'm coming across," says Mum. "I'll get your dad settled then I'll be right over."

"Mum, no, get some rest. I'll be fine." But she's already hung up.

I stride along the shiny corridors towards the hospital's revolving doors and greedily gulp in the cold, clean air after the heat of the hospital. It's getting dark and as I walk to the car park, I notice daffodils opening up along the side of the pathway. Something inside me lifts, but immediately falls again.

I wander around the multi-storey in a daze, unable to remember where I left my car. I try to retrace where I was when I parked up this morning, but can't think straight. *My husband has been carrying on with my sister.* I've forgotten to get my ticket stamped by the HDU staff, so I'll have to pay to get out of here. I don't even know if I've got any change and the card machine is always out of order.

I arrive home, relieved to discover that Adam hasn't returned yet. I need to be in and out of here before he gets back. If I see him, then I won't be responsible for my actions. To think I was arguing to bring that baby here. No wonder he went off on one. If Sacha dies, then Adam may be legally forced to take responsibility anyway, and not just as an uncle. I accept that I've never truly known my husband. *But Sacha.* I can't believe she'd do this to me.

Really, I should pack Adam's things and change the locks. It's him, after all, whose behaviour is breaking our marriage up. But I haven't got the strength right now. I need to get away. I need to think. *Then* I will fight.

I throw what I need into a case and drag it to the car. I stride back inside and scrawl the word *bastard* on the pad by the telephone. Hopefully, he'll get the drift. I leave the house again and slide back into the driving seat and let the tears fall.

It's at times like this when I'm glad to have kept my financial independence. Adam knows nothing of the savings I've stockpiled over the years, and I have my salary paid into my account rather than the joint one. But I'll ensure I get my share for helping him with his business. I do all his admin, accounts and marketing on an evening, when I should put my feet up after being out working all day. I'll log into the business account as soon as I sort somewhere to stay.

. . .

I find myself at the Hilltop Lodge Hotel, a few miles from where we live. Adam and I attended a wedding here last year and I remember it has a gym, spa, restaurant, and some self-contained lodges in its grounds. After the two months I've just lived through and with what I've learnt today, I deserve some self-indulgence.

It's the end of February, and midweek, so I get a good deal on a two-night stay in one of the lodges. The receptionist gives me the option to extend so long as they stay quiet at the weekend. Even better, the lodge has a hot tub. I book a table in the restaurant, and for a few minutes, I almost forget my predicament as I drive through the woodland in the dark, occasionally stopping to study the map they've given me. In less than two hours, I've gone from a bedside vigil at my sister's side in the high dependency unit, to a luxury lodge with a hot tub.

When I find 'Lakeside,' I sit in the darkness of my car for a few moments, checking in with the enormity of my latest decision. I've left Sacha on her own. She might be a lot of things, but she's still my sister. And she still could die. It will be hours before Rebecca gets there. She always gets the kids settled first. *And* I've left my husband. We've been together for nearly ten years and I've left him without giving him the chance to explain his side of things. I just couldn't face seeing him after what I've heard.

In response to its beeping, I tug my phone from my handbag. I've missed calls from everyone. Mum. Adam. Rebecca. And a stream of text messages.

Adam. *What are you playing at? I've found your note, if we can call it that.*

Rebecca. *Where the hell are you?*

Mum. *I've just got back to the hospital. Feeling terrible for blurting it all out over the phone, but I didn't think I'd be coming back today. Please let me know you're OK love.*

Mum's messages are always long. I drop my phone back into

my bag and lug my case towards the lodge. A light flicks on as I approach the entrance and insert the key card. I gasp as I survey my surroundings. Wow. I wander from the lounge to the kitchen, to the bedroom to the bathroom. Wow. But then I sink onto the sofa in the lounge area. My sister is lying in a coma, pregnant with a baby that might be my husband's. *How could they do this to me?* And how did I think I could run away from it all by coming here?

I pull my phone from my bag again and switch it off this time. No one knows where I am, and I need some space. I eat the banana I threw into my case, then rummage around for my gym kit, swimming costume and a change of clothes.

I pound on the treadmill like my life depends on it, trying to outrun all that's going on. I work harder in the gym than I normally would, expending as much pent up anger and anxiety as I can. Another half an hour swimming up and down the quiet pool does wonders for my state of mind. By the time I'm dressed again, and have blow-dried my hair, I'm feeling clearer, and starving for the first time in a while. I make my way from the spa area along the rustic corridors, following the signs saying *restaurant,* as my feet sink into the thick pile of the carpet. I'm a million miles from reality and that's exactly how I want to feel.

"We're very quiet here tonight," the waitress tells me. "You can choose where you'd like to sit."

I look around, my eyes falling on a loved-up couple to my right. "Over there please." I point to a table at the other side of the restaurant, as far as possible from them, where I can look out of the window, instead of at them.

"Can I get you a drink?" She stands over me as I sit, her pen poised above a notebook, her blonde hair clipped neatly in a bun. I bet she has a nice, normal life. Not a philandering husband, a brother-in-law who's jumped off a cliff, a pregnant sister in a coma and a terminally ill father. When I make a list of it all like this, I imagine people would accuse me of making it all up.

"A large Pinot Grigio please. No, in fact, make that a bottle." I'm a bugger when I'm feeling like this and always go straight for the wine.

"Certainly." She plucks the menu from its stand and slides it in front of me. "I'll leave you with the food menu."

Really, I feel like wine more than food right now, but must be sensible and keep a clear head. One bottle of wine is more than enough in an evening and shouldn't affect me too much as long as I eat a meal with it.

"So is it business or pleasure?" The waitress speaks in her tinkly voice as she slides a glass towards me and pours a little of the wine for me to taste.

"Neither." I hope my tone conveys *mind your own business.* The last thing I want to do right now is make small talk. I take a sip from the glass. "Yes, that's fine thank you."

She fills my glass halfway; the pale liquid making a satisfying glugging noise. "I'll be back shortly to take your food order."

Stress normally steals my appetite but not today. I practically inhale my meal. I sit for a while, sipping at another glass of wine and staring out of the window into the darkness. The couple have gone thankfully, as they were getting on my nerves even from the other side of the room, as were a group of men, clearly business associates, talking loudly and animatedly. I need peace right now. I need to work out how to handle all this.

23

Squinting in the sunlight, I wonder where on earth I am when I first wake up. A lamp is blazing away at my side, the curtains are undrawn, and I'm laid fully clothed on top of the bed. As I haul myself up, I recall bringing a second bottle of Pinot back to the lodge and regret this decision immensely. I stagger through to the kitchen and fill a glass with water. I'll feel more human after something to eat and a shower. Then I'll let Mum know I'm OK.

There's a knock at the door of the lodge. "Here's the continental breakfast you ordered Madam."

"Thank you." I take the basket from the same waitress who served me last night's wine and close the door. She looks younger in the cold light of day. I could get used to living like this though.

Then, with the force of a blow to the head, I recall what Mum told me yesterday about Adam and Sacha. It feels dreadful just to place their names side by side. *Adam and Sacha.*

When I switch my phone on, I'm greeted by a flood of missed calls and messages. Adam's initial ones are full of anger but then mellow and become more desperate. He wants to talk to me. Tough. Rebecca is calling me selfish for taking off, and for worrying Mum and Dad. Who's she to call anyone else selfish? If it wasn't for her...

As I read the last text message Mum has sent, my heart misses a beat. *Call me straight away. Your sister has woken up.*

"It's me." My voice echoes around the silent lodge.

"Thank God Christy. I've been frantic about you. Where on earth have you been all night?"

"I stayed at a hotel. I needed some space. And didn't realise my phone had died." I take a deep breath. "I'm sorry to have worried you Mum." And I am. She has enough on her plate. And Dad. But the rest of them can go and boil their heads. Especially Adam.

"Are you alright love? I should never have told you everything over the phone like that."

"I guess so. Right... Sacha. She's woken up?"

"Yes." Mum is evidently trying to disguise the excitement in her voice for my sake. "She's sleeping again now, but it's normal sleep, not coma sleep." She stops and takes a deep breath. "Anyway, she recognised me as soon as she opened her eyes, and she squeezed the doctor's hand when he asked her to."

"That's a good sign." My voice sounds hollow. I should be over the moon. And I would've been jumping around the room if it were not for what I found out yesterday.

"I really think she's going to be OK," Mum goes on. "They're taking her for a scan soon, and they're going to scan the baby again too."

The baby. Someone I was coming to care about as the niece or nephew I was yet to meet, but now could be my stepdaughter or stepson. And to think, I was considering looking after it myself. What an idiot.

"I'm sorry to mention the baby." Mum must sense my misery. "This must all be really hard for you."

"That's an understatement."

"Have you spoken to Adam yet? The more I think about things, the more I'm convinced that everything has been blown up into something far more than it is."

"No. But I guess I'll have to at some point. I need to find out what's been going on. And what he has to say for himself."

"Of course you do. But you must go easy on Sacha for now. She's certainly not going to be up to being quizzed for a while."

"What do you take me for Mum?" I sigh. "Of course I'm not going to start questioning her. But I'm sure the police will soon enough."

"So what's your plan now Christy? Are you coming to the hospital later? I could do with getting back to your dad."

"Where's Rebecca?"

"She stayed here overnight, and I stayed at her house. I was so tired after yesterday that I couldn't have driven back to Bempton. So your dad's been on his own since after the inquest. I arranged for the carers to call in last night and this morning, but he'll be ready for me to go home by now."

"I don't know Mum." I feel as self-centred as hell, but am not sure how to cope with visiting Sacha after what's come to light. "Look, give me a couple of hours. I need to get my head together... and talk to Adam. I'll let you know what I'm doing then."

"She's still your sister Christy. You need to talk to *her* before you jump to any conclusions."

"What do you think happened between them Mum?"

"Oh love. You and Sacha have always been so close. There must be a grain of truth in what Adam's been saying, but I can't imagine your sister carrying on with him. I just can't. And your dad agrees with me. We had a long chat on the phone last night."

They would say that. I can't blame them for trying to make the best of the situation though. "I'm off for a shower and something to eat Mum. I promise I'll ring you soon."

I pull up outside Rebecca and Greg's smart detached house on the outskirts of Leeds. Before I confront Adam, I want to find out what Greg knows. Mainly, Greg works from home so should be here.

He and Adam seem to have become almost conjoined lately and have established a relationship that appears independent of merely being married to Rebecca and to me.

"What are you doing here?" Greg is unshaven, his hair looks like he's had an electric shock, and the baby is crying from behind him. "Shouldn't you be at the hospital?"

"Not just now. Can I come in?" I try to peer beyond him. "Where's Rebecca?"

"She's gone to bed. She was up and down at the hospital all night with Sacha waking up. Maybe we can all start getting back to some sort of normal. Stop revolving our lives around your sister."

"Do you reckon?" I don't smile back. "So are you going to let me in, or do I have to stand on your doorstep all day?"

He widens the door. "I suppose so. I'll just grab Zach."

I follow him through to the sunny kitchen where the baby is bawling from his pram. The house is in its usual state of dishevelment, clothes, shoes, and toys everywhere. Another reason I've never wanted kids. And never will. "Are the girls at school?"

"Yes. That's why Zachary's in his pram. The walk usually gets him back to sleep."

"It doesn't sound like that to me." I glance at the baby in his arms and am reminded once again of the one that's growing inside my sister. One that might also be my husband's.

"Do you want to hold him? I'll make some coffee. I could certainly do with one after the amount of sleep I've had."

The baby stops bawling, and the house falls silent. "No, you're alright. No point disturbing him now he's settled. I'll make it." I walk towards their coffee machine, hoping I can remember how to use it.

"You really haven't got a maternal bone in your body, have you Christy?"

"I didn't think Adam had either." I turn from inserting the coffee pods to study Greg. "Now, as it turns out, he could be the father of Sacha's baby."

"I think," Greg's expression is hard to read as he looks down at Zachary, "that as far as this family is concerned, we should accept that *Neil* is the father."

"Just by that comment alone, Greg, you seem unconvinced. And we're all aware that Neil was firing blanks." It's an awful term but I need to make my point. "What do you know Greg?" I slide two cups between the nozzles. "You and Adam seem to have some sort of bromance going on all of a sudden. He must've talked to you about it all."

"I don't know anything. Yeah, it was a surprise to find out Sacha was expecting, but it's nothing to do with Adam."

"How can you be so sure?"

"Cos he wouldn't do that to you." His voice rises in a way that people's often do when they're lying.

"You would say that."

"It's true. You just need to talk to him. He's as upset as you. He even turned up here last night to see if you'd been in touch."

"How convenient. You mean he turned up here to get pissed with you?" I add milk to the cups and take them to the island in the centre of their vast kitchen, perching myself on a breakfast bar stool facing him.

"It was a hell of a day yesterday." Greg adjusts his position on the stool, balancing Zachary in one arm, leaving his other arm free to drink his coffee. "The inquest took it out of all of us. You were lucky to get out of going."

"Mum told me Adam was thoroughly interrogated."

"Yeah." Greg stares into his cup. "It was heavy going. At least they saw sense in the end."

"So do *you* believe Neil chucked himself off that cliff as well?"

"Well, I've never thought for one minute Adam pushed him, if that's what you're getting at?"

"But there's no denying the two of them didn't get on. Not at all. And then there was the argument. Why didn't he tell me the whole story about that?" I observe Greg's face for signs that he is lying. He's never good at eye contact, so it's a difficult sign to measure. "I was left to find out from my mum after the inquest."

"I don't know. I wasn't there when it happened, was I? I've told everyone a million times. Neil was nowhere to be seen by the time I found Adam that night."

"I want to know what you know, Greg." I repeat my request. He seems uncomfortable beneath my constant gaze. "It's more than you're letting on. What's been going on between my sister and Adam?"

He sips his coffee. "You should have this conversation with your husband, not me."

"You would say that. What hold has he got over you that you'd keep secrets like this for him?"

"I've no idea what you're on about. We're just brothers-in-law. That we enjoy a drink and get along is a bonus."

"It's more than that, though. What about the investment you made into Adam's company last year?"

"That's just business. It was a sound opportunity and had the added benefit of helping Adam out."

"Has no one ever told you that family and business don't mix?"

"I disagree. Things are working out very well on that front. Anyway, you should be more grateful. His business might have folded without me investing, and him then being able to take that contract on."

"I couldn't give a toss anymore. I have my own job. In any case, Adam and I are unlikely to stay together, especially if he's proven to be the father of Sacha's baby. I'll be long gone if that turns out to be the case." The coffee burns the back of my throat, but at least my hangover has subsided slightly.

"Why don't you leave things alone Christy? It's unfortunate that Neil killed himself, but…"

"*Unfortunate?*"

"Perhaps knowing about Sacha's baby would've stopped him. We all should accept Neil's the dad and leave it at that."

"We'll see what Sacha tells us, shall we? Now that she's woken up."

"Rebecca says she could be brain damaged." Greg's tone is bordering on nonchalance. "Apparently, she can't string two sentences together. I've heard that the longer someone is in a coma, the more likelihood of damage there is."

"That's not what our mother is saying. She reckons Sacha is responding well. So if you and Adam won't give me my answers, Sacha will." God, he sounds almost as if he wants her to be brain damaged, as he puts it.

"We've still got to get to the bottom of that as well. Who put Sacha where she is in the first place? At least we know what happened to Neil now. He did what he did to himself. But Sacha didn't."

"There's no CCTV, no witnesses and it's been over a month now." Greg rocks Zachary from side to side as he speaks. "If there was anything to find out, they'd have it by now. Are you sure you don't want to take your nephew Christy? I don't think you've ever held him, have you?"

I shake my head. "When I've drunk this, I'll get going. I need to talk to Adam. And I'm convinced they'll get the driver eventually for what happened to Sacha. If there's one thing life has taught me, it's that what goes around nearly always comes around."

24

ADAM SIGHS and sinks to the bottom step. "It's Neil's bloody baby. For God's sake Christy, Sacha will tell you exactly the same thing, if and when she can."

"So, you'll do a DNA test when it's born?"

"Of course I will." The light from the stained glass window in the front door casts colours across his face.

"Has *anything* been going on between you and my sister? *Ever?*"

"Never. I promise you. I'm not like that."

"So why did you say what you said to Neil? About Sacha? Offering to make her pregnant?"

"I wanted a rise out of him."

"Oh, you got that alright." I lean against the hallway radiator, comforted by its heat. I'm feeling fragile again after the wine I drunk last night, and for not really sleeping properly. *And a fall,* I nearly add, until I realise how insensitive it would sound.

"I didn't tell you about it because I'm only too aware of what damage I've caused. If it wasn't for me, Neil might never have taken his own life." Adam drops his head into his hands, and something gives way within me. Perhaps he *is* telling the truth.

"I've got to live with what I've done, which is punishment enough. But to lose you as well. I can't lose you Christy."

His face bears a hangdog expression and he sounds almost tearful. Adam never cries. His attitude is the total opposite of the arrogant one he displayed the other day. My leaving seems to have tripped a switch within him.

"It seems a bloody strange thing to say. That you'd offer to get someone's wife pregnant. Your wife's sister at that."

"It was a joke."

"Jokes are funny Adam. Is anyone laughing?"

"Of course not."

"And why did you lie about the fight with Neil? You told no one that you'd actually retaliated after he hit you. You made it sound as though you'd walked away."

"Because I knew how terrible it would look. I was the last one to see him alive, wasn't I? Anyway, Christy, it's all over now." He raises his eyes to mine for the first time since I walked in here. "They've returned a verdict of suicide. I'm not the father of your sister's baby, and I've had nothing to do with Sacha in that way. What I said was to get at Neil. That's it. I wish I could convince you I'm telling the truth."

"There's no smoke without fire." It's true. I don't want to believe the worst of Adam, but all this has come from *somewhere.*

"The DNA result will prove it to you."

"It might show you're not the father, but not that you don't have designs on my sister or that nothing's ever happened between you."

"At least you've downgraded me from having an affair with her to fancying her. And neither is the case."

I want to trust him. Deep down, I want to get my stuff from the hotel and come home. I want everything to be back to normal again, especially now Sacha has woken up. But the doubts are gnawing at me and I can't ignore them. Faithfully married men don't make jokes about impregnating another man's wife. Innocent people don't fight with others moments before their death. And who mowed Sacha down on the day of Neil's funeral?

I look at my husband, staring intently back at me. I've always been able to see the boy he used to be in his face, and the older man he'll become. I thought I knew him as well as I know myself. I so want to believe him. But something is stopping me and I can't ignore it.

It's mid-afternoon by the time I park up at the hospital. Mum does not look impressed when she notices me standing in the doorway of the high dependency unit. I beckon to her to join me in the family room. Sacha doesn't appear any different from the last time I was here. She's still fast asleep.

"I thought you'd have been here ages ago." Mum sinks to the plastic sofa as I fill a glass with water from the cooler. "I told you I needed to get back to your dad."

"I'm sorry. You should've just gone."

"We agreed that someone would be here with Sacha."

"Things are different now. She's woken up, hasn't she?"

Mum rubs at her eyes and yawns. "Where've you been?"

"I went to talk to Greg and then Adam."

"And?"

"Greg's claiming not to know anything other than what he told the inquest."

"Well, he does know nothing as far as I can tell. Get me one of those will you?" Mum points at the cooler. "The air's so dry in this place. And Adam?"

"He swears blind he was just goading Neil and there's nothing for me to worry about. He's even offered to do a DNA

206

test to prove he's not the baby's father." I fill a cup and pass it to Mum.

"There you go then. He wouldn't be offering to do that if he was guilty of anything, would he?"

"He seems genuinely remorseful about his part in Neil's suicide, but..." I sip at the water.

"But what? He *is* genuinely remorseful. The way Adam treated Neil is something he has to live with now. That won't be easy."

"Oh, I don't know Mum. I've just got a bad feeling. And we still have no idea who or what put Sacha in here. Then there's Dad. It's just all so..." I sit on the sofa beside her.

"I agree love." She swaps her water from one hand to the other and drapes her arm around my shoulders. "But we've all got to stick together. We need to get Sacha and the baby through this and take care of your dad. It's horrendous how things ended up with Neil, but nothing we say or do can change a thing now."

"I just can't forgive Adam for his part in it all."

"He's going to have a harder time forgiving himself, let me tell you. He looked like he had the weight of ten suitcases on his shoulders after the inquest."

"So what are we supposed to do now?"

"We carry on. But you need to let this go. This suspicion you've got about Adam and Sacha, it'll eat you alive if you let it."

"I'm going to insist on the DNA test Mum. That's if I stay with him. I don't know what I'm doing at the moment."

"Well, right now, I need to get back to Bempton, and I need you to take your turn here until Rebecca gets back tonight." Mum puts her cup in the bin and reaches for her handbag.

"But Sacha's come out of her coma. Surely we don't need to do shifts like before?"

"We do for the time being. She's still got a way to go. At least until she's moved back to a normal ward."

"Sacha's always been your favourite." I sniff, knowing I sound pathetic, but I don't care.

"That's absolute rubbish. Sacha thinks Rebecca's my favourite, Rebecca thinks Sacha's my favourite, but I love you all the same. If it were you in that bed, I'd be right at your side too."

"I'm sorry Mum."

"The truth is that I'm torn between being here and being with your dad, and I need your support right now." Mum turns to me. "These last few months of his life, well, they're passing quickly, and he's needing me more and more as the cancer progresses. Besides, I want to be with him. We haven't got much time left."

"OK." Suddenly I feel terrible and vow to spend some time with my dad as soon as I can too. "I'll stay until Rebecca comes back."

"That's my girl." She pats my hand. "And are you staying at home tonight?"

I shrug. "All my stuff is at the hotel. I'll see how I feel later."

"Keep me posted. And don't go switching your phone off this time."

I sigh as I sink into my all-too-familiar place at Sacha's bedside. A couple of the monitoring machines have been taken away, so there's less beeping than I'm used to. Usually I would reach for my sister's hand, so she knows I'm here. But no matter how hard I try, I can't shake it out of my head that her baby is my husband's. And for that reason, hers is the last hand I'd want to hold. She's so peaceful that she still looks to be in her coma. If I hadn't been told otherwise, I wouldn't be able to tell any difference.

"How's she doing?" I ask the nurse at the desk.

She jerks her head up from her writing. "Pretty well, considering. The CT scan shows the swelling's gone down some more and she's been responsive when awake. She opened her eyes for a few minutes before."

"Really?"

"Yes, whilst you were in with your Mum. We're very pleased with her progress. I think she just needs to rest now, then hopefully we'll be able to get her moved to a general ward."

"She's been doing that for the last month – resting, I mean."

"She had a lot of injury to recover from. But she's doing great. She's one tough cookie, your sister."

I stare at her chest rising and falling beneath the sheet, then my gaze travels to her bump, another tough cookie. "What about the baby?"

"We've done a scan, and all is progressing as it should. We've taken an ultrasound image if you'd like to see it?"

I nod and she rises from the desk, sliding something from behind her monitor. "The only thing I need to warn you," she smiles, "is that the gender of this baby is incredibly obvious from this picture."

I take it from her, half expecting the jumble of black and white blobs to somehow show a likeness of my husband. I smile despite my suspicions. "Yes, I see what you mean."

"Meet your nephew." The nurse's voice is the brightest I've heard since Sacha was brought in here. I suppose it would be now that Sacha's heading in the right direction. "Keep that one if you like. Show it to her when she wakes again."

"Has my mum seen it yet?"

"Yes, but she wanted to leave it here, so Sacha could see it as soon as she's more alert." The nurse looks across Sacha as she checks one of the machines, her expression darkening. "Did the police investigation get any further with finding out how this happened to her?"

I shake my head. "No witnesses, no CCTV, nothing. We're

hoping Sacha might be able to tell us something when she comes around more."

"Let's hope so." The nurse writes on a chart at the foot of Sacha's bed. "She and the baby have been extremely lucky. There have been times over the last month, when it could've easily gone the other way for them."

My phone beeps in my bag and the nurse returns to her station.

I love you Christy. Please come home tonight.

I text back. *I don't know what to do. I can't think straight.*

I'm so sorry. I've been such an idiot.

That's putting it mildly.

I don't fancy your sister. I never have.

It's just such a strange thing to say. What you said to Neil that night.

Like I said before, I've got to live with that, haven't I?

So have I.

Does that mean you'll come back then?

I think for a moment. I've paid for the hotel for another night. All my things are there. And I still haven't decided on a way forward. I'm best to allow myself more space, and Adam has no right to make demands of me.

I won't be back tonight. I need more time.

Why? How much time? For God's sake, Christy.

Just give me some space.

What I don't tell him is that before I return home, I need to hear what Sacha has to tell me. And if that takes a few days, well, it's a very nice hotel.

Despite my misgivings, I can't conceal my excitement when I notice Sacha staring straight at me a few minutes later. "Sacha! You're awake." Something fires inside me. No matter what mistakes she may or may not have made with my husband, and *mistakes* is putting it mildly, Mum's right. She's still my sister and I want her to get better, of course I do. We'll deal with everything else later. I reach for her hand and she squeezes it.

"It's good to have you back sis." Tears fill my eyes. I've dreamed of this moment for the last month and I feared it would never happen. "You gave us all a fright."

She points at the beaker on the table beside her.

"Am I alright to give her this?" I call to the nurse.

"Yes. She's already had a couple of sips through the straw. It's good to get her swallowing again."

Sacha lifts her head from the pillow and purses her chapped lips around the straw. When she leans back again, I take my lip salve from my bag and rub some onto her mouth. She smiles. It's a small smile but a smile, nonetheless. She points towards her belly. "Baby?" Her voice is a croak, but it's a sound I wondered if I'd ever hear again.

I slide the scan picture from my pocket. "Sacha, meet your baby." I hold it in front of her, wondering if she can see she's having a son. "Everything's fine."

She raises her head again and studies the picture for a moment, looking as though she's struggling to focus. She drops back onto her pillows and her eyes fall closed again. I want to talk to her. Find out what she remembers about her accident. Ask her if there has ever been anything going on between her and my husband. Tell her they've returned a suicide verdict for Neil. But I have to be patient. There will be time for all that soon.

"Is there any sign of anything permanent?" I whisper to the nurse as she checks Sacha's monitors a short time later.

"Only a baby." She chuckles but then stops and says, "it's too early to be certain. Everything's looking good, but things such as memory loss might show themselves once she becomes more alert."

～

"You look like you could do with a coffee," I say to Rebecca when she arrives at the foot of Sacha's bed that evening.

"It's all this." Rebecca gestures towards Sacha. "And three kids. I'm just snatching sleep when I can. I hope that family room's free tonight."

"It shouldn't be like this for much longer."

"I don't see why we're keeping up with this now. Especially since she's out of her coma."

"That's what I said at first. But Mum wants us to carry on until she's moved out of this ward."

"Mum should focus on Dad. Sacha's taken enough time and attention from him."

"She'd do the same for you."

"You've changed your tune, haven't you?" Rebecca tugs a chair from the pile in the corner and places it beside mine. "Greg made it sound like it was curtains between you and Sacha... and you and Adam."

I sigh. "I don't know what to think Rebecca. Adam has denied everything. I want to believe him, but I'm more interested in hearing what Sacha has to say when she's up to talking."

Rebecca sits down heavily and hangs her shoulder bag behind her. "That's *if* she's ever up to talking. She's been in a coma for over a month. We've no idea how she'll be yet so don't get too ahead of yourself. I can't imagine her getting back to normal."

"Ever the optimist, aren't we?" I glance at Rebecca's puffy face. She's got a long way to go before she loses her baby weight. In times of difficulty, she comfort eats, not like me and Sacha. Instead, we're prone to losing our appetites when we're stressed out.

Other than her baby bump, Sacha has lost even more weight, but we're told she's getting all the food she and the baby need through the drip.

"Just keeping it real," Rebecca replies.

"Anyway, what's most important is that Sacha remembers some details to help catch the maniac who put her in here."

"I can't imagine she'll remember much," Rebecca replies. "She's been out for the count since it happened. It was dark and raining and it sounds like the car came out of nowhere."

"If it were an accident, as you're making it sound, the driver would have tried to slow down. They'd have slammed on when they saw her, surely?"

"Maybe they didn't see her. It was foggy that day as well, wasn't it?"

"Even if they didn't, they'd have stopped afterwards. You don't hit nine stone of person and keep on driving."

"Well, I think you're hoping for too much." Rebecca drags a bag of sweets from her bag. "Whoever the driver was is long gone." She offers the bag towards me.

"No thanks. Anyway, I'm going to make a move."

"Are you going home? I hear you stayed away last night."

"Nope. I'm stopping in a hotel. I paid for two nights so I might as well go back there. Leave Adam to stew in his own juices after how he's behaved, for a bit longer."

"Fair enough," she sniffs. "I'm keeping out of it all. I've enough of my own worries."

Perhaps I should find out what her worries are, other than Dad, but I can't be bothered. Rebecca is so negative and draining that it's always a relief to part company with her. Sometimes I can't believe we're even related. "I'll leave you to it then." I get to my feet and squeeze Sacha's hand. "See you tomorrow." Then I turn back to Rebecca and say, "I hope you get some sleep tonight."

"It's alright for some." She doesn't seem able to disguise the venom in her voice. "I wish I could swan off to a bloody hotel for the night."

25

I'm staying off the wine tonight as I've felt ropey all day. It's been hours since Adam's tried to contact me, which is puzzling as he sounded desperate to make amends earlier. Perhaps he's just doing as I asked and giving me space. *Be careful what you wish for,* Dad has always said. *You never know what you might get.*

Sacha waking up might have changed things for Adam. If there *was* something going on between them, maybe that's why he's gone all distant on me, worried about what Sacha might be about to impart. It was mid-afternoon when I last received a text from him.

I place my knife and fork in the centre of the plate. At least I've eaten half of my meal. I reach for my phone. Straight to Adam's voicemail. Strange. His phone is never, ever switched off. He's meticulous about it as clients contact him at all hours of the day and night.

I return to my lodge and switch the TV on. But I'm distracted. No way am I going to settle. It's all going on at the moment and I'm no closer to getting the answers I need to make any decisions. I try Adam again. His phone is still off. I wonder if he's gone to see Greg like he did last night. I can't stand all this. Without really planning to, I find myself back in the car, which I point towards home. Yes, I need space, but I need answers more.

I'm stopped short by the presence of Greg's car outside our house. His kids are at school in the morning, so I can't imagine him having them out at this time of night. It's nearly ten o'clock. He must've got someone to sit with them. At least, I hope he has, or Rebecca will kill him.

I linger in the car for a few moments, staring at my house. I can't talk to Adam with Greg hanging around. Although, there's a chance I'll actually get more answers by confronting them together.

Adam has not completely closed the lounge blind so I can see the shape of someone pacing up and down in front of the window. I get out of my car quietly, and don't push the door shut as I normally would. As I approach the porch, raised voices are echoing from inside. I strain to listen, but the voices are muffled from where I'm standing. I creep into the hallway, beyond thankful that the alarm is off – normally it beeps whenever anyone comes in or out of the house. I wait for a moment, trying to slow my breathing, desperate to learn what they're arguing about.

"You seem to have conveniently forgotten that you owe me mate." Greg enunciates the consonants in *mate* as he speaks. "I saved your bloody arse last year."

I can just about make out what Greg is saying. I edge closer to the lounge door, praying they don't discover I'm here.

"You can't deny that. And we've come this far, haven't we?"

"You can't keep lording that one over me." Adam now. "And anyway, all that was before my marriage started to fall apart. Things have changed Greg. I had nothing to lose before."

"Christy will come back. What else is she going to do?"

There's a note of sarcasm in Greg's voice. "You can talk her around, then all this will blow over. I've had enough of it all - we've just had a bloody new kid. And there's our bloody father-in-law dying to get through yet."

How dare he talk about my dad like that? Somehow, I resist the urge to storm into the lounge and thump him.

"Actually Greg, you don't know my wife like I do. When she gets something into her..."

"The baby thing is the *least* of our problems right now."

"It's not you that's being accused of anything."

Shit. What does that mean? *The baby thing.* Why are they talking about that?

"Admittedly, it's complicated things. But if we hold our nerve," Greg again. "We can let this pass. We got through the inquest and we can get through the rest of it."

The rest of what? I am dying to burst in there and demand answers, but really, I need to wait - whatever I'm going to hear needs to be first hand.

"I'm not losing my wife because of *you* Greg."

I should be touched by Adam's sentiment. But I'm shaking like I've never shaken before. I wish I'd never come here. What is that saying, *ignorance is bliss?* Perhaps it's true. What has Greg got on Adam? What has Adam got over Greg?

"It's too late to change our stories now. We need to stick to what we've said. If it were to all come out, I've got more to lose than you. But you will lose, Adam. You will lose."

What is Greg on about? What has *he* got to lose? I don't get this. Any of it.

"You've done nothing but threaten to pull your money out for the last two months Greg. Do you want to ruin me? Don't you think things are bad enough for all of us?"

"Perhaps you're just going to have to let Christy know."

I can't stand here anymore listening to them talking in

riddles. "Let Christy know what?" I throw the door open and look from one startled face to the other.

"How long have you been here?" Greg's face is pinched with anger, which is unusual for someone who's normally easy going with me.

"Long enough."

"What have you heard?" Adam's tone is gentler than Greg's.

"Enough to be sure that you two are a pair of liars. What have you got to hide? Both of you?"

"Nothing." Adam looks down at his bare feet. "It's just all this stuff with your sister."

"So you are the father? Come on, Adam, I want the bloody truth. You owe me that much." I turn to Greg who doesn't appear to have shaved or combed his hair since I saw him yesterday. "And what has all this has got to do with you?"

"Absolutely nothing. This is between you and him. And Sacha."

"So why are you here Greg?" I let the door fall closed behind me and step into our cosy lounge. On a normal evening, Adam and I would be curled up on the sofa, sharing a bottle of wine with the fire crackling in front of us. At least we would have been before things went so badly wrong. "What were you talking about?"

"Business stuff." Greg leans on the mantlepiece. "You had no right, sneaking around, listening to our private conversation."

"Can I remind you that this is my house?"

"So why didn't you come in like a normal person?" Adam drops into the armchair like a stone.

"You were speaking in raised voices as I parked up." I was suspicious enough before, but I really am now. I feel even more certain that Adam has been up to no good. But whatever it is, they're not coming out with it. Then I remember Rebecca is at the hospital. "You haven't left your kids on their own surely?" I ask Greg.

"Like you care about our kids." This sneering Greg is one I haven't met before. Adam, since what happened at Christmas, seems to have mellowed somewhat, other than when we argued about us taking Sacha's baby on. Another reason to be suspicious. And he's always got a haunted expression – he's as guilty as sin... of something. And I'll get to the root of it somehow.

"I care about them being left alone at ten o'clock at night."

"They're with Rebecca, actually."

"But she's at the hospital." This conversation between Adam and Greg must have been so 'urgent' that he's made her leave.

"She came home. She'd had enough. We've all had enough."

"So – Sacha's on her own? Great."

"She's a grown woman Christy. And she's getting better isn't she? Rebecca says they've been talking."

"Really? About what?" I watch Adam carefully, but his expression isn't giving anything away.

"How the hell should I know?"

I'm not going to get anywhere with these two. I look around at my lounge, which needs a damn good tidy after my being away. There's no way I can come back here yet. Not until I get my answers. Is Adam the father of Sacha's baby? Who put her in the hospital? And was the verdict of the inquest the correct one?

Sacha can answer the first question – I will *make* her tell me the truth. And she may remember something to go some way toward answering the second question. As for the third, perhaps we'll never truly have the answer. But I can't accept that Neil committed suicide. It would be the easiest thing to believe, but something inside niggles at me to keep pushing.

Sacha's sitting up in bed when I arrive at the hospital the next morning. She has more colour in her face and someone has plaited her hair. Apart from the still visible marks from the stitches she had in her head, she looks almost back to her usual self.

"She's doing great, aren't you?" The nurse smiles as she unhooks one of the remaining monitors. "So great, that she'll be moving to a general ward later today."

"Wow. That's good news." Perhaps I'll be able to question her at last.

"The doctors will take the final decision on their ward round later, but as far as we're concerned, she's well enough to be moved."

I sink onto the chair beside Sacha as the nurse moves to the next bed. "So, aren't you the miracle woman? Has anyone told Mum and Dad you'll be moving?"

She shakes her head, the force of the movement clearly making her wince.

"Mum will probably be back over later. Poor thing. All this driving backwards and forwards. Hopefully not for much longer, eh?"

Sacha nods.

"Is the baby OK in there?" I point at her stomach, speaking almost through gritted teeth. "Can you feel him moving around yet? It must be weird, having another human being inside you."

She nods again and her hand flits to the bridge of her belly.

"Who's the father Sacha? Just say the name. One word. I need the truth." I glance at the nurse to check she isn't listening. She's talking to a relative from one of the other beds.

A look that I can't read passes over Sacha's face as she croaks, "Neil."

I watch her closely. "I don't believe you sis. Nobody does."

She stares back at me, her eyes not leaving mine. It's as though she's imploring me to accept what she says. *Why won't anyone tell me the bloody truth?* It's so frustrating. I could scream, and I've no idea what to do about it. For now, I'm just going to keep talking.

"Do you know they're saying Neil jumped? At the inquest, I mean?"

She nods once more.

"Adam was apparently in hot water for a while." I stare at my hands where specks of nail varnish remain from the manicure I had five weeks ago. I *never* normally let my nails get into this state. "I wasn't at the inquest - I stayed here with you – but the truth about his fight with Neil came out, as well as the things Adam had said to Neil that night. He got a right grilling."

"I know." There's clearly nothing wrong with her level of understanding. Then she closes her eyes. Nice one Sacha. When the going gets tough, pretend to fall asleep. I'm not going to get anywhere here. I'll come back later. In the meantime, I'm going to extend my hotel stay over the weekend and make use of the gym and spa again.

26

MUM'S SITTING with Sacha when I arrive back at the hospital. By now it's dark again, but I'm feeling calmer after unleashing some frustration in the gym, having a late lunch and sleeping for a couple of hours. I went to the high dependency unit when I first arrived, but the nurse redirected me here, to Ward Thirty Six. "I hope your sister continues as well as she has so far," she'd called after me.

"Thanks." I turned to smile at her.

I can't shake this hollowed-out feeling and right now, I feel like a fraud, just being here. I love my sister, but part of me hates her too. Even more because she won't tell me the truth. That baby is not Neil's, and I can't wait for a DNA test to find out. I wonder if they do them on babies *before* they're born. I will research that later.

"Sacha remembers car lights." The suddenness of Mum's words cuts into my thoughts. "Don't you love?"

I jerk my head upwards. "From the night you were hit, you mean?"

She nods. "Fast."

"Did you see who was driving? How many people there were in the car? Whether it was a man or a woman?"

She shakes her head. "I wish."

Mum pats the chair at the side of her. "Come and sit down Christy. Rebecca's already been grilling Sacha today about the accident, hasn't she love?" She takes her hand. "In fact, I had to tell her to change the subject. Sacha's had enough of it now."

"Have you let the police know she's out of the coma?" Once they get involved, that should push things forward.

"Rebecca's rung them. She says they're giving Sacha a couple more days recovery time, then they're going to visit and take a statement."

"Hopefully she'll remember more about what happened by the time they come." I can't talk to Sacha about the baby in front of Mum, so I ask after Dad instead.

Mum's face clouds over. "To be honest love, I shouldn't even be over here tonight. Pamela from next door is checking in on him every so often until I get back."

"Really? Has he got worse?"

"It's ironic, isn't it?" Mum lifts her glasses and rubs her eyes. "The minute Sacha starts getting better, your dad suddenly goes downhill. It's almost as though he's been hanging on."

"Going downhill? How? Why?" Sacha is also looking at Mum with troubled eyes.

"It's the pain. The MacMillan nurse warned me this would happen. Without the chemo, the cancer is taking hold of him faster. They've upped his morphine today, but that only makes him even more sleepy. I can barely get a conversation out of him now." She forces a smile. "Once upon a time, I'd have been glad of the peace but now, I miss his company."

"I noticed how sleepy he was at Christmas. He was bad enough then." *Christmas.* It makes me feel sick to think about it. "Poor Dad. I must get over to see him."

"He'd like that. But give it a few days. He might have got used to this new level of morphine by then."

"OK." I don't want to say anything to Mum, but it hits me he could die without me seeing him again. I can't risk that. I expect Sacha is worrying about the same thing. It might give her extra fight to get out of here quicker.

"The best thing you can do right now," Mum goes on. "You and Rebecca, that is – would be to take care of things here with Sacha so I can look after your dad. I'm run ragged with all this driving. It's not as though I'm getting any younger either."

I watch as Sacha squeezes Mum's hand.

"It's since the inquest," Mum sniffs, and dabs at her eyes. "He's been deteriorating since then. I should have insisted he stayed at home, but he wouldn't hear of it. He said he wanted to be there to represent Sacha."

"That's Dad all over," I say.

Mum continues. "Now, like I've said before, it's as though he's been waiting for Sacha to be alright, and now he's letting go. I thought we'd have more time. It's only been a few months since he discontinued the chemo."

"They said he'd only have a few months Mum." I look away, not wanting her to see the tears pooling in my eyes as well. Us all crying around Sacha's bed in the middle of this bustling ward is not ideal. All around us TVs are robotically droning, and other visitors are arriving for the evening visiting slot. We can only visit at certain times now, which I guess will make things easier for everyone. Until they discharge Sacha, then I don't know what will happen or whether she'll even be able to manage at home. Under normal circumstances, I'd have insisted she stay with me and Adam. But that hardly seems like a feasible option.

"What a few months we've been through. I wanted to make them special for your dad."

"I'm sorry." Sacha says in a voice that's so much smaller than usual.

"It's not your fault." Mum lets go of her hand, then slides her handbag from the back of her chair. "What have you done to cause any of this?"

Maybe more than you could imagine, I want to say.

I glance at Sacha; her eyes are full of tears. "Dad," she says, grappling for Mum's hand. "You go."

"You need to get yourself right." I say to Sacha in a mock-stern voice as we watch our mother walk towards the ward's double doors. "Then we'll drive you over to see him."

"Not Rebecca." It's difficult to ascertain from her tone whether she's stating a wish or asking a question.

"What do you mean? *Not Rebecca?*"

She doesn't answer, but closes her eyes instead.

I leave soon after Mum. Sacha's falling asleep anyway. It feels strange heading to the hotel instead of home for another night. But not returning home possibly gives me more leverage. It shows Adam that until he tells me straight, he risks losing me. I'm puzzled though. I assumed he'd bombard me today after the altercation last night with Greg. There's been one text from him, that's all. Over an entire day.

None of it is what you think. That's all he had to say. Talking in riddles, as usual.

At least I got the chance earlier to ask Sacha about the baby. She said *Neil* straightaway, but there was something about her expression that will not stop me pursuing this. I must be patient. The truth will find its way out. It always does.

The weekend passes in a blur of Rebecca and I taking it in turns to visit Sacha. I call Mum several times to receive updates about Dad and make the most of the gym and the swimming pool at the hotel. I eat all my meals in the restaurant, very much aware of my self-indulgent behaviour, but not giving a damn.

Adam is remaining strangely quiet. When I finally give in on the Sunday evening and ring him, the conversation is like getting blood from a stone.

"So why haven't you been in touch Adam?" I stare out of the lodge window at the darkening lake as I wait for his answer. This is a place we could have stayed at together, but he's ruined all that. It's the last day of February which I'm pleased about. The days are quickly lengthening now, and this is a winter I'll be relieved to leave behind.

"You told me you needed space Christy." There's a weariness to his voice. "Make your mind up, will you?"

"Have you sorted your differences with Greg?"

"There's nothing to sort. It was a business thing."

"Oh, come on Adam. It sounded like more than that. Much more."

"You probably only got wind of a fraction of our conversation."

It sounds more like Adam is asking me a question here. I don't answer him. It's better if he's left to speculate over how much I heard, or in this case, didn't hear. Enough, though, is enough. Greg and Adam have got more over one another than merely a financial arrangement.

"Sorry about your dad," he says. "It must be rough for you."

"Yeah. On top of everything else." Adam has always been good at changing the subject.

"You should visit him for a few days."

Those are not the words of someone who wants his wife back home. I'm now more suspicious than ever. "Why a few days, Adam? Are you trying to get me out of the way?" I imagine him sitting at Sacha's bedside with his hand on her swelling belly. The whole thing is driving me insane.

"Don't be daft. It's just that, you'll regret it if you don't take this time to be with him."

"We've promised Mum we'll take care of Sacha."

"She's getting better now, isn't she?"

"I guess so."

"I've got to go Christy. There's someone at the door." And with that, he's gone, leaving me more confused than ever.

As I feed coins into the coffee machine in the hospital foyer, I spot Rebecca. She looks straight at me, quickly looks away and carries on walking as though she's trying to avoid me. She appears to have aged two years in two months. If that's what having a baby does to a woman, I'm glad I'm not bothering.

"Rebecca!"

She turns towards me. "Sorry. Didn't see you there."

I frown at her, hoping that my face conveys my thoughts. "What's up with you?"

"Nothing." She sighs. "Everything."

"Do you want one of these?" I point at the machine.

She nods.

We take our coffees to a bench at the edge of the waiting area. I'm sick of the sight of this place. It's been my second home for nearly five weeks. I recognise most of the porters and reception staff. Many of them say hello to me now.

"How's Sacha doing?" I ask Rebecca. "I'm on my way in?"

"Fine. I haven't been there long – I'm knackered." She crosses one denim clad leg over the other. I notice she's back in jeans for the first time since having Zachary.

"Will she be up to talking to the police by now? We could do with getting that out of the way."

"I don't know." The tone of Rebecca's voice dips.

"I thought you said they'd be here in a couple of days."

"They did. But they said they'd ring first. I guess they'll come when they're ready."

"OK. Listen. I'm glad I've got you on your own at last." I sip at my coffee, grimacing. Machine coffee is always worse than I think it's going to be. "What's going on between Greg and Adam?"

"What do you mean?"

"I went home the other night and caught them arguing?"

"About what?"

"I've no idea. They wouldn't tell me. That's why I'm asking you. I want to know what you know about things." I watch as she lifts the paper cup to her lips, noticing a slight shake of her hand.

"Nothing. I mean, I was aware Greg was calling around to your house obviously, but I assumed he was checking up on Adam. After splitting from you, I mean."

"We're not *splitting*. I've no idea what's happening yet. We're just having some time apart."

"Well, whatever. It's nothing to do with me."

"If you sit any higher on that fence Rebecca, you'll get splinters in your backside."

"Bloody hell, Christy, wind your neck in. It's probably just business stuff. Greg put a lot of money in last year."

"Don't we know it?"

"Then obviously they're coming to terms with the inquest verdict."

"What do you mean by *coming to terms?*"

"It can't be easy, especially for Adam, knowing what Neil did and how he'd treated him – he knows as well as we do, Neil jumped off that cliff and he probably drove him to it."

"Is that what you think as well?"

"Adam was bloody awful to Neil on Christmas day. Don't you remember what he said when he raised his glass. *To family... and Neil.*"

"That's nothing compared to what he's admitted saying to him later."

"About Sacha?"

"Yeah."

"Like I said, I'm keeping out of it. We've all got our own troubles to deal with, haven't we?"

We sit in silence for a moment, sipping our coffee. She's so closed, is Rebecca. I can't remember us ever having an in-depth discussion. I'd be interested in what she thinks. I need to know what she knows. And I wonder if the problems she's referring to involve Greg's disagreements with Adam. Why won't anyone tell me anything? It's so frustrating, I could scream.

"You were there that day, Rebecca. At the inquest, I mean. Were they right to grill him?"

"Adam?"

"Who else could I be on about?"

"They didn't grill him that much. You know how Mum can exaggerate at times."

"No, she doesn't. What are you on about?"

"Why do you even keep raking over this? It's finished now. It's been confirmed that Neil committed suicide, and that's all we need. I can't understand why you won't leave it alone."

"What about Sacha? We don't know for sure who the father of her baby is, nor do we have any clue about who put her in here."

"She had an accident, for God's sake! It was dark. It was raining. And she was dressed in black that day."

"I reckon someone ran her over and left her there. On purpose."

"Rubbish."

"Well, that's what I think. And I won't rest until..."

"Leave it to the police, Christy. For God's sake, why can't you count your blessings." Her voice rises and several people glance over at us. She pauses and lowers it again. "Look. You've got a good life with a husband who loves you. We've got to the truth about Neil. Sacha has survived her accident, and it *was* an accident, and her *baby* is safe."

I notice she emphasises the word baby in a way which puzzles me. She almost spits the word out. Sacha said before that Rebecca would see another baby in the family as competition for Mum's grandmotherly affection. I thought Sacha was being dramatic, but I can't imagine what else Rebecca's attitude could be put down to.

"Blessings!" I laugh, but it's not a genuine laugh. "We've got a terminally ill father. I've got a husband who really, I think probably *pushed* Neil to his death, and a sister who might be carrying my husband's baby."

"You've really got to let this go, Christy. Blimey, this coffee is awful. You're going to make yourself ill."

"I'll be insisting on a DNA test," I continue. "And no, I won't let this go. Would you?"

"I've got to get home to the kids." She stands without looking at me. "I've totally had enough of all this. I just want a quiet life with my husband and my children."

"Make sure you chase up the police, will you?" I call after her. "Don't forget, Rebecca."

She hurries away without turning back to reply. It's as though she can't get away from me quickly enough.

27

MUM JOINS me in the conservatory, handing me a cup of tea before sitting in the chair opposite. "The house seems so empty without him."

The stillness of the bungalow is eerie after the drama we had at Christmas. It's the first time I've been back since.

"It certainly does." I sigh and look out of the window, which I opened before Mum came in. The morning air that wafts over my face lifts my spirits slightly. Her garden is full of crocuses and daffodils, and the newly arrived birdsong is a welcome sound. The life of the garden is in stark contrast to what we're facing here. I've been staying with Mum for the past three days, having decided not to continue forking out money for the hotel. I'm glad to be here. Mum will never admit to it, but she shouldn't be on her own at a time like this.

"He really didn't want to go into the hospice." Mum follows my gaze to the garden. Dad loved gardening. It's one of the many things Mum's going to have to take on after... "It's the word, isn't it? *Hospice.* You don't go into one and then come out again."

"Some do." I think of Adam's mum. She enjoyed staying

there. Said it was more like a hotel. "Some people use them for respite."

"But that isn't the case with your dad." She lowers her gaze as she sips her tea.

"It's a lovely place though Mum. And they're taking amazing care of him from what you've said."

She pulls a hanky from her apron and presses it against her eyes. "It feels even worse because the last few months have been so *awful*."

"What's happened has definitely made it even harder." Guilt twinges within me, but if I search inside myself, my conscience is clear. Maybe it's because I'm pushing so hard when everyone else wants to sweep our family's issues into a dark corner. I'm only guilty of trying to get to the truth. Other than that, nothing that's happened in this family has resulted from *my* actions. Which is more than can be said for some.

"Are you still able to collect Sacha from the hospital today?" Mum tucks the hanky up her sleeve and sniffs. "At least she'll get to see your dad before..."

"Yeah. I'm going to set off shortly. I want to be with her when the police get there."

"That's good of you." Mum smiles through her misery. "I'm pleased she won't have to face it on her own. That was a strange carry on, wasn't it?"

"What do you mean?" My ears prick up. I wonder if Mum is going to say out loud what I've been thinking.

"Rebecca definitely said she'd been in touch to inform them of Sacha coming out of the coma. I heard her say it myself."

"She told me she'd followed it up as well." I'm pleased that Mum is questioning it too.

"But when I rang them yesterday to see if they could come before she was discharged, they knew nothing about Sacha having even woken up. There's been a real lack of communication there. I'm not sure whether we should put a complaint in."

I'm back on the long road between Bempton and Leeds, for the fourth day in a row. At least I won't have this journey for a while, once Sacha is staying over here with me and Mum. We've agreed that her staying at the bungalow is the best way forward for now.

Everything is on one level, which will make Sacha getting around on her crutches so much easier, and she can use Dad's wet room shower. More importantly, she and Mum can look after each other. Rebecca's face was a picture when Mum said those very words in front of her. Pure jealousy.

Adam, true to his word, has been giving me *space*. In fact, I've barely spoken to him since I've been staying with Mum. I can't decide if I'm comfortable with this, or more wary about it. However, until I get some truths, I might as well stay in Bempton. It's where I should be, and work have been really understanding. Head office has got someone in temporarily to cover the shops I manage. And I can't deny being closer to Sacha might just help me get my answers, starting with her interview with the police.

"I'm DC Lisa Fowkes, and this is my colleague, Sergeant Fay Atkinson."

A DC and a Sergeant. They've sent the big guns. Like me, they must still suspect something more than a mere accident caused Sacha's injuries. Somebody is out there, knowing they have run my sister over. Not only that. They nearly killed her. And her baby.

"I'm Sacha's sister, Christy, and this," I point, "is obviously Sacha." Me and the nurse helped her dress this morning. She looks strange wearing Mum's clothes. But with her growing bump, it would have been pointless picking any of her own clothes up. Mum's a size fourteen so her jogging bottoms and the zipped hoodie she would normally lounge around in, are a comfortable fit on Sacha. Although it was no easy task trying to get her dressed. Not with one leg and an arm still in a cast.

"Is it alright if we sit down?" DC Fowkes nods towards the chairs stacked by the window. "And are we alright to talk in *here?*" She looks around at the other beds. The ward is quiet compared to what it was when Sacha first arrived. There's a lady in the bed opposite who has dementia, and the lady in the bed next to her has been taken for a shower. The one at the other side has taken herself out for a smoke. The other two beds are empty.

"We're alright in here, aren't we ,Sacha?"

She nods.

"And I'm OK to stay with my sister whilst you talk to her, aren't I?"

"Of course." The sergeant speaks this time.

"Right." DC Fowkes flips a notebook open and presses the top of her pen. "Firstly, let me apologise for not having got here sooner. We were informed someone would contact us when you were well enough to talk to us Sacha. I'm glad you're on the mend, by the way."

"Yes," Sergeant Atkinson adds. "You're looking considerably better than the last time we saw you. Is everything OK with the baby?"

She probably realises she's safe to ask that question. Beneath Mum's pink hoody, zipped up and snug on Sacha, it's obvious from her bump that everything is very much OK.

"Yes, thank you. It's a he, and he's fine."

"I think a bit of miscommunication has taken place

somehow," DC Fowkes continues. "You said your other sister had been in touch with us? Twice?"

"Yes. And she was told you'd visit in a couple of days. That was last week."

"We've no record of her having been in touch. And they log every communication. So," she shrugs. "I'm not sure what happened."

"Would you be able to check into that?"

"Yes. Of course. Anyway, we're here now and hoping, Sacha, that you can tell us what you can remember. This happened to you on the day of your husband's funeral, I believe?"

"Yes." Sacha looks down at her hands. "I'd gone for a walk to clear my head."

"You were at the King's Arms pub in Farndale, weren't you?"

"That's right. Neil's dad, Joe, had arranged the wake."

"And Neil's death has been recorded as a suicide since, hasn't it?"

"Yes," I reply, slightly annoyed with how direct she is about something so huge for our family. "At the Hull Coroner's Court."

"OK. Thank you for that." She smiles at me. "Sacha, can you recall what time you left the pub that day?"

"I can't remember what time it was." Sacha pushes her hair back from her face. "I only remember how desperate I was to get away from there."

"Why was that?"

"Well, it was a difficult enough day, anyway. Obviously." She laughs a hollow laugh. "But since my husband died, I'd discovered I was pregnant, and I hadn't told anyone."

"Go on."

"Well, my other sister Rebecca guessed, as I wasn't drinking and had begun to get a belly. She decided to broadcast it to all and sundry at the funeral, and..." Sacha's voice trails off.

The DC looks at me, as if she expects me to continue Sacha's tale.

"There were allegations at the wake over the baby's parentage." There, I've said it now and I'm watching Sacha very closely indeed for her reaction.

"You mean who might be the father?"

"Yes." Sacha's avoiding my gaze – I'm sure of it. "The baby is Neil's," she says. "But we'd been told we couldn't conceive without fertility treatment, so people were putting two and two together, and making eight."

It's the longest sentence I've heard Sacha speak since she emerged from the coma. There's absolutely no denying how well she's done. Physically, she'll probably be back on her feet in no time. Psychologically, who knows?

"So the baby is definitely Neil's child?" DC Fowkes asks.

"Of course it is."

"OK. We'll park that for now. Let's go back to that afternoon. Do *you* know," DC Fowkes looks at me, "what time Sacha left the pub?"

"Not for certain, but possibly around two pm. We didn't start worrying until a good ninety minutes had passed though. We'd accepted she probably just needed some time to herself."

"Were you not able to contact her when she didn't return?"

"She'd left her bag, and her phone behind. So no. But we didn't notice it straight away. We were giving her the space she needed."

"So you left in a rush?" DC Fowkes looks from me to Sacha, who doesn't reply, then back to me. "You must have done not to even pick up your phone and bag."

"It was about an hour and a half," I continue, "at least... before we got the news report. I sensed straight away it was my sister they were talking about."

I'll never forget that day. Waiting with Mum whilst Sacha was in emergency surgery. Then, the two of us waiting at her side, willing her to fight after being told the next twenty-four hours were critical.

"Which way did you walk Sacha?" DC Fowkes's voice is gentle.

"I don't know. I've been trying to remember. I just needed to get out of that pub and away from Rebecca, my other sister. You know what it's like when you need to be on your own." She looks from DC Fowkes to the window and squints in the bright light. "I'd had the month from hell. When all that carry on started up at the wake, I'd had enough."

"So you don't remember how you ended up on the B514 out of Farndale?"

"I can't understand why you'd be walking there anyway Sacha," I say. "There isn't even a footpath, is there?"

"No," replies DC Fowkes. "And it's single track in some places."

"I remember noticing it was getting dark, and thinking I should probably go back," Sacha continues. "I thought my parents would start to worry, given the situation. And Christy."

"What happened next?"

"I realised I didn't have a clue where I was, or even how I'd ended up there. I was wandering around in the road like an idiot, looking for signposts. I remember being worried at how narrow the road was."

"Go on."

Sacha's expression is pained, as though she's having to dig deep for the memories. "I can recall a car stopping in the road. I was so relieved it had seen me."

"Can you remember anything about the car?"

"It was big. I think it was a dark colour. The main thing I remember was its headlights blinding me."

"Any idea of the car's type?"

Sacha shakes her head. "I'm sorry. I wish I had."

"What about the driver? Man? Woman?"

"I've no idea. The car possibly had its full beam on, as though it was dazzling me on purpose."

"Did you try to get out of its way Sacha?"

"I must have done. Anyone would, wouldn't they? I can't remember. Only a loud screech. And then... nothing. Not until I woke up here." Her voice trails off.

"But the car was *definitely* stationary in front of you? Before it set off again?"

"Yes. Definitely. I remember that clearly. It's the lights that have stuck in my mind."

"And would the driver have seen you?"

"Well, they were shining their lights on me, like I said. So they must have done."

"Can you think of anyone who would want to have done this to you, Sacha? To hurt you?"

"No." Her voice is small. "I'm wondering if whoever was driving thought I was someone else. Or if they were out of their mind on drugs, or something."

"Is there any way of being able to catch them?" I shuffle in my seat. "After over five weeks?"

"The problem we've got is where it happened," Sergeant Atkinson says. "There's no CCTV on that road. We've picked Sacha up on several cameras that afternoon, but that does nothing to lead us to the car. Especially not without a more detailed description of it."

"There is of course," DC Fowkes says, "every chance that the driver will have an attack of conscience and come forward."

"Or there'll be someone in their life who they've confessed to – or will confess to," Sergeant Atkinson adds. "It's a big secret to live with."

"I hope so." Sacha is slipping down the bed, so with her good arm and leg, hoists herself back up. "What if I was targeted? What if they try again?"

I look at her. She's right. I never thought about it like that. "But who the hell would target you Sacha?"

"I wish I could tell you. I've completely lost five weeks of my life, and I've still got a long way to go."

"We'll do everything we can." DC Fowkes stands, and her colleague follows. "Starting with looking into these two phone calls your sister Rebecca says she made. And we're thinking a reconstruction could help with our investigations." She smiles at a lady from one of the other beds as she's wheeled back onto the ward. "A member of the public might have seen something – a car driving erratically, for instance. We'll keep you updated, of course."

"We're both staying with our parents for a while," I tell her. "Over in Bempton. Our dad is end of life."

I'll be so relieved to see the back of this hospital. I've had nearly six weeks of airless heat, the stench of disinfectant, and the fear that I'm going to catch something.

"I'm very sorry to hear that." She stacks one chair on top of another, and Sergeant Atkinson returns them to the corner. "You've certainly had a lifetime's worth of trauma in the last couple of months."

"At least I'll be safe over there," Sacha says. "No one will know where I am. Please try to find the driver of that car, won't you?"

28

AFTER CALLING in at Sacha's house, then at my own, to pick up a few things, we're on the road. I was half hoping Adam would be in when I called. I want space, but I also want to talk to him. His silence is unnerving on so many levels.

I've shoehorned mine and Sacha's stuff into my Mini Cooper, and Sacha has pushed her seat right back to accommodate the cast on her leg and her crutches.

"You OK?" I ask her. "I'll try not to go too quickly over any bumps."

"I'm as dosed up on paracetamol as I can be," she replies. "They said I can't take anything stronger because of the baby. Anyway, I'm getting better, aren't I? Which is more than can be said for Dad. I can't wait to see him, but at the same time, I'm dreading it."

"You'd better prepare yourself." I glance at her, then back to the road. "You've obviously not seen him for a while. He really isn't good. I saw him the other day before he went into the hospice."

"Has Rebecca been over yet?" There's an edge to Sacha's voice every time she mentions Rebecca.

"Not since he's been moved. I imagine she'll get across in the next day or so."

"I suppose."

"She was at the hospital most nights whilst you were in a coma, did Mum tell you?"

"Really?"

"What happened to you hit her hard. Everything has. As a family we've really been through it, haven't we?"

"Yeah, but it's far from over."

"You can say that again. And the way things are going, there might be a divorce to look forward to as well." I glance at Sacha again, watching for a reaction. Nothing. "Has Adam been in to see you since you woke up? Whilst I've not been there, I mean?"

"No. Why would he?"

"Because you're his sister-in-law. In fact, it's strange you've never mentioned what's going on between me and him. Mum must have told you something."

"Only that you've been having problems and you've been staying in a hotel." Her tone hardens. "It's just... I don't want to talk about Adam, Christy. I'll never forget how he treated Neil before he died."

"There's more to all this than anyone's telling me." Sacha has no escape from me right now. She's cornered, here in my Mini. We need to finish this conversation before we arrive at Mum's. There might not be another chance for a while. Once we get there, everything must revolve around Dad and supporting Mum.

"More to what?"

"OK, I'll spell it out, shall I?" I take a deep breath. "Why would my husband tell your husband that he is able, and willing to get you pregnant?"

"*What?*"

Her shocked reaction heartens me, but I continue regardless. "According to Adam, when he spoke at the inquest,

240

Neil died believing there was something going on between the two of you."

"Me and Adam?" Sacha visibly stiffens. "If that was true, why is now the first time I'm hearing about it? Why didn't you say anything before?"

"I've been wanting to talk to you for ages. But I've had to keep quiet up to now. Even if you have been carrying on with my husband, you're still my sister and I wanted you to get better, not to pile more stress on you." It's true. If I'm honest, I could probably forgive Sacha more than I could forgive Adam. "Besides, Mum would have killed me if I'd started questioning you before you were up to it."

"Well, you should've done. I could have put your mind at rest earlier." She rests her hand on my arm as I drive. "Christy. I would never, ever do that to you. You've got to believe me. It was Adam."

Something inside me plummets. "What was Adam?"

"Look. I hoped never to be forced to tell you about this but..." Her voice is wobbling.

"Sacha. Just bloody tell me." I swerve the car into a layby off the A64 and yank the handbrake on. Then I swivel in the seat to face her.

"It's all stopped now, but last year." She pauses. "Last year, Adam seemed to, well, to be honest, he developed a bit of, I can only call it, a fixation with me."

"With you?" I was right about this. Right not to believe him. "What do you mean?"

"It was after we'd had a bit of a heart to heart one night."

"You had a heart to heart? With my husband? When? Where? About what?"

"It's not what you think at all." Her voice is low, and despite the crushing misery, I trust what she's saying. "It was purely platonic." She moves her plait to her other shoulder. "On my part, anyway. Neil was staying over at Joe's one night, so I was on my own. As usual. He'd drunk too much and was well over the limit. Adam had been at Greg's, and Rebecca had told him about the problems Neil and I were having. Anyway Adam turned up at my house without warning."

"He said nothing to me about having been at your house. Where was I?"

"You were away on a course."

I deliberate for a moment. "That must have been in October then." I was in London. It was the only course I went away for last year and remember it well. I'd really struggled to focus, as it was when Dad had decided not to continue with his treatment. I do a mental calculation to see if October tallies with the dates of Sacha's pregnancy. Not quite. Something inside me lifts.

"Yes, I'm sure it was in October. Anyway, Adam said he was *passing* on his way back from Greg and Rebecca's. Apparently, he'd noticed my car outside, and not Neil's, so thought he'd call in to check I was OK."

"And?"

"I thought it was strange, but that night, I was glad of the company, if I'm honest. I ended up having lots to drink. We both did. I didn't mean to Christy, but I was at such a low ebb that night."

Oh God. What's she going to tell me? *Didn't mean to what?*

"I spilled everything to him. Everything. Dad, Neil's drinking and unemployment, the fertility problems, our arguments... I shouldn't have done, but he was there. If it hadn't been him, it would've been someone else."

"Did you sleep with him Sacha?"

She shakes her head vehemently. "No. God, no. Never in a million years would I do that to you. And as for him, even if you and he had never met, I wouldn't be interested in him. But he tried. He *really* tried. I had to literally throw him out."

"You're joking me, right?"

"Look you wanted to know. I hate having to tell you this. You'd be better off not knowing."

"You should've said something before." I go quiet for a moment, struggling to process what my sister has told me. "Maybe I can let it go... if it was a one off. If he was drunk, then..."

"Christy." Her voice is firmer than before. Less apologetic. "I'm going to be completely honest with you because if I were you, I'd want the truth. It wasn't once. It was over and over. Adam kept turning up, he kept messaging me..."

"Did you ever tell Neil about it?"

"No. But I'll never know what he suspected. Your husband drove me insane. He wouldn't take no for an answer. I've kept all the messages just in case I ever had to prove anything to you."

"How could he? Our marriage was OK. I mean, things had got a bit *samey* but..."

"It's him Christy. Not you. And if it hadn't been me, it would have been someone else he'd gone after. None of it was rational behaviour."

"So what was he saying to you?"

"Oh Christy. I hate to do this."

"Go on. I need to know." Cars are whizzing past us, each one causing my car to shift in the wind. "What he's said to you will decide whether I go back to him."

"He told me he's always wanted a baby. That you were *depriving* him of something important to him, and that all that mattered to you was your career."

"That's not true. I've hardly even worked since December. And as for the baby thing. *Why didn't he mention it to me?*"

"He said you didn't talk to one another, and he even said he didn't love you anymore. This must be hard to hear sis. I'm sorry it's me having to tell you."

"But he was in love with you? Is that what you're saying?"

She stares straight forward. "I did nothing to encourage him. Not a thing. I wasn't any more friendly with Adam than I would be with any other man I came across. It was as though he became obsessed. I've no idea what made him think I'd be interested in him."

"It sounds as though there really was something in him telling Neil that he'd be willing to get you pregnant."

"Perhaps on his part, but as far as I'm concerned, I wouldn't touch him with a bargepole."

"So you promise me," I point to her belly, "that baby is not Adam's."

"Not in a million years." She looks straight into my eyes. We have the same eyes, Sacha and I. Like our dad's. Rebecca's are like Mum's. "I wouldn't have let him anywhere near me. Ever."

"I want to see these messages Sacha."

"I don't blame you. But they'll hurt. At least they'll show you what kind of man you're married to."

"Not for much longer." As the days draw on, I'm realising I really don't know the man I've been married to for the last ten years. And how can I stay with him when he's been stalking my sister?

Mum's out when we get to the bungalow, committed to spending as much time as she can with Dad at the hospice in the time he's got left. Thank God she's no longer torn between him and Sacha. I'm glad we can be here with her. For the first time since before Christmas, I feel calmer and easier. More importantly, I trust my sister. I do want to see the messages though. I'll need proof of things to begin dealing with Adam.

With Mum out of the way, I help settle Sacha onto the sofa with her leg raised up on a stool, one cushion under her arm, and another behind her back. "I'll do you a deal," I say to her. "I'll make you a brew and a sandwich, and you get these messages up for me. Then, we'll put the entire sorry thing to one side and focus on Dad for a few days."

"Done." She smiles at me, but it's a weak smile. "I'm sorry to do this to you, I really am."

I sip at my tea as I read the first few messages. Sacha's watching me, concern and guilt etched across her face. But I feel certain it's guilt of a different type than I was accusing her of. Guilt at what I'm discovering rather than anything she's done.

It was so good to spend some time with you last night, Adam has written. *I'm glad you were able to confide in me.*

I probably said too much, Sacha has replied. I look at her. Her innocence still doesn't explain who the father of the baby is. Her message goes on, *Please don't say anything to Neil.*

Likewise. Christy wouldn't approve of my advances towards you, either. I'm sorry. I thought you were feeling it too.

No.

Is that it? No? I've fancied you for ages. You must have noticed.

Stop it Adam. You don't know what you're saying. Are you still drunk or what?

I know exactly what I'm saying. And you feel the same. You're just scared about Christy and Neil and how they'll react.

You're deluding yourself and I'm ending this conversation. It didn't happen. Last night didn't happen. Sort it out Adam. Don't you dare hurt my sister.

I can give you what your husband can't. We could even just sleep together until you get pregnant.

"I'm sorry." Sacha says again. "This must be awful for you. I promise, nothing happened. Nothing. He just wouldn't leave me alone."

I continue scrolling through. Adam's messages get longer and longer. He never sends me messages of more than a few words. Then, they're usually *pick some milk up, will you?* Or *I might be a bit late back.* Nothing like the infatuation he's displayed towards my sister, here in all its black and white glory.

"Are these the only ones? Has he only messaged through text? No social media or anything?" What I'm doing is like picking a scab off a wound, but at least I'm getting to the truth.

"He did start on social media. After I blocked him on text, that is. I'd ignored him at first, but that didn't stop him so I had to block him instead."

"Bloody hell." I would never have suspected that my husband could carry on like this. "Are you sure, really sure, you didn't do anything to give him the wrong idea?" I stare through the window and down Mum's street. It's inconceivable that last time I arrived here on Christmas Eve, I didn't have a clue that anything was amiss with my marriage. What an idiot I've been.

"I've always been friendly with him. But no more than with anyone else's husband. He kept turning up when Neil was out. But I've got to be honest..."

"What?"

"When I got back home the day after Boxing Day, that was it. I didn't hear a thing from him until the funeral."

"Why do you think he suddenly stopped?"

"After what happened to Neil, I guess. And the part he had to play in his death."

"That would make sense." We sit in silence for a few moments as I try to gather my thoughts. "So that was the reason you didn't take me up on the New Year's Eve invitation?"

She picks up the sandwich I've made for her then puts it down again. "Well, one of the reasons. And it's why I left it to you to keep in touch with me around that time. I'm sorry I didn't tell you sooner."

"At least I know now."

"I thought that by keeping my distance, I might be helping you and Adam work things out." She pauses for a moment. "What are you going to do Christy?"

I sip my tea, watching the carriage clock inner workings twist backwards and forwards on Mum's mantlepiece. "Nothing yet. Adam's gone quiet on me for the time being, thankfully. Which gives me the chance to focus on Dad whilst I decide what to do next."

29

SACHA IS SETTLED in front of the TV and I've been pacing the bungalow, not really knowing what to do with myself. I find myself in Dad's office, which piles more misery onto my current woes.

The sudden ring of my phone makes me jump. Adam. I deliberate over whether to answer the phone to him. But now Sacha has told me the truth about what was going on last year, I'm interested to find out what he's ringing me about. Not that I'm going to let on what I've discovered. Not yet. There's enough to cope with right now.

"It's me."

"What do you want?"

"Where are you?"

"In Bempton. I'm staying here for a few days." I sink into Dad's chair and glance around the room. He's probably never going to come in here again.

"You never said you were going there. Even when I suggested it."

"Why should I?"

"Are you with Sacha?"

I chew my lip. "Why do you ask?" I can't believe this is one of the first questions he's asking me.

"Just wondering. Have the two of you talked yet?"

"Yeah. We've talked." My eyes fall on a photo of Sacha, Rebecca, and me. What I'd give to get those carefree days back again. When the worst thing in life was being grounded, and the only loss was pocket money for not doing our jobs. In the photograph, I'm about to leave primary school, Rebecca's still in the infants and Sacha's somewhere in the middle.

"So you've given up this ridiculous notion that I'm the father of her baby."

"I guess so." It's true. But I haven't given up on anything else. It's time to shake Adam up a little. "The police came to see us before we left the hospital."

"Did they? Why?"

"To ask some questions."

"About what?" The tone of his voice rises.

There's more to come, I'm certain of it.

"What do you think?"

"Have you been in touch with Greg or Rebecca?" He asks. "Do you know whether they've been to the hospital at all?"

"Nope. Greg hasn't visited full stop."

"I need to talk to him. And he's stopped picking up." Ah, so that's the main reason Adam is ringing me after barely bothering lately.

"Why do you need to speak to him?" I think back to the partial conversation I overheard last week. Greg definitely knows something too.

"I've decided to pull out of this business deal - give Greg his investment back. He's had too much leverage over me for far too long. When I've sorted that Christy, we'll talk. I'll tell you everything."

"About what? Why can't you tell me everything *now*?" I was right. I was bloody right.

"I've a few things to deal with," he says. "Then we'll speak again, I promise."

"I'm not one of your business associates." I'm furious. I've let him take charge in this conversation and need to claw back control. I should never have answered the phone to him. "Look Adam. I said I wanted space. My dad's at death's door. I'll ring you in a few days. Please respect that and don't ring me in the meantime."

"*A few days?* But..."

I hang up, imagining the confused expression on Adam's face. He's not used to not getting his own way. It must have infuriated him when Sacha sent him packing last year. But if he can pursue my sister so brazenly in the way he has, it makes me wonder what other women he's gone after. I don't trust him one bit anymore. And not only with other women. I'm going to get proof of what a snake he really is.

"Adam's rung." I tell Sacha. "He reckons he's going to tell me *everything* in a few days. What's that supposed to mean?"

Sacha sits up straight. "Everything about what?"

"You tell me."

"I've no idea Christy." She shakes her head. "I really haven't."

"Whatever it is, he's talking of Greg having something over him, whatever that means. Sacha, if you know anything else, you need to tell me." I search her face for answers.

"Like I've already said, there's absolutely *nothing* between me and Adam. There never has been and never will be." She looks me straight in the eye and that's good enough for me. For now.

～

"Keep it down. Sacha's asleep on the sofa."

Rebecca is evidently here to stay, judging by the bags she dumps in the hallway, followed by the baby, strapped into his car seat. With Dad in his final few days, I can really, really do without the kids here right now. The dog bounds through the hallway into the lounge. If Sacha is still asleep, she won't be for long.

"I picked the kids up early from school. I heard you and Sacha were here, so thought I should be too."

"Auntie Christy." Freya launches herself at me, and is shortly joined by Matilda. Her hug feels good, despite my initial irritation at seeing them.

"Which room are we in?" Greg grabs a bag in each hand and grins at me. He's a snake as well. "Same one as before?"

"Mum's sleeping in there." I'm unable to even meet his eye. "Sacha's got Mum's room as it's got the wet floor shower. Plus Mum can't bear to sleep in her own room now Dad's not here."

"But that little room." Rebecca juts her chin out and faces me, her hand placed on one hip. "It's not big enough for us five."

"It's a good job I'm in there in that case, isn't it?"

I smile at her with mock-sweetness. She always swans into Mum's house like she owns the place.

"So what are we supposed to do?" She's pouting in the same way she was in that photo of us all in Dad's office.

I smile again. "There's always the airbed. Or a hotel."

"With three kids and a dog? Don't be ridiculous."

"Stop thinking about yourself for a change, Rebecca."

"I don't see why your Mum and Sacha can't share a room." Greg drops the bags back to the floor.

I glare at him. "Don't you think Mum needs her space right now? Anyway, I'm not arguing about this. I can't be arsed."

"Bloody Sacha. I'm sick to death of everything being about her."

"I'm listening to you, Rebecca." Sacha calls from the lounge. "Ouch! Get this bloody dog off me."

I dart into the lounge where the dog is leaping all over her. I can't imagine his over exuberance is too welcome with a broken arm, leg and pregnant belly.

"Talk to your mum when she gets back," Greg says to Rebecca as he takes hold of the dog's collar and closes the lounge door. "We're going to no hotel. You've as much right to be here as them."

"Why couldn't you come on your own?" I look past Greg to Rebecca. "Why bring your bloody entourage? Did you not consider this might be too much for Mum to cope with at the moment?" The girls are clattering around in the kitchen, no doubt looking for biscuits or similar.

"For your information." Greg faces me. "Wendy wants us here. All of us. God, why must you be so frosty all the time?"

"Hmm, I wonder," I retort. "It might have something to do with all the crap that's been going on behind my back." I follow them towards the dining room. "Anyway, you can expect a windfall soon Rebecca. It sounds as though Adam wants to return Greg's investment."

"Why would he do that?" Rebecca swings around to face me, looking puzzled. "It was a big decision on our part to put all that money in last year. I thought Adam needed it."

"He reckons Greg is holding him to account over something." Greg has perched himself on the edge of the breakfast bar. I glare at him. "And I want to find out what."

"Adam has no right speaking about our business to *anyone*." He clasps his hands together on the counter.

"I'm not *anyone*. I'm his wife. So what's going on Greg? What dirt have you got on my husband?"

"Nothing's going on. And I don't know anything." But Greg looks rattled. "I'll give Adam a ring. See what he's on about."

· · ·

After helping Sacha to the loo and settling her back onto the sofa, I set about making something to eat.

"I've spoken to Mum." Rebecca strides into the kitchen. "She's on her way back. Dad's apparently too done in for anyone else to visit tonight."

"Where are the kids?"

"In Mum's room, watching a film. Zach's asleep. Anyway, Mum said she'd go back into her own room and share with Sacha, so that's sorted at least."

I shrug. "As long as you get your own way Rebecca. Are you going to help me in here or what? I'm not here to wait on everyone."

"I've got the kids to keep an eye on, haven't I? Mum said to defrost some chicken and throw it in the oven with a casserole mix. She said she'll sort the rest when she gets back."

"No, she won't. She's putting her feet up when she gets back here."

"Such a martyr, aren't you?" Rebecca peels a banana from the bowl on the breakfast bar. "Saint Christy." She laughs. "Have you sorted your marriage out yet?"

"Leave me alone, will you?" Then I remember something. "By the way, why did you tell us you rang the police twice about Sacha waking up, when you clearly hadn't rung at all."

Her face tells me she's taken aback. "To shut you up. You were constantly on at me about it."

"I'd have rung them myself if you'd been honest."

"I've got other things going on in my life apart from Sacha."

I reach into the cupboard behind her for a jug. "What I don't understand," I pause and try to gather my thoughts, "is why you bothered sleeping at the hospital whilst Sacha was in a coma, if you've *so much to do*." I stare at her. I'm thinking I know my sister even less than I know my husband. *What's going on?*

"That was different. It didn't seem like she was going to

wake up, did it? But yet, she did." Her expression is not one I'd expect from a person whose sister has woken from a coma. It's verging on disappointment.

"Go easy on her, won't you? It's brought it all back, about Neil, I mean, even being here, in this house."

"Do you know what? I'm sick of hearing Sacha, Sacha, Sacha. Our dad's dying. Can we not focus on that?"

I suppose she's got a point about Dad. But there's an arrogance and hostility in her since she arrived here that I can't put my finger on. I still get the feeling there's far more going on that I've yet to find out, and I also get the feeling that Rebecca is very much in on whatever it is.

30

THE HOUSE IS IN SILENCE. I'm more tired than I was when I got into bed. The baby has cried several times during the night, and Sacha's been clattering about in Mum and Dad's en-suite on her crutches.

I stare at the fresh paint and new curtains. It's a cruel irony that Dad won't get to enjoy this lovely new house they bought before he was declared to be terminally ill.

I can't bear to lie here with the torrent of thoughts turning themselves around and around in my mind. My head aches with the wine I drank last night whilst we were all flicking through old photo albums. It was wonderful, yet painful to see Dad looking healthy and happy in them. Even Rebecca seemed to enjoy them, though Greg looked bored stupid.

I'm going to focus on Dad over these next few days, as well as looking after Mum. I can put my marital problems on ice until then. Knowing Dad won't be here for much longer has manifested itself as a physical pain in my gut.

I sit up in the comfortable bed, suddenly anxious about not seeing him before he passes away. I'm going there right now. On my own. I pull on jeans and a t-shirt, brush my hair and slide my feet into pumps. Then I grab a banana and a bottle of water from the kitchen, and I'm good to go.

I don't want Mum to stop me, and I don't want anyone to say *wait, I'll come with you,* so I creep from the house, hoping no one hears as I start the car in the silent street. I get to the main road, shuddering as I pass the point where Neil died. What happened seems like only yesterday, and yet like a lifetime ago.

There's no denying how beautiful it is here. The grass of the clifftops shimmers in the sunshine, and spring flowers offer their colour whichever way I turn. The sky and sea reflect each other, both appearing bluer for this. Birdwatchers are already filling up the viewing platforms.

I'll go for a walk on the beach in Bridlington after I've visited Dad. The waves and the sea air will do me good. Especially on a day like this. This is a place of beauty. However, it's become a place of death for our family.

It's nearly half-past eight when I arrive in the hospice car park, though it feels later somehow. Visits are allowed around the clock, within reason, so there shouldn't be an issue with me being allowed in so early. Especially since I'm his daughter. Still, I stall for a few moments and pluck my phone from my handbag. I switched it off last night, to ensure I was unaware if Adam tried to ring again. If he had, I would have been angry that he wasn't respecting my wishes. If he hadn't, I would have blamed him for not fighting to save our marriage. Really, he could hardly win either way. I only hope he doesn't turn up here. I wouldn't put it past him though.

As it happens, Adam's only tried to contact me twice. He's rung once and sent a text.

Hope you're OK, it says. *We'll talk soon. Tell your dad I'm thinking of him. And I'm glad your sister's out of hospital.*

He has to mention Sacha, doesn't he? Pillock. I fling the

phone back into my bag and step out of the car, grabbing my jacket.

The hospice is a sunny building with a radio playing at low volume in the reception area. As when I looked around with Mum, I'm taken aback by the atmosphere of the place. I think I expected more of a sense of death - if that has a scent. Salt and lilies, perhaps. Instead, there is a smell of 'new-ness,' coupled with a sense of calm.

"Good morning." The woman at the desk looks up from her computer.

"I'm here to see my dad. Stuart Brooklyn."

"Ah yes." She smiles. "Have you been before?"

"Only to look around with my mum. I haven't visited since he came in. Can you tell me how's he's doing please?"

"Well, I'm the administrator, so I'm afraid I can't tell you personally, but if you'd like to take a seat in the lounge, I'll get the sister on duty to come and have a chat before we take you to your dad."

I follow her through two sets of double doors into an airy lounge overlooking the garden. The chairs are as inviting as the room itself. It's full of colour and I hope Dad will be up to sitting with me for a while. It'll do him good to get out of his room.

"Take a seat. Can I get you a coffee?"

Such was my rush to leave the house this morning that I didn't have one, so I accept her offer gratefully. The hospice clearly knew what they were doing when they appointed this lady as their administrator. She's got an air about her that has already settled my anxiety. I clutch my bag to my chest as I sink into a chair and stare out at the garden.

It's another lady that brings my coffee. "I'm Sister Beverley." She holds her hand out. "I'm looking after your dad today."

"I haven't seen him since he was brought in." I take the cup from her. "So I was wondering how he's getting on."

"You're one of three daughters, is that right?" She smiles at me. "I met your sister yesterday. She had quite a following with her. We had to say no to the dog though."

Irritation rises in me. Followed by questions. *Why didn't Rebecca mention she'd been here yesterday?* Greg's visited my dad, before even Sacha and I have been able to.

"Anyway," she continues. "There's not been much change in your dad since yesterday. He's sleeping a lot now and as you might already be aware, we've had to increase his pain relief since he first arrived. He's very comfortable though."

"Is he talking much?"

Sister Beverley shakes her head. "I'm afraid not. Since the doctor increased his morphine dose, he's become unresponsive."

"So, what about eating? And going to the loo?"

"He's got a catheter fitted. As for eating..." She shakes her head again and looks almost apologetic. "He's not well enough for food. He's getting all the fluids he needs to keep him comfortable though."

"Will he stay at the same level with the morphine? Will I be able to talk to him at all?" Tears are stabbing the backs of my eyes. I didn't expect him to be completely out of it. Fancy me thinking he could get out of bed and come in here for a coffee with me!

Sister Beverley reaches out and pats my hand. I expect she has to deal with upset relatives every single day. "You can talk to your dad as much as you want sweetheart. He'll know you're at his side. You might not get much of a response, but he's still in there and is listening to everything you say to him."

"How long will it be?" Why am I asking. *Do I even want an answer?*

"We just can't say. Probably a few more days. Maybe less."

I stare at the thick oatmeal-coloured carpet. *Days!* It's

happening. I honestly thought this was months away, but it's happening now. "Can I see him?"

"Of course you can. I'll take you through."

I'm shaking as I follow her along a carpeted corridor until she stops and taps on a door. I thought I was prepared for all this, but I don't think I am.

"Good morning Stuart," she says. "You've got an early visitor."

From the tone of her voice as she talks to him, I half expect Dad to be sitting up in bed. But he does not appear like he ever will again. However, he looks to be comfortable, like she said, and peaceful.

"Will he ever talk to me again?" I can't fight the tears any longer now in front of him. "Will he wake up, or is this it?"

"He apparently opened his eyes a couple of times when your sister and mother were here yesterday, so he might. But like I said, he can definitely hear you – he's just very sleepy with the pain relief." She checks a couple of his monitors. "I'll leave you to spend some time together, but we're just along the corridor if you need anything."

"Should that be open?" I point at the window above him. "Won't he get cold?"

"Your mum says he likes it to be slightly ajar." She checks the thermometer on the adjacent wall. "It's fine. He won't get cold. The heating's on low too."

I sink into the armchair beside Dad and take in the surroundings. As in the lounge, double doors lead into the garden, and Mum has dotted some family photographs around. Dad's new slippers are tucked under the bed and his dressing gown hangs forlornly from the hook on the back of the door. Slippers and a dressing gown which he's unlikely to wear again.

"Oh, Dad." I take his hand in mine, hoping he'll give it a squeeze like he normally would. He's lost so much weight, he barely makes a dent in the pillow. "What are we going to do with you?" Really, I mean, *what are we going to do without you?*

"We were looking at old photos last night." My voice is loud in the silence. "You gave us such a happy childhood, Dad. The best."

I witter away some more, reminiscing about holidays and trips out. In between my tears, I tell him how we're looking after Mum and always will. I tell him how Sacha is getting better all the time, and I also tell him, though he will already have been told, about the grandson he's never going to meet. I resist the urge to mention my split with Adam. Under normal circumstances, Dad would be on the phone to me, telling me to *get it sorted.* Once upon a time, he and Adam got on well together.

I can't stop staring at him, taking in every contour of his face whilst grief threatens to swallow me whole. I watch his chest going up and down, knowing it won't for much longer. This is agony. I can't bear it.

And suddenly, I can't breathe. I cough and try to get a big inhalation. I've not suffered a panic attack for years. I need to get out of here. Snatching up my coat and bag, I rush towards the double doors into the garden and pull them behind me. I gasp in the pure air of the sunny March morning and lower myself onto a bench moistened with dew, noticing the plaque. *For our Mum, Patricia. Gone but never forgotten.* A sob catches in my throat.

It takes a few minutes to settle my breathing. I stare across at a *forget-me-not* garden that's been created. This really is a lovely place, but so very sad. I know they offer respite here, but most people who arrive will not leave again. Well, they will, but...

I glance up at the window of my dad's room. I'm sure I heard a voice. I stiffen and wait.

"It's me." The voice is so familiar that for a moment, I think

Dad's woken up, and is talking to himself, or wondering where I've gone. "I thought I'd drop in. Whilst you're still with us."

It's Greg. *What the hell is he doing here?* I thought that by getting here early, I could spend some time alone with my dad. Now it looks as though they're *all* here. Perhaps I should just go. No. *Why should I?* I tug my jacket on. I'll wait out here until they've gone. I imagine the kids will be with Mum, so Rebecca and Greg shouldn't stay long.

"You see, there's something I want to tell you, Stuart. Something I need to share. Whilst it's just me and you."

Greg's here on his own. How odd. Why isn't Rebecca with him?

"So what I'm about to tell you. I literally must get it off my chest mate. And you, well, you can't exactly repeat it to anyone, can you? But I'm told you can hear me." He clears his throat. "You see, no matter what anyone thinks of me, I do have a conscience." His voice cracks. "I feel so bad about what's happened Stuart. I really do, and I'm sure if I just tell someone..."

Oh my God. He's crying. My dad's at death's door and self-pitying Greg is in there crying all over him. I lean forwards to stand from the bench, then something stops me. I may find something out if I sit and just listen. Let's see what he has to get off his chest. It might even have something to do with Adam.

"So I need to say it out loud. What I've done. What Rebecca has done. Call it a confession if you like. Confessing a sin makes it go away, doesn't it? It absolves a person."

What Rebecca has done? What's he talking about?

"See, we've got away with it Stuart. I'm not sure how, but we have. With the police, anyway. Now we can put everything that's happened over the last few months behind us. Perhaps after you've gone, life will settle down and we'll all get back to some kind of normality. Sacha can have my baby and..."

Wait. Did he just say *Sacha can have his baby?*

"So there you have it Stuart. Yes. I'm the daddy. We didn't mean to start carrying on with each other, but well, you must remember what it's like when your wife is pregnant and knackered all the time?" He laughs out loud. "You must remember."

I can't believe he's just laughed. And I literally can't believe what I'm hearing. I hope to God no one else can hear Greg talking and laughing and comes in to check. He needs to keep talking, and I need to hear what else he has to say. *He's the father of Sacha's baby.*

"So Sacha gave me what I wanted, if you know what I mean, and then I gave her what she wanted. Win-win. To start with, at least. But then she broke things off between us. Said she wanted to make a go of things with Neil. Said she had betrayed her sister. Then she called me a mistake. Have you any idea what that did to me, Stuart? To be referred to as a *mistake?*"

Greg would never normally talk to my dad with this sort of familiarity. And I hate the way he keeps using his name. I'm so glad now about the open window which I challenged the nurse over. I can hear every word he's saying.

"When I kept getting in touch with her," Greg's still talking. "Sacha called me a lot of other things besides a mistake. She made me hate myself, to be truthful. But I hated Neil more. Weak, pathetic Neil. I've no idea what Sacha saw in him. You weren't that keen either, were you?"

I imagine my dad lying there, probably desperate to speak. This is not what he should be exposed to in his final days. I should go back in and stop Greg, but the compulsion to find out if he has anything else to say is too great.

"So Stuart, as you might imagine, it was pretty convenient to find him and Adam scrapping on that clifftop on Christmas night. Suddenly an opportunity presented itself to get Neil out of the way, so that Sacha might want to continue things with me. I never planned to push him, but I couldn't resist it when I got the chance."

It was Greg. Greg pushed Neil to his death. He didn't fall. Nor did he jump. He was pushed. By his brother-in-law. I wrap my arms around myself, rocking back and forth on the bench as though trying to comfort myself. And Greg's still talking. I've no idea what else he could possibly be about to confess. Not after what he's already said.

"Adam's just as guilty as I am." I freeze as Adam is mentioned. "He could have stopped me if he'd wanted, Stuart. But he just watched as I sent Neil on his merry way."

Oh my God. Adam has known all along. They even grilled him in the witness box about it. How could he keep a secret of that magnitude?

"And Adam knew why," Greg continues. "He'd found out weeks before that Sacha and I were sleeping together. But he obviously couldn't say anything."

Why, *obviously*?

"I'd told Adam I'd take him down with me if he tried. And tell Christy about the obsession he had towards Sacha. He was hounding her for weeks, she'd told me all about it. Then there's the big wedge of money I've invested in his business. He knows as well as I do that I saved him from going under. So, you see, it was in his best interest to keep schtum. The whole thing's a mess really, isn't it Stuart? Families – who'd have em? You're probably well out of it."

I'm as still as the statues in this garden. I wish I'd recorded all that he's said on my phone. How will I prove it? Will anyone even believe me? It might all hinge on persuading Adam to…"

Greg's still talking. "I'll admit that I've been an idiot Stuart. I'd had a few to drink Christmas night – we all had. I shouldn't have done what I did to Neil, but it was cut and dried at the time. However, if I'm honest, I've struggled to live with it, like I said – I have got a conscience.

Then, to add insult to injury, whilst Rebecca was in labour with Zach the next day, she told me she'd found out about me sleeping with Sacha. She reckons she'd suspected for a while. The bottom fell out of my world, let me tell you. Especially when I'd already decided to let Sacha go, and focus on my family."

No wonder Rebecca's been so hostile these last three months. The poor thing. It wasn't *my* husband carrying on with our sister. *It was hers.* How could Sacha behave in this way? To either of us? I owe Rebecca an apology. And some.

"Rebecca didn't just tell me though." Greg's voice rises and again, I'm worried in case the hospice staff will get wind of what he's saying to my dad. This obviously is not normal behaviour from a person visiting someone on his deathbed. "Rebecca was literally snarling at me in that delivery room. All this in front of the midwife too. Anyway, I decided it was best to mostly leave Sacha alone after Neil had died. Less risk of me saying something I might regret. In any case, she pretty much stonewalled me and acted as though nothing had ever happened between us."

I'd like to find out what Sacha has got that makes her so bloody special. For both our husbands to be pursuing her. She's not innocent in all this.

"Then Rebecca got wind that Sacha was pregnant. You must remember this Stuart – at Neil's funeral. I've never seen my wife so livid. Ever. She's said herself that it was like a red mist fell over her. After all, she had a very good idea that I was the father."

God. The plot thickens. And I find myself now praying Dad is out of it after all. I don't want him to be taking all this to the grave with him. Part of me wants to go in there and tear Greg limb from limb. But that's not going to achieve much. I'll sit this out and then go for my walk. Calm down and work out what to do.

"So, Stuart, I'm sure you don't need me to spell out what happened next. Even if Rebecca reckons not to remember much about what she did."

What she did? What did she do? It is the second time Greg has alluded to Rebecca being involved.

"Can you remember, Stuart, when Rebecca disappeared from the wake for a while? She said she needed to sit in the car to make a phone call. Well – I know my wife and I had an odd suspicion she would go after Sacha."

I think back. I can vaguely remember Rebecca leaving the pub. I recall she'd said something about needing to check the kids were sorted. But there were so many people around that I had no idea how long she was gone for. I tug my jacket more tightly around myself, wishing now that I'd borrowed Mum's big coat.

"After Zach's birth, Rebecca was starting to come to terms with Sacha and I having slept together, but the pregnancy thing tipped her over the edge," Greg continues. "Plus, it was the first time she'd seen Sacha since Christmas, which also flipped Rebecca's jealousy switch. She'd spent much of the day accusing me of staring at her."

I must say, I was shocked at the time with Rebecca for drink driving – she's normally so law-abiding. But I was even more shocked at what she did to Sacha. It cost a few quid to get that car straightened out afterwards, let me tell you."

It sounds like Rebecca mowed Sacha down and left her for dead in the road. Her own sister. I swallow hard. I feel sick. If I'm sick out here, he'll hear me. What am I going to do?

"Afterwards, all bloody Rebecca did was weep and wail about what she'd done. It's been a nightmare and there's been several times she's nearly confessed. I can't take care of three kids on my own if she ends up in prison. Things are best left as they are. Let it all blow over. As far as anyone is concerned, Neil committed suicide, and Sacha was merely the unfortunate victim of an unsolved hit and run. Don't you think Stuart? Leave things as they are?"

No chance. I rise from the bench. He's going to get what's coming to him. Greg looks as though he's seen a ghost when I appear at the doorway of my father's room. "You'd better say your goodbyes Greg." I smile at him. "You and your wife."

31

SACHA

IF I TURN out to be half the mother mine is, I'll be happy. Even with all she's facing right now, she's run me a bath and has helped me get into it before setting off to visit Dad, taking Freya and Matilda with her, so Rebecca can get Zachary sorted. She even brought me a cup of tea before she left. Sometimes I could weep with gratitude towards her.

Zach's crying echoes along the hallway – a sound that would have normally upset me but now makes me more excited for when I'll meet my own baby. Despite the circumstances of his conception, I have to allow myself to be happy about this. None of it is his fault.

My right arm and leg are hung over the side of the bath, and I'm thankful that my broken limbs are on the right hand side. There's no way I could have had a bath otherwise. I lean forwards for my tea, enjoying the scent of the lavender bubbles. I'm going to have half an hour here, then I'll get sorted and get along to see Dad. I need to see him as often as I can in the time he's got left.

Hopefully Christy will take me and Rebecca – I'm not sure where Christy has gone this morning. Greg seems to have disappeared too, so I'm wondering if they could be cooking something up together. I'm trying not to read things that don't exist in situations but right now, in this family, it's difficult not to.

At least Christy believes me about what went on with Adam. I hope they work it out but it's hard to imagine them being able to come back from the way he was with me last year.

I place my cup on the side of the bath, listening to the bubbles that pop all around me. It wasn't ideal, having Mum have to get me in the bath, but like she said, it's not like I physically have anything too different to her, apart from my growing belly. I'll have to manage to get out with my crutches – I'm too stubborn to call Rebecca in to help me.

Right on cue, the bathroom door swings open. I jump as it crashes into the sink. Rebecca bursts in.

"What the..."

She marches towards me, slipping on the towel Mum's left on the floor for me. This intensifies the already venomous expression on her face. I watch in confusion as she wrenches my crutches from where Mum's left them for me and hurls them against the tiled wall.

"Put them back." My voice shrieks around the bathroom. "I need them to get out! What the hell's got into you?"

"I've just had Greg on the phone. It seems everything's out." She stands over me, her hand resting on her hip, her lip curling.

"What on earth are you talking about?" I try to hoist myself up and glance around for the nearest towel. Not that I can reach for anything in my current predicament. If only there was someone else in the house. Rebecca's fury is making me feel incredibly vulnerable.

"If me and Greg are going down, you needn't think you're just going to get on with your merry little life. No chance." She steps towards me.

"No!" I yelp as she grabs my cup and throws hot tea into my face.

"You might as well know…" Her voice sounds strangled as she throws the empty cup against the tiles as well. It shatters across the bathroom, and shards land in the bath with me. Mum will go mad. "That I know what you did."

I try to shrink back as Rebecca steps towards the bath. There's nowhere to go. She's totally lost it. I can only imagine she's found out about Greg and me from last year. I desperately try to get my arm and leg inside the bath out of her way, but quick as a flash, she's got hold of them. "No, please, they're healing." My screeching voice echoes around the walls. "Please don't hurt me anymore. Stop… aargh…" Pain shoots through me as she bends my arm against my naked chest. The room swims around me. I'm going to black out. No. Not in the bath. I'll drown. I try to hook my good foot around the chain for the plug to let the water out, but I can't reach it. "Get off me Rebecca. Please, please get off me." I can hardly get my words out. The pain she's causing me is…

"It's time I finished what I started with you." She jumps on top of me in the bath. I'm in agony as her weight crushes down onto my stomach.

"No," I wheeze. "Please. The baby."

"You're going to pay for what you've done to my family you bitch."

I scream out again, the sound drowned out as she forces my head beneath the water. I choke under her weight as the water seeps down my throat. I can hardly move. *Please God. Help me.* The words bounce around my mind as I squirm and struggle to get my head above the water's surface again. Momentarily I do, and my sister's bellow echoes into my ears as she forces me back down again. The water gurgles around me as I accept what's happening. I'm going to die. My sister is going to kill me. Here in my mother's bath. Mum's going to lose her daughter, her husband and her unborn grandson within days of each other. I'm losing the fight. I never stood a chance against Rebecca. The light's fading. Then suddenly there's a whoosh of water and the weight disappears from on top of me. My head is hauled above the water, but I still can't get any air in.

Time slows. I watch as I'm hauled from the bath and placed on the bathroom floor. I expect the chill of the tiles, but I don't feel a thing.

"Breathe. For God's sake Sacha. Breathe." It's Adam. What's he doing here? "What have you done!" He yells at Rebecca who is panting against the wall, blood pouring from the back of her head where she must have hit it. I'm at peace as I look down on the situation from the corner of the bathroom. Detached from it all. I watch as Adam rolls me onto my back and begins chest compressions. Then mouth to mouth. This is it.

"Come on. Come on." I don't know if it's Adam's voice, or Neil's. Adam raises his head and looks at my chest. Rebecca gets up, but he shoves her back. Somewhere in the distance, a baby is crying.

I watch as I'm rolled onto my side and suddenly realise that I'm lying naked in front of my brother-in-law. All my weight looks to be placed on my broken arm and I'm bleeding from where pieces of the cup have cut me. I should be in agony but can't feel a thing.

Adam's voice grows louder. "Sacha please! Wake up." All is still for a moment. I don't know how much time passes. I become aware of moving from one corner of the bathroom to the other. I'm near the window. I could float up and away. Into the sunshine outside the window. There's a voice again. Then more crying. Then the weight of desperate hands on my chest as I gurgle, cough and then throw up tea and bathwater all over the bathroom floor.

"Thank God." Adam wipes away tears with the back of his hand as I gasp to get air in through the liquid that remains. "I thought she'd killed you." He reaches for a towel, which he drapes over me. "I'll get an ambulance here. Just you hang in there, alright Sacha?"

He swings around to Rebecca as he slides his phone from his pocket. "Don't you even think about moving." His voice is a snarl. "It'll be a long time until you see the outside world after what you've just tried to do."

32

SACHA

I stare at the horizon, enjoying the warmth of baby Oliver strapped in the sling, snuggled into me. We've come through so much together. Sometimes I'm overwhelmed by the two miraculous escapes we've had.

As it's December again, most of the seabirds have migrated. There are just a few gannets remaining. Dad taught me the names of all the birds around here when I was a girl. The last time I sat on this bench was Boxing Day last year, just hours after Neil's body had been recovered from the foot of the cliff. Tears rush to my eyes at the memory. It's Christmas Eve again, so nearly a year to the day.

The film wrapper of the red and white roses I've placed next to the bench flutters gently in the breeze. Today's winter sunshine could not be any more in contrast to the freezing grey gloom of that day, when I was last sitting here.

Greg's been remanded to Hull prison and Rebecca to Wakefield. There was a chance they might get bail, as Adam did. But thankfully, the judge accepted the threat they posed to all the witnesses, especially to me and Oliver. They won't be locked up forever, but I should have plenty of time to either get away and start afresh in a new place, or make sure I'm protected from them, when it gets to their release.

I rest my face on the top of Oliver's head, breathing in his scent whilst listening to the waves below us. It's inconceivable to equate the horror that happened here, not even a year ago, with the tranquillity that is to be found here today, and the love I feel for this tiny person who's already been through so much with me.

I always believed that Neil would never have ended his own life. Admittedly, our marriage was in trouble and he was a mess, but I could never accept he would leave me so painfully and abruptly. It breaks my heart to imagine the words he'll have heard from Adam and Greg in the moments before he died. Doubting my fidelity would have cut him right through. And a more terrifying death, I cannot imagine.

On a freezing cold night, being thrown from a three hundred foot cliff in the dark. What was going through his head as he hurtled through the air? People speculate in conversation with me that his heart may have stopped as he fell. I hope so. I can't bear to consider him being aware of the impact as he hit the bottom.

I'm having counselling to get over the trauma of my two brushes with death and also to come to terms with my part in things. It's no excuse, but my head was all over the place when I was sleeping with Greg last year. With the pressure we were under, Neil and I were poles apart, and Greg was there. Again and again and again.

I suppose, on some level, I'd hoped for pregnancy to result from our affair, and can't believe now that I could have been so heartless and stupid. If I ever felt guilty about Rebecca whilst I was going to bed with her husband, I did a good job at the time of pushing it away. She's more than adequately taken her revenge on me since, though. It's haunting to think how close Oliver and I were to having our lives cut short by her in March.

What she's done to me was far worse than what I did to her. But the biggest victims of all this are Freya, Matilda and Zachary. Both their parents are on remand and likely to get custodial sentences. Rebecca had every conceivable charge thrown at her, but the main ones are four counts of attempted murder. Mum's told me the kids are staying with Greg's parents. They're lucky they didn't end up in care.

I was in hospital for days after what she did to me in Mum's bathroom, and she robbed me of the chance of seeing my dad before he died. The only time I've seen Rebecca was at his funeral. We didn't speak; she was handcuffed to an officer in any case. I couldn't bear to be near her.

Yes, I slept with her husband. Yes, I became pregnant. I'm not proud of my behaviour, not at all. I deserved for her to fall out with me forever. To fly at me in a rage. But to drive her car at me and leave me in a coma for four weeks. No, I did not deserve that. Nor did I deserve her leaping on me whilst I was in the bath and nearly drowning me. Thank God Adam turned up when he did – that's all I can say.

I've been told that because of the circumstances and because of her postnatal condition, her defence will argue for *grounds of diminished responsibility.* But according to Mum, no matter what, Rebecca has said she'll never come near me again. That won't stop me getting some sort of order against her though.

Adam and Christy are somehow finding their way through all this and are having couples counselling. At first, I wondered if Christy might be faking their reconciliation. After all, she wanted to ensure that Adam told the truth about what had happened on that clifftop, even though he would also incriminate himself for perverting the course of justice.

It turns out Greg had been blackmailing Adam – not only

with his stake in Adam's business, but knowing that Adam was stalking me. I should never have confided in Greg about Adam's obsession, but when you're sleeping with someone – well, these things come out. You think you can trust a person. How blind and naïve I've been.

It also turns out that Adam knew about Neil's death at Greg's hands – but nothing about Rebecca running me down. I can't imagine him keeping that knowledge a secret. It seems only Greg knew the truth about that. Until Christy heard him unburdening himself to our dad. Thank God she did.

Christy's working through forgiving Adam for his behaviour towards me and luckily, doesn't blame me for it. In fact, mine and her relationship is as strong as ever, and between us we take care of Mum too. Which is why I'm here now. She's holding up well, considering what we've all put her through this year, and after losing the love of her life. Mum and I are going to get through this first Christmas together. We've put the tree up so Oliver can enjoy looking at the coloured lights, and we're going to go for a long walk and have a quiet day. There'll be memories, there'll be tears, but we must keep moving forwards and putting ourselves back together.

Christy's now talking about becoming a mother, something I never thought I'd hear. Adam's unlikely to get a custodial sentence, but they're waiting to find out before they decide for certain.

When I consider how much everything has changed since last Christmas Eve, I can hardly get my head around it. We still had Dad, and where there was life, we had hope. He was still trying to keep going. Neil was alive, and I had no idea I was pregnant. I've cheated death twice since I lost him - both times at the hands of my little sister.

Would I turn the clock back to a few months before I had the fling with Greg? Would I do things differently? If only I'd known then that miracles can and do happen.

I kiss the top of Oliver's head and he looks up at me. He has gorgeous eyes, exactly the same as Neil's. No DNA test was ever needed - with every passing day, he becomes more and more like his father.

For details of my other titles, visit my author page on Amazon. All my books are in Kindle Unlimited.

Before you go...

Join my 'keep in touch' list to receive a free book, and to be kept posted of other freebies, special offers and new releases. Being in touch with my readers, is one of the best things about being an author. You can join via https://www.mariafrankland.co.uk

If you want to read my next psychological thriller, find out more about Frenemy on Amazon.

BOOK DISCUSSION GROUP QUESTIONS

1. Sacha left her question unanswered at the end of her final chapter. Discuss.
2. What sentences do Adam, Greg and Rebecca deserve for their behaviour in the novel?
3. Discuss the truth behind whether a patient can hear when in a coma. What effect can talking to them can have?
4. Which character(s) were you most rooting for in this story? Where did your sympathies lie?
5. Discuss the situation from the point of view of Stuart and Wendy. Should they have been more 'selfish' in Stuart's final months?
6. How does the predicament of longing for a baby feed into the behaviour in this story?
7. Imagine the conversation that might have taken place in the aftermath of the pregnancy revelation between Sacha and her father-in-law, Joe. What might he have said to her?
8. What events could have changed Neil ever being on the clifftop in the first place?

9. What, do you suppose, might have been the attraction towards Sacha from her brothers-in-law?
10. To what extent did Neil fit the stereotype of someone at risk of committing suicide? How could he have been helped?
11. Consider what Adam and Christy's future might look like.

IN HIS SHADOW

Prologue

It takes between four and ten days after death for a body to reach putrefaction. In March, in a warm spring cellar, I would expect things to be doing their worst towards the earlier end of that spectrum. Today is day eight.

The odour of death assaults me as soon as I step into the hallway. I reach forward for the light, which blows no sooner than I have touched the switch. No! The fuse box is in the cellar. I should have done this before it got dark, but I've been putting it off all day.

I edge through the kitchen, burying my nose and mouth into the neckline of my jumper. The smell is like nothing I've ever encountered – bad eggs, curdled milk, sewerage, and decaying meat all rolled into one. As I reach the cellar door, I pause, trying to get some breath into my lungs without my senses connecting to my inhalations.

The walls between this house and the terrace it backs onto are so thin, they might as well be made from papier mache. Once a shop downstairs and a large residential dwelling upstairs, it seems the developer took the cheapest option and built something barely stronger than a stud wall between the two resulting homes.

I listen for signs of life from the house behind.There shouldn't be any, but a slim chance exists that the last person I would want to see could turn up there. Nothing. Only the gasps of my own breath. Beads of sweat soak the skin beneath my jumper. Instinctively, I release my chin from it, inadvertently succumbing to the inevitable stench that now has its chance to launch its assault, causing my stomach to lurch and my mouth to fill with saliva. I swallow, hard. Although, I could get away with throwing up now, unlike a week or so ago. In fact, it could be viewed as an expected reaction.

I reach out for the door handle and slowly wrap my fingers around it, allowing the chill of the steel to cool my sweating palm. If only I could leave things as they are. But there's no way. I'll have to deal with this. Before long, passers by will able to smell what I can smell as they walk along the street outside.

I don't know how long I stand, rooted to the spot, steeling myself as I sway through indecision – do I throw the cellar door open, or edge it ajar an inch at a time?

Before I've even got it halfway, a swarm of plump bluebottles fly at my face. I jump back, yelling, spitting them out and swiping at them. There's no way I can go down there. No way.

There's only one course of action I can take. The one we agreed on.

Available on Amazon

INTERVIEW WITH THE AUTHOR

Q: Where do your ideas come from?

A: I'm no stranger to turbulent times, and these provide lots of raw material. People, places, situations, experiences – they're all great novel fodder!

Q: Why do you write domestic thrillers?

A: I'm intrigued why people can be most at risk from someone who should love them. Novels are a safe place to explore the worst of toxic relationships.

Q: Does that mean you're a dark person?

A: We thriller writers pour our darkness into stories, so we're the nicest people you could meet – it's those romance writers you should watch...

Q: What do readers say?

A: That I write gripping stories with unexpected twists, about people you could know and situations that could happen to anyone. So beware...

Q: What's the best thing about being a writer?

A: You lovely readers. I read all my reviews, and answer all emails and social media comments. Hearing from readers absolutely makes my day, whether it's via email or through social media.

Q: Who are you and where are you from?

A: A born 'n' bred Yorkshire lass, hurtling towards the ripe old age of 50, with two grown up sons and a Sproodle called Molly. (Springer/Poodle!) My 40's have been the best: I've done an MA in Creative Writing, made writing my full time job, and found the happy-ever-after that doesn't exist in my writing - after marrying for the second time just before the pandemic.

Q: Do you have a newsletter I could join?

A: I certainly do. Go to https:www.mariafrankland.co.uk or click here through your eBook to join my awesome community of readers. I'll send you a free novella – 'The Brother in Law.'

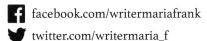 facebook.com/writermariafrank

twitter.com/writermaria_f

instagram.com/writermaria_f

tiktok.com/@mariafranklandauthor

ACKNOWLEDGMENTS

Thank you, as always, to my amazing husband, Michael, who is my first reader, and is vital with my editing process for each of my novels. His belief in me means more than I can say.

The next big thank you goes to my brilliant book cover designer Darran Holmes, who always manages to capture the design I have in my head from a simple cover brief, and also to Sue Coates, the photographer who took my author photo.

A special acknowledgment goes to my wonderful advance reader team, who have taken time and trouble to read an advance copy of Last Christmas and offer feedback on the book.

I will always be grateful to Leeds Trinity University and my MA in Creative Writing Tutors there, Martyn, Amina and Oz. My Masters degree in 2015 was the springboard into being able to write as a profession.

And finally, to you, the reader. Thank you for taking the time to read this story. I really hope you enjoyed it.